STAR VOYAGER ACADEMY

WILLIAM R. FORSTCHEN

STAR VOYAGER ACADEMY

This is a work of fiction. All the characters and events portrayed in this book are fictional, and any resemblance to real people or incidents is purely coincidental.

A Baen Book

Baen Publishing Enterprises
P.O. Box 1403
Riverdale, NY 10471

ISBN: 0-671-87608-2

Cover art by Gary Ruddell

First printing, July 1994

Distributed by Paramount Publishing
1230 Avenue of the Americas
New York, NY 10020

Printed in the United States of America

Semper Fidelis?

"This Academy is under the command of the United Nations," said Senior Commander Thorsson. "It was established as a training school for cadets who would eventually serve either aboard United Nations ships, United Military Command or Solar System Defense. When you took your oath of enlistment, that is whom you made it to."

There was a nervous stirring in the room.

"To a bunch of hidebound bureaucrats," Matt mumbled coldly.

"What was that, cadet?"

Matt stood silently, looking up at Thorsson.

"I said, sir," Matt announced, his voice clear, filled with the drawl of a deep spacer, "that I made my oath to a bunch of bureaucrats. They don't understand us, they don't understand the colonies and they don't understand space."

He said the words evenly, not showing any defiance, but not willing to back down either. An angry mutter swept through the room.

Thorsson stared at him.

"You've got guts, cadet. Now I'll only ask you the same question I ask of all my cadets: *will you live up to your oath?*"

"Until Earth forces me to break it; then we'll all be choosing sides. But until that day, sir, I live by what I promise."

FOR MEGHAN MARIE FORSTCHEN,
Born July 28, 1993

May some of the dreams in the book come true in the world
you will someday know

✧ Chapter I ✧

The view from the forward docking port was simply magnificent. The Earth curved away beneath him, the entire United States visible below. On the distant horizon, which shimmered with a brilliant turquoise blue, the crescent moon was breaking the horizon.

There was only one problem though — and Justin Bell looked around desperately for a bathroom, a paper bag, anything so that he could get decently sick to his stomach.

"Did you bring your own space sickness patches?"

He looked over at a young woman who floated up alongside him.

Justin shook his head weakly. He started to hiccup as beads of sweat broke out on his forehead.

She smiled at him in a mischievous way, her long

1

shiny black hair floating around her pale oval face like a halo.

"My name is Tanya Leonov. I'm from Russia, Saint Petersburg. I think we're in the same company," and she extended her hand.

Just looking at her made him even dizzier, since she was floating upside down. Or was he upside down and was she right side up? He was too sick to even care.

"I'm Justin Bell, United States, West Lafayette, Indiana," he croaked out weakly.

Her eyes widened slightly.

"Your father, was he Jason Bell?"

He nodded glumly, knowing what was coming.

"Hey, I saw the holo film about him." She paused and a sarcastic smile lit her features.

"You don't look anything like the kid that played you in the movie."

She stared at him closely, as if he was a specimen in a jar, and he could almost see the disappointment in her eyes. After all, his father was the late and famous Jason Bell, the man who was first to Neptune, the hero who died saving over five hundred people aboard the space transport *Condor*.

He could imagine what this girl was thinking when looking at him — embarrassingly skinny, an overactive case of acne, a cowlick of hair that wouldn't stay in place, and worst of all a pair of old-style glasses that made him look like an owl since he wasn't old enough yet for corrective eye surgery. Surely this was not the son of a hero.

"Your first time in space?" she asked.

"Um-hum." He was afraid to open his mouth to say more.

"You'll get your space legs eventually," she said sympathetically.

"I hope so," Justin croaked weakly, forcing down a hiccup.

"Well, look at it this way, Justin. If you don't, you'll get washed out of the academy and sent home. They can't waste time on space-sick cadets. Even those who won appointments because their father was a hero."

He tried to come up with some sharp reply. He fought down a temptation to simply let go, get sick, and make sure it was aimed in her direction. He had heard real horror stories about people losing their lunch in zero gravity. The stuff would float all over the room and coat everyone and everything. As if she had read his mind, Tanya reached out to a handhold on the wall and pulled back several feet. Behind her the blue horizon of Earth filled the viewport, highlighting her floating black hair.

She reached into her pocket and pulled out a peach.

"Care for a snack?" she said, still smiling with that mischievous light in her eyes.

"Oh God."

Desperate, he turned away and tried to think of something else, anything else. He knew, however, that it was hopeless; when you're going to get sick, nothing in all the universe could possibly help. No matter how hard you tried to think of something else, that horrible stomach-churning feeling would just continue to build up until it finally exploded.

He drifted over to a viewport and looked out, praying that it might divert him from thoughts of his stomach. The blue-green Earth was far below, great banks of clouds hiding most of the Amazon Basin. It was hard to believe he was down there only hours ago, waiting to board the Rio elevator tower and take the long twenty-three-thousand-mile ride up to geosynch orbit. It already seemed a lifetime ago. As he looked over at the final terminus station of the tower, half a dozen kilometers away, he found himself wishing more than ever that he could somehow get back to it, grab the next car and head back down to home.

The trip up to space on the tower was nothing more than a very long elevator ride; the days of chemical rockets lifting into space were now long over. Until the gravity started to drop off, he had even been enjoying himself. After all, a ride on the space tower was considered one of the most exciting trips anywhere in the solar system. Besides the usual Earth-to-space traffic, it had become a major tourist attraction in itself, with tens of thousands riding up every day to stay overnight at one of the hotels anchored at various points along the way. A new sport had even started with the opening of the tower: space diving, with people riding up to the thousand-kilometer mark then jumping back off with a heat shield on their backs. He had even seen a team of divers heading down. Now that was nuts, as far as he was concerned; but given the chance, at the moment he was certain he would gladly have taken even that method of getting back down to terra firma. Terra firma: it reminded him of Curly from the old Three Stooges of the mid-twentieth century, talking about a little less terra and a lot more firma.

Everyone else on board the shuttle car on the way up was excited, shouting, laughing, hundreds of brand new cadets heading up to the Academy, having the time of their lives, and Justin Bell had whooped it up and shouted along with them — at first.

They had floated aboard the orbital transfer shuttle, which would take them to the Academy, everyone in high spirits, and he had even turned a few exuberant zero-gravity somersaults. And then the first hiccup hit.

He wiped the cold clammy sweat from his forehead and stifled a groan as the vertigo started again. Down or up in space had no real meaning, and at the moment he felt as if he was falling up and sideways. He grabbed hold of the railing by the window and hung on for dear life, closing his eyes and praying that it would pass.

A cold flash went through him; he felt the sweats breaking out all over his body. He swallowed hard and then swallowed again, forcing the horrible moment back down.

"Cadet, are you going to get sick?"

Weakly he looked over his shoulder and vaguely remembered the freckled face of the redheaded cadet floating beside him. It was his squad's senior cadet advisor for the summer session. He could only remember who he was thanks to the name tag sewn on to the cadet's white class A dress uniform.

Brian Seay, the upperclassman advisor for second

squad of Company A, class of 2080, looked over at Justin. Brian was in a cold rage, his features flushed to a dark crimson. One of the twenty cadets in his squad was already sick, another had lost her I.D. information disk, and yet another had announced that he was dropping out of the Academy and wanted to go home on the next available flight. The small room assigned to the squad aboard the shuttle craft was in chaos.

The zero-gravity sticky boots assigned to the cadets were missing and everyone was floating back and forth about the room. It was a favorite prank upper-classmen played on rival squads of new cadets, more affectionately referred to as scrubs. What was making it a real nightmare though was the fact that some really great upperclassman prankster had hidden the entire supply of anti-space sickness patches which were to be handed out to all cadets before boarding the transport ship. Two whole companies of new scrubs, four hundred students, were thus floating around inside the transport, many of them feeling less than well at the moment.

"Scrub, do you have your space sickness bag?"

Justin nodded weakly.

"Then damn it, scrub, get it out."

Justin fumbled for the pouch that had been issued him when he boarded the shuttle and pulled it out of its foil liner.

"All right, scrub," Brian growled with disgust, "the head's down the corridor. Let's get you there and for heaven's sake don't throw up without your bag or you'll have to clean it up yourself!"

He grabbed hold of Justin and pushed him. Justin floated across the room and out into the space transport's main corridor.

"Move it, scrub, move it! The Academy's really scraping the bottom of the barrel if they're taking jerks like you who throw up five minutes after getting into space!"

Brian floated alongside him, leaning into Justin's face, shouting at him.

They entered the corridor. Brian grabbed hold of a handrail, stopped and then reached out to grab Justin. From other rooms down the corridor cadets, in various stages of despair, were shepherded out into the hallway by their senior advisors. Lines were forming up at bathroom doors. The crowd groaned and moaned, like the damned that they were, no one even caring if they were waiting to get into the male or female bathrooms. It was definitely first come first served.

Justin, hand over his mouth, waited. A red light above the door in front of him snapped to green and a cadet emerged, her face looking like pale wax, a most unpleasant sour smell coiling around her.

"Right in there!" Brian shouted, nodding towards the door on the other side of the corridor.

It was only a couple of meters away, but even if his life depended on it, which he felt at the moment it most certainly did, Justin could not figure out how to cross those two meters, let alone how to use the zero-gravity toilet.

He had always imagined that weightlessness would be the thrill of a lifetime. The whole idea of going into space had been the most important goal of his life. At least that was what he had been told was his most important goal, his destiny some had called it. This wasn't anything like he imagined.

One of his earliest memories was the night his father had come home after his two-year mission to Neptune and taken him out into the cold winter fields behind the farmhouse. They spent hours watching the night sky, sipping hot chocolate to keep warm, and talked of space. He was seven, and it was one of the few times his father and he ever really talked. They sat outside watching the stars and the orbital bases and solar power beaming satellites moving overhead until he fell asleep in his father's arms.

His dad had been a shadowy figure in his life. Someone who showed up, stayed for a week, sometimes a month and then was back out the door, carrying his old beat-up tote bag.

He remembered some of the fights as well, his dad wanting the family to move to Mars, his mother demanding that they stay on Earth so she could continue to teach at the university in town, saying that a frontier outpost on Mars was no place to raise a family.

Yet when his father left, there were always the tears and his mother sitting alone at night on the back porch, watching the stars come out.

The morning after their shared vigil of watching the night sky, his father was gone, returning back to the icy darkness and silence which in his heart Justin knew his father loved even more than his family. Three weeks later he was dead.

In his bedroom, framed on the wall, was his father's Medal of Honor and beneath it a letter from the President of the United Nations, declaring that Justin Bell, as the surviving child of a Medal of Honor winner, was guaranteed acceptance to the United Nations Space Academy when he reached the age of sixteen.

It had caused no end of conflict. His mother came to hate space, even though the teaching of aerospace engineering at the university was her field. There was the other side of her life which he knew she wanted him to follow, and thus be safe. She had come from a long line of Indiana farmers, going back over two hundred years before the time of the Civil War. They had lived on the land, surviving the Great Depression of the 20th Century, and the political upheavals of the early 21st. Her family had wanted him to stay, to forget about his father's universe, to go to Purdue University, where his mother taught, and stay on Earth and perhaps even run the farm.

But there was the other side, the Bell half of the family. Grandpa Bell had taken over so much of being a father to him, and always there was the pride in his family, the tales told on the back porch while the stars came out in the evening sky. They were three generations of space explorers, starting with a shuttle jockey in the old American space program, and Justin was expected to be the fourth.

His grandfather would talk softly, his voice filled with pride as he pointed out the planets, telling how Bells had explored the Moon, Venus, Mars and Neptune. At least once during each of those visits his grandfather would reach into his wallet and pull out a faded photograph of himself as a young man, part of the first United Nations expedition to Mars in 2026, flying with the legendary Thor Thorsson.

"Bells have always been part of the frontier. We flew with the old United States program, and now we fly with the United Nations and someday we'll go to the stars. That's your destiny, Justin. Two hundred years ago they used to call it a manifest destiny to form this country, and I believe in the same thing today: it's our destiny to go to the stars."

He somehow felt though that his grandfather would look at him and feel disappointment, suspecting that Justin took too much after his mother's side of the family, and that space was simply not in his blood.

He really wasn't sure, even now, how he felt about all of this. An Academy posting was put into his hands, signed by the President of the United Nations and by Thor Thorsson, who was now head of the United Nations Space Academy. Over a million sixteen-year-olds from Earth and all the colonies applied each year to the two-year prep program which would lead into the four-year officers training, and only sixteen hundred were accepted. They were the best, the brightest, and the toughest, something he definitely did not see himself as being.

Some said it was unfair that the children of medal winners were given a guaranteed admission, but then again, in order to win the Medal of Honor in space one had to lose his life in the process of attempting to save others in an act far above and beyond the

ordinary call of duty. It was felt that this was pay-
ment back by a grateful society.

He felt as if all eyes were upon him right now. In
the holo movie about his dad the famous child actor,
Ricky Cochran, had even played himself. The last
scene in the movie was young Ricky looking off into
space, holding his father's Medal of Honor. Ricky
had even looked like a proper son of Jason Bell's,
tanned, smooth-skinned, attractive and without the
bulky glasses. That scene in the movie still haunted
him. The truth was that the night after the award
ceremony he had fled to his room, pulled down the
shades and then cried himself to sleep, the Medal of
Honor tossed into a far corner of the room.

His going to the Academy was assumed, by
Grandpa Bell, by all the other Bells, by his teachers,
and everyone else in town. Yet he felt so out of place
in it all.

As for the guys at school, their reaction was the
worst. To them he became the space geek, the weak-
ling, the wimp who would cry every time they cornered him after school and roughed him up for the
fun of it, taunting him with the promise that he'd
flunk out of the Academy and come back to them
for yet another working over.

The son of a hero, it did seem like a joke. He was
so unlike his lost father, a man who grew even stronger, more heroic, more legendary the longer he was
dead. Though the adults wouldn't say it, those he
went to school with took delight in pointing out just
how unlike the "real" Academy students he truly was.
And down deep he knew they were right; the thought

of space terrified him. To others it might seem like a romantic adventure, the high frontier of the 21st century, where millions were now working and living. But to him it held an inner terror, the vast open void, the cold, the silence and the vacuum which could kill in an instant. There had been a report issued after the *Condor* incident, something his mother and family friends had kept hidden from him. He had, however, finally stumbled across it in a computer file. The photographs filled him with horror, especially the one that showed what was left of his father. It showed just what space could do to a person.

Far too many expected him to go, and to back out was even more frightening than going. But what made it worse was the simple fact that he wasn't even sure if he could cut it, since the Academy was known to be the hardest school in all the solar system. It was a six-year program. Barely one in five managed to graduate. Of those who didn't graduate, quite a few were actually killed in the process.

The schoolwork would be tough enough. Though he was a good student he didn't really consider himself to be the best, even though his teachers kept saying that if he only applied himself he could do just about anything. There was the physical side as well: he was never very good in sports and the guys at school took delight in letting him know. Part of the Academy training involved close-in hand-to-hand combat in a variety of environments. The prospect of that training was not very amusing.

The night before he left he had sat on the back porch of the farmhouse with his mom. The wind was sighing through the cornfields, a sound he so loved to hear, the night air alive with fireflies and the songs of crickets. For the first time in years he heard his mom talk about his dad. How they had met when both were graduate students at the University and how down deep she was afraid of space even though the designing of the machines that crossed it was part of her work.

"Your father and I loved each other," she sighed. "We still do. It's just that his heart was up there, and mine was down here. I guess, Justin, you're sort of in the middle. I know you're afraid. It's all right, even your dad was afraid at times. Just try to do your best and if it doesn't work out, that's okay. You can always come back to Earth and find your life here and no one, least of all me, will think the less of you. I think you need to go, just to find that out."

Then she started to cry and left him alone to look up at the stars and wonder if this was what he really wanted to do, or if he was just living out the life that a long-dead parent had left for him.

And now he was aboard the shuttle to take them out to the Academy, located in lunar orbit. The dream of a lifetime was here at last, and all he wanted to do was die.

"Get in there, scrub!" Brian shouted, and grabbing hold of Justin, he pushed him towards the open door into the bathroom.

Justin floated across the corridor. Arms flaying, he tried to grab a handrail next to the door and missed. He bounced off the opposite wall and came straight back at Brian. Suddenly, he knew with a terrible certainty that it was too late, far too late to attempt another bounce across the hallway and back to the sanctuary of the bathroom.

Seay's eyes grew wide.

"Barf in the bag, you jerk, in the bag!"

Justin fumbled with the bag and put his mouth over the opening.

The explosion erupted—and to his horror it blew right out the other side of the bag. He had a distant memory, his father told him how it was one of the oldest jokes in the fleet, cutting holes in the bottom of the barf bags and then putting them back in their packets.

He knew with a horrified certainty that a senior cadet's spotless class A dress white uniform was about to get ruined. He remembered as well the old advice he had heard from his father — "never, absolutely never get your senior cadet pissed off at you, no matter what!"

Brian's eyes grew wide with terror. The senior cadet saw what was coming straight at him, but there was no way to avoid it.

Gasping, Justin Bell slowly floated down the corridor, sweat beading on his face, his eyes still popping out like a catfish who had just been hauled in for supper. What he just accomplished triggered a chain reaction down the hallway. All the other scrubs lost it, heaving into their bags, all of which had holes in the bottom. Senior cadets screamed in rage and horror as the hallway filled up with a most unpleasant substance. In the zero gravity the stuff floated around, covering the walls, floors and everyone floating around in a smelly sticky goo. The air filtration system, its sensors picking up evidence of the disaster, kicked into high gear, a torrent of air swirling down the corridor, sucking up the gallons of spray. Scrubs who failed to grab a handhold spun through the air, wailing in agony as they plopped up against the vents and were stuck there like flies pinned to the wall, a misty spray swirling in around them, covering them in a multihued slime.

At least for the moment Justin felt a little bit better as he hung on to a side rail, gasping for air. And then he looked back at the mess he had just made of Brian Seay. With a sick horror Justin knew he had made the worst mistake in the world for a scrub, a brand-new cadet — he had made an enemy for life out of an upperclassman. It was a great way to start his career at the Academy.

❖　❖　❖

With a groan Justin awoke and again felt a moment of panic. The holograph movies of people sleeping in zero gravity had always looked so nice and peaceful. But it sure didn't feel peaceful at the moment. It was like a bad dream, he thought, where you suddenly fall off a cliff and you come awake with a start. It was the same here, that endless sensation of falling.

He gripped the sides of his sleeping bunk net and hung on for a moment. At least the space sickness patches had finally been located, hidden inside a ventilation shaft, and the medicine was helping things a bit. He felt absolutely drained though, having pulled his first punishment assignment of his career, to help change the clogged up air filters. It was a task which

had caused him to lose it half a dozen more times
until there was simply nothing left to give to the all-
demanding god of nausea.

The other bunks were empty. Gathering up his
courage he unsnapped his sleeping net and slipped
out of his bunk. He reached out and grabbed a pair
of zero-gravity shoes, which would stick to the floor.
He, along with most of the other scrubs, suspected
that it was Sharon O'Malley, the squad leader in the
next room, who had hidden the boots, just to watch
the fun, when she made such a big show of "discov-
ering" them stashed away in a storage locker. Popping the boots off from their holding slot on the wall,
Justin slipped them on and stepped down onto the
deck. With clumsy exaggerated steps he slowly made
his way out of the room and into the lounge. A small
crowd was gathered around one of the viewports.

"Feeling better, Justin?"

Madison Smith, the one other American in his
squad, looked over at him and flashed a sympathetic
smile. Her bright smile, which crinkled up her dark
round face, was warm and friendly and she walked
across the room to join him.

He still felt a bit shaky and she offered her hand to
help steady him. He smiled wanly and refused. Walking with zero-gravity shoes was something he had to
master on his own.

"You'll get the hang of it," she whispered with a
conspiratorial wink.

"I feel so stupid," he blurted out, glad to see that
unlike Tanya, she wasn't going to set him up.

"My parents used to take me on vacations to

DisneySpace Resort, so I got the hang of it early. In a couple of days you'll have your space legs."

"I hope so," he sighed.

He looked around the room. No one else had noticed him, everyone was glued to the viewports.

"Senior Cadet Seay said that we're waiting for one more cadet to show up and then we're off for the Academy."

She looked at him with eyes that sparkled with excitement. At the mention of the word Seay he quickly looked around, but the senior cadet was nowhere in sight and he breathed a sigh of relief.

"In fact he's coming in now and everyone's watching the show. Let's join them."

With clumsy steps he followed her across the room, leaning on Madison at one point when he didn't quite catch the sticky bottom of his shoe to the deck floor and almost fell over. She gave him a playful squeeze on the arm and steadied him. As they approached the viewport window he saw that Tanya was with the rest of the group. She looked over her shoulder at him and again gave that mischievous smile.

He couldn't help but notice that she certainly looked attractive. Her long black hair was tied into a simple ponytail to keep it from floating into her face.

"Ah, here he is now," she announced. "We were just talking about you."

Several of the cadets in the group looked over at Justin. He felt himself flush with embarrassment and also a touch of anger. It was obvious that Tanya had decided to single him out.

"Good shooting, Justin," one of them said with a

laugh. "Hit the senior upperclassman first day out."

The group broke into a gale of laughter, Tanya with a dramatic flourish and contorted features imitating the great moment.

The cadet who had spoken extended his hand.

"Pradeep Singh from Bombay. I think we've been assigned to room together."

Justin smiled weakly and shook Singh's hand.

"Where I came from we were taught to hit our target on the first shot," Justin said quietly, and he relaxed a bit to realize that his reply had turned the laughter in his favor. A sudden hush came over the group and all eyes turned from Justin to the far corner of the room.

Brian Seay was floating in the open doorway and Justin realized with a cold dread that Brian had heard his retort. The senior cadet turned around and left the room, the door closing behind him.

"Oh, just great," Justin groaned.

"I'll take all bets Seay makes sure straight-shooter here gets washed out before the summer session's ended," Tanya said.

The group was quiet, several of them nodding in agreement.

Justin tried to form a reply to Tanya, to find just the right way to tell her to get lost, but he couldn't. The quick retort was never one of his strong points. He tended to take things in, and ponder them for a while before replying. He knew that twenty minutes from now he'd have just the right snappy response made up, but by then, of course, it would be meaningless.

"That ship's a beautiful sight," Madison said, and to Justin's relief the group turned back to look out the window, forgetting about his troubles.

"It's a Yukon Clipper class," Justin said, recognizing it immediately. "They haven't made them in nearly forty years. The last model of the D class solar wind sailing ships came off the docks back in '41."

"Looks like a junk scow," Tanya replied.

He had to admit to himself that it did. Barely a scrap of paint was left on its sun-blasted hull, and the sensing arrays on it were absolute antiques; but to Justin, it was simply magnificent. On a clear night down on Earth, it was easy to track solar sailors setting out on their downwind runs to Mars, the asteroid belt and the gas giants beyond, their thousand-square-kilometer set of sails catching and reflecting the sunlight. Occasionally they stood out as brightly as the Solar Energy Power Stations that ringed the planet. Now at last he was seeing one up close.

He still found it remarkable that ships cruised the solar system using the pressure of sunlight to fill their sails. It was almost like the ancient clippers and frigates of the 19th century. With their mylar panels set to catch the solar wind, the ships hauled heavy bulk cargos that were too expensive to move using ion and nuclear pulse rockets.

In a way Tanya was right, though he hated to admit it. The solar sailing ships were the tramp vessels of the space age. A nuclear pulse engine ship could make it to Mars in two weeks and Jupiter in six. In that same time a solar sailor would just be building up speed and at best would be a couple of million clicks out. But once it got going, riding the solar wind, it could go as fast as ion drive. It was just that they were so darn slow to start up and slow down. The one advantage, of course, was that the solar wind was free while the engines and fuel of a nuclear pulse rocket cost a bundle.

The ship was scarred. Its paint blistered off from years of blazing sunlight and the scouring of thousands of micrometer impacts. It had a worn down and battered look to it, its communications dish punched with dozens of tiny holes. It should have long ago been sent to the space museum, but it was still flying the lanes and working. Underneath the living quarters, half a dozen ore canisters were slung, filled most likely with ten thousand tons of raw titanium from the asteroids, ready to be converted into the newest ships. Sticking out like the legs of a spider were the long furling arms for the sails, each of the dozen masts more than a hundred meters in length, the sails wrapped tightly around them except for a single square kilometer panel which the pilot was using to drop off the final few feet per second of momentum for docking.

The pilot was obviously a master. He was coming in to dock, barely using his thruster controls. The last sail finally started to furl in, winding up on the mast. Justin watched with admiration, his space sickness momentarily forgotten.

A slight but noticeable shudder ran through the transport as the solar sailor achieved a hard dock. The show was over. The crowd started to drift away back to their rooms to get some sleep. Justin watched them go.

This was his first night in space and now that they were on the dark side of Earth, the heavens above seemed to blaze with a million stars. Maybe it was old stuff for most of the others. He had heard Tanya boasting about having lived on the Moon for a year, and how her great-grandfather was a famous cosmonaut. Even Madison seemed not too interested in the view, other than the momentary excitement of the solar sailor coming in to dock.

I'm in space, he thought with wonder. *A hundred years ago only a handful could have said that. I'm in space and tomorrow I'll step foot into the Academy.*

The mere thought of it sent a cold shiver down his back, a shiver he wasn't sure was that of fear or excitement. He realized that it was both.

He leaned back out and pressed his nose to the window. The Academy shuttle had waited for this last arrival, since it was forbidden for solar sailors to dock with the skyhook tower, or with any orbital habitats. The last cadet to join up for the class of 2080 was on board and Justin was suddenly curious, never having met a solar sailor before. He reached over to the communications and information panel on the wall, punched up a quick question and got directions to where the ship had docked.

✧　　✧　　✧

Matt Everett looked around his room one last time. For years he'd dreamed of escaping it. Now that he was leaving, most likely forever, this final look tugged at his heart. The walls were plastered with pictures of Earth, an Earth he had only seen from orbit, or as nothing more than a blue-green flicker of light a billion kilometers away. He'd only taken a couple of the pictures down to go with him — the sunset over a tropical beach, a snowstorm in a pine forest and the picture of his parents.

He could hardly remember them now. The holo image was taken only a couple of days before the meteor collision which had nearly destroyed *Corona Wind*. In the photo he was standing between them, barely reaching his father's belt, both their hands resting on his shoulder.

He heard the door into his room slide open. He fought down the slight misting of his eyes and turned around.

"Well, laddie, we docked. Time to move along now. I've got to get over to the orbital unloading docks, get these ore canisters dumped and foodstuffs to load in. Solar storm's kicking up, sail pressure's expected to be up nearly a hundred percent. I wanna catch the high wind and be off."

Matt looked at his uncle and forced a smile. He knew it was as tough on him as well. All his life there had always been Uncle Dan, who'd taken over as mother and father and captain of the family ship.

Matt wanted to say something, but knew he couldn't. There was, after all, the unwritten code. Sailors were supposed to be a quiet lot, loners who could stand the endless watches and never have need to say a word. Emotions? Those were a luxury for gravity-dwellers, the people down on the planets or aboard the big orbiting space stations. A true spacer never let anything upset him.

He forced a wry smile. With the centrifugal spin

shut down for docking he hung motionless in the zero gravity. The service robot floated up alongside Uncle Dan and fixed Matt with a quiet gaze, its electronic eyes almost looking lifelike. It was hard to think of "bot" as not being alive. A pet for someone growing up aboard a sailing ship was impossible, and Dan had picked up the bot with the claim that it could help keep the place clean and serve a watch, but Matt knew Dan really got "him" as a companion and substitute friend.

"Matt, one more game of chess?" the bot asked.

"Gotta go, bot," Matt said quietly.

"Oh."

The machine tilted its bowl-shaped head and looked around the room.

"Your favorite pictures are down."

"That's because I'm leaving ship. You know that."

"Oh." The bot was silent for several seconds as if digesting such a strange thought as someone leaving. Solar sailors floated the space lanes between worlds, each journey stretching out a year or more. No one had really left the ship since the bot had come aboard ten years ago, except for quick stops at space stations or mining ports.

"When will you return? We've got a schedule to keep around here."

Matt looked at the bot, a lump in his throat. Of course the machine knew that he was going, part of its job was knowing everything aboard the *Corona Wind*. It had helped him study for the Academy exams, which had been administered via the commlink systems and celebrated with him when word arrived of his acceptance. Matt couldn't quite figure out if the machine was just acting on its program to make believe that it had emotions, or if it was genuinely upset and confused.

At times the bot would act as if he was still a child, offering a piggyback ride, challenging him to a spelling contest, or offering to read a story, behaving like a kindly grandfather who could not accept the fact that his favorite child was growing older.

"It'll be six years, maybe never," Matt said quietly.

The bot looked up at Dan, who floated in the doorway, and then back to Matt.

"I'll miss you, Matt," the bot said.

Matt looked at the machine, unable to reply. It was the first time he had ever heard it use the personal pronoun, I.

Dan huskily cleared his throat.

"Come on, laddie. Academy ship's waitin' for you. I've got cargo to offload. Now shake a leg and get off this ship."

Matt nodded and forced a weak smile.

"So long, bot," he said, and he patted the machine on its shiny mechanical head.

"Game of chess when you get back then," the bot replied.

Matt unclipped his bag from the floor and floated for the door. His uncle extended a callused beefy hand.

"Make the family proud of you. Four generations of us as spacers. Ten generations of water sailors before 'em. Remember, you're a sailor and a colonial, so don't let those damn Earthsiders get the better of you. If it comes to a fight of honor, then I'll understand. But your job is to avoid trouble, get through your training and come back a leader. And don't get your nose into this business about the Mars secession and separatists movements. It's not your problem to worry about right now."

"But they're right, Dan. I'm not going to back away from no fight with a damn Earther."

Dan took hold of Matt by his shoulders and looked into his eyes.

"Listen, son, there's a time to fight, and there's a time to get ready to fight. Your job now is to get ready. The Academy will give you the best training to be found anywhere in this system. Your dad wanted to see you an Academy graduate and so do I. If it ever does come, a fight with Earth one day, we'll need trained people. Academy trained people are priceless and we need more of them who are colonials, like yourself.

"Get through the Academy, learn everything you can learn and keep out of arguments. If you don't, they'll have you out on your tail before you know what hit you, and then what will you be, nothing but another damn colonial. If you want to serve the cause, get an education first. So keep your mouth shut and your ears open. Some of those quick lads you'll meet will try to trip you up. Others of them aren't so bad. Now promise me that. No matter what happens, you'll stay in the Academy."

Matt finally nodded a reluctant agreement.

Dan smiled and patted him on the shoulder.

"Take care of yourself, laddie."

"Good-bye, uncle."

Dan took his hand, and held his gaze for a second. He nodded, and then turned away.

"Come on, you damned bot, we've got work to do."

The old man floated across the room to the far door, the machine clicking along behind him. Matt watched him leave the room. He took a deep breath and fixed his features. In the last hour he had allowed himself more emotions than he had shown in years. Why, it just wasn't decent. After all, he had to carry the reputation of all solar sailors and live up to what Earthsiders pictured deep spacers and colonials to be like. He knew they'd think of him as a yokel from the outback, but he also knew that they would expect him to be tough.

Before popping the airlock door he double-checked the seal attachment. People who didn't double- and triple-check things didn't live too long in space. The seal was secure.

"Well good-bye, old ship," he whispered, patting the bulkhead before punching the open button.

The door hissed back. A wisp of cool air from the shuttle swirled in, feeling clean and fresh, a welcome change after eight months straight of recycled air. The condensers aboard the *Corona* were getting shaky, and the air was taking on a decidedly mildewy smell, but then again everything aboard the *Corona* was shaky at best.

An upperclassman in a white uniform was waiting.

"Cadet Matthew Lee Everett?"

"That's me."

"Say 'sir' when addressed by an upperclassman."

"That's me, sir."

She held a small laser emitter up before his right eye.

"Look straight at the laser please."

Several seconds later she lowered the device, which checked the pattern of blood vessels in the back of his eye, and was far more accurate than finger-prints for identification.

"All right, colonial boy, identification confirmed."

"What did you call me?" Matt asked quietly.

"You heard me, colonial boy, and when you address me, it's sir," she snapped in reply. She looked at him as if expecting a reply.

He remembered what his uncle had just said and took a deep breath.

"Yes, sir."

"You're assigned to Company A, second squad, now shake a leg and report to your squad commander, Senior Cadet Seay. This entire ship's been waiting for you to dock so we can go on to the Academy."

She looked back over her shoulder.

"You said you're with his company?"

"Yes, sir."

"Then show him the way, scrub."

She turned and pushed off back down the corridor without another word.

Standing on the other side was a one-man reception committee. His features were deeply tanned, obviously an Earther, but Matt could see in an instant the greenish tinge of someone who'd been getting his space legs the hard way. The Earther was tall, skinny, with a major case of acne scarring his features, and most curiously of all he was wearing a pair of glasses, something Matt had never seen before in real life. The Earther forced a friendly smile and Matt grinned at him as he floated through the airlock, turning so that he approached upside down.

"Matt Everett is the name, and the things I've seen you Earthers will never know," he began.

"The name's Justin Bell."

"You look a bit downtrodden, Justin."

"I've had better days," Justin said, again smiling weakly.

"Ah well, not to worry, not to worry, even old spacers get sick sometimes, what with all the gravity changing and such," Matt laughed.

"You took long enough to get here."

The two looked over at the far door where Brian stood, hands resting on hips.

"Come on, you damn scrubs, ship's kicking up pulse drive in ten minutes. Get back to your quarters and strapped in for acceleration. Now move it!"

Brian turned and started back down the corridor.

"Well, bucko, I think this Academy is going to be an interesting place," Matt said with a grin. "Now let's get a move on, like the upper said."

✧ Chapter II ✧

"It's beautiful," Justin Bell whispered, his nose pressed to the viewport.

Matt, Madison, Tanya, and even Brian Seay nodded in silent agreement.

"Home for the next six years," Justin said quietly.

"Maybe," Brian snapped.

Justin started to reply but thinking better of it, he turned back to watch the show.

The pilot of their shuttle expertly rolled his ship so that it was lined up for a close fly-by of Deep Space Station 23, more commonly known as Star Voyager Academy.

It was hard to judge the true size of the Academy ship since it was so vast, but Justin, like all the others, already knew that the cylinder was over a kilometer and a half long, and 310 meters in diameter. It spun slowly on its long axis, thus creating an artificial gravity inside, an experience which Justin was eager to get back to.

As they drifted down the length of the ship, viewports slipped by and Matt was able to get occasional glimpses inside the ship. For a brief moment he saw an exercise room, attached to a pylon that extended out an extra hundred and fifty meters from the main ship. Placing the room that far out from the center increased the rotation speed, jacking up gravity inside the room to nearly 1.5 that of Earth.

In twenty-meter-high golden letters down the length of the ship was the name of his new home — United Nations Space Academy, the U.N. flag painted beside the name. As the pilot turned his ship for final line-up on the docking port, Earth rolled into view behind the station, small enough now that Matt felt as if he could reach out and cover it with his hand.

He could just barely make out the midwest of the United States, a hundred thousand kilometers away. It looked like rain for today. He wondered if Andy, the hired hand who took care of the farm, was in the fields hauling in the hay they had cut together only three days ago. It already seemed like a lifetime ago. The Academy ship blocked the Earth out from view as they turned into final approach. The Moon filled a good quarter of the sky on the other side of the Academy, which circled it in high lunar orbit.

"All right, scrubs, strap into your seats for hard dock. Now move it."

Justin looked over at Matt and gave a weak smile.

He was still feeling a bit queasy, but now was not the time to think about it.

There were a lot of other feelings coming up as well, the worst one of all was the fear. He felt awkward, out of place. The others, led by Tanya, were already fitting together as a group while he seemed very much on the outside. When he first met Matt, less than a day ago, he thought that surely here was the leader of the group. But Tanya instead assumed that role and most of the others in the squad were already poking fun at him over his outlandish clothes and equally strange dialect.

Common English had evolved as the language of space in the 21st Century, at least as far as near Earth operations were concerned. It was based on American English, but had a fair smattering of Russian, Japanese, German and French thrown in. For those colonials living in the outback region of Mars and beyond, however, new but very obvious changes in the language were already starting to take place.

The Martian colonials considered it to be a political and cultural statement to not adhere to common English, their dialect already as distinctive as Outback Australian compared to the King's English of London. It was even more true of those living in the outer orbital colonies, the various religious and utopia-experiment colonies drifting in remote solar orbits between Earth and Mars, and those working in the Asteroid belt and beyond. The changes had become even more evident with the growing strength of the separatist movement and Justin found that Matt's jargon was a full reflection of the disdain that many in space had for Earthers in general, and for the anti-space political faction in particular.

Justin wondered just how he would stand on this issue of language. His ancestry led him towards space, but he wondered if he was not an Earther after all and if coming to this Academy was one hell of a mistake.

He realized now just how much space scared him. The vastness alone was unsettling, along with the knowledge that just on the other side of a half inch of titanium hull and a meter of slag rock shielding was instant death, a death that would be most unpleasant. He could do his best, never screw up, never make a mistake, and it could still get him. And if he ever did screw up, even if just for a second, it definitely would get him.

He felt a slight bump, and a computerized voice announced that airlock to the Academy ship was secured.

"All right, scrubs, form up and let's get going!"

Justin hoisted up his small bag of personal gear, careful not to lift it up too quickly, otherwise his sticky shoes might lose their grip. Following the others in his squad, he started out into the main corridor where several hundred other scrubs were forming up, and starting to move towards the docking door which was already wide open. Everyone was excited, chattering, laughing, their senior cadets shepherding them along. They cleared the triple barrier of the doors and he took his first step aboard the Academy.

The corridor was vast, airy, the walls a brilliant spotless white, light panels filling the corridor with a warm cheery glow. There were even plants growing, strange-looking ivy creepers with brilliant blue flowers, and the scrubs moved past them gingerly, attempting to keep their footing on what was supposed to be the "down" side of the corridor. One of them lost his footing, floated up and banged against a plant, crushing part of a vine, and his senior cadet let loose with a stream of angry shouts, pulling the thoroughly bewildered scrub back down to the floor. The group shuffled along, turning down a side corridor which opened out into a dome-covered courtyard.

Justin looked up and gasped with astonishment. The room felt like a cathedral and the happy exuberance of the crowd gave way to quiet whispering. The dome overhead was made of a clear reinforced diamond polymer, a still somewhat rare diamond glass forged in zero-gravity solar-powered furnaces and nearly identical in composition to the material used to make the skyhook towers. The fifty-meter expanse of the dome revealed the splendor of space above the group, Earth floating to one side. The sight of it gave him a strange sort of feeling, as if his eyes were suddenly going to mist up.

He looked over at Matt, who seemed to be taking it all in stride.

"So what do you think?" Justin asked.

Matt smiled.

"Ever been out my way before?"

Justin shook his head.

Matt looked over at Justin, ready to launch into an expansive story about derring-do and adventure. But there was something in Justin's look that stopped him. It made him feel a bit funny somehow. This Earther was all out of place, balanced wrong on his gravity sticky boots, his features pale, a look of confusion in his eyes. He almost felt sorry for him.

But there was another factor as well that made him stop. He knew that Justin was awed by the view. For Matt such views were ordinary everyday events; rather it was the crowd that was getting to him. In his entire life he had never been in a room with more than fifty people, and that was considered a major shindig of the first order out in the asteroid mining camps. For months at a time the only real faces he talked to were Uncle Dan and bot; the rest were mere holo images radioing in from passing ships.

People on Earth thought being a solar sailor was all high romance and adventure . . . it wasn't. It was damn boring 99% of the time and lonely 100% of the time. That was the big secret and in this jostling crowd he felt very much alone indeed.

He leaned over to Justin and lowered his voice.

"Frankly . . ." He hesitated, ashamed to admit it, and stopped.

Justin looked at him, forcing a nervous smile.

"Frankly, I'm scared half to death."

A grin lit up Justin's features and Matt was rather surprised when Justin extended his hand.

"Same here," he said enthusiastically, "maybe not about the same things though."

Matt nodded and shook Justin's hand.

"I guess we're in this one together," Matt blurted out. "I mean, if they flunk me out, where the hell do

I go? Uncle Dan's already turned around and started looping Earth for a return trajectory to Mars. I mean, I'm stuck. It'll be a year or more before I can hook up with him again."

"Hey, if they kick me out, I've got to go home to all those 'I figured you wouldn't make it' cracks. Most of the guys thought it was a joke I even got accepted."

"You have a lot of friends?" There was almost a note of envy in Matt's voice.

"Yeah, a couple. Not too many," Justin replied softly.

The mere thought of having a bunch of guys and even females to hang around with was a strange thought for Matt. He did have friends in a way. The only problem was that unless another ship was running awfully darn close by, like under ten million kilometers, two-way conversations were difficult because of the delay in radio signals getting back and forth.

He'd even fallen in love once, with Gloriana Rameriez, a girl his age, her family running the solar clipper *Santa Maria*, hauling bulk cargo on the Jupiter run. Their ships had passed close by a couple of years back and they had started to talk with each other over the commlinks. They'd even met face-to-face, for a whole thirty hours standard when her ship and his docked together at Mars orbital base three. He smiled at the memory. Of course Gloriana's grandmother had kept a very strict chaperoning throughout and all they had managed was a quick good-bye kiss as he shoved back off with his uncle for a downwind run to Europa, hauling heavy construction equipment.

A month later she broke up with him for a guy on Mars. The only good thing was that if he had ever tried to marry her it would have meant her spidery-looking grandmother would have been part of his family, a thought which made him shudder.

He pushed the memories away, and allowed himself to look around. There were hundreds of people here, including hundreds of girls. He wanted to ask Justin about that, just how do you talk to one face-to-face, not the usual game of bragging, which Gloriana understood and played along with, but to really talk.

Matt noticed that the room had gone quiet and that a cone of light was now shining on a podium in the center of the amphitheater, a lone man walking up to it dressed in white overalls, the standard class B uniform.

The man looked quite old, nearly bald with a thin wreath of white hair, his features all wrinkled up. But he moved with a spry fitness, a real spacer who could easily handle zero gravity.

A call for attention echoed through the room and Matt noticed that Brian was standing stiffly, hands pressed down to his side, and he followed suit. Justin was already standing rigidly, looking with open admiration at the old man who gazed out at the crowd.

"Welcome to the United Nations and Colonies Star Voyager Cadet Training Center, which we around here simply refer to as the Academy. My name is Thor Thorsson."

There was a round of excited gasps from the group. There wasn't a person on Earth, or for that matter in the entire solar system, who didn't know that name. He was the only person to have fought with and destroyed an alien Trac ship, and for that alone he was legendary.

Thorsson was the founder and senior commander of the Academy. He had flown nearly every ship that could be found in space and had sat on the board of the United Nations Committee for Space Affairs for nearly thirty years, a position that he continued to hold, in addition to his other responsibilities.

The old man smiled and looked around at the group.

"Are you folks a bit scared?" he asked, his Norwegian accent still evident, though he had left home for Mars fifty years ago.

There were nervous chuckles all around and Thor smiled.

"First time I went into space was all the way back in '20 for a stint on the old American space station. Four years later I was on my way to Mars. I was out of my mind with excitement."

He smiled softly.

"And scared to death."

Justin instantly liked him, and felt as if Thor was almost having a private conversation with him alone. The last time he had met Thor was at the memorial service for his father, nearly nine years ago. The man had towered over him then and he was too afraid to speak, especially with all the holo cameras focused on them when Thor had presented him with his father's Medal of Honor and the admission certificate to the Academy. The only thing he could clearly remember was that Thor started to cry, something that had struck him as strange, since he was, after all, a famous hero.

He looked closely at the man, finding it hard to imagine Thor Thorsson ever being afraid of anything, let alone a trip into space. What caught him the most, though, was that the man now seemed smaller, almost tiny compared to the legendary giant that he remembered.

"Tomorrow morning, classes will officially start for the summer orientation session, what we around here call 'scrub summer.'"

He smiled again and then lowered his head for a moment as if remembering his own first days at school so long ago. He raised his head again and this time his features were set in sober lines.

"Every year the Academy accepts sixteen hundred students who are sixteen years old for the two-year preparatory program which will lead to full admission to the Academy. Six companies of new cadets have already arrived and you two companies are the last of the lot, the class of 2080. You are the best of the best. For every scrub standing here, nearly a thousand very disappointed candidates are back at home. To be selected to the top pilot and military school of the entire solar system is a high honor."

Justin couldn't help but look around at the others, some of whom were smiling in a satisfied way, others with dead serious looks in their eyes.

"At the end of this summer session, one-third of you will be going home, so look around, because some of your new friends won't be here by the beginning of the next semester. That's why we call it scrub summer, to see how many of you we can scrub off the list."

Justin gave a nervous side glance towards Tanya, who was looking straight back at him and smiling. It'd been a long time since he really didn't like somebody, but Tanya now definitely fit the bill. It was obvious that she was looking at him as if he were already lost.

"That'll only be the first hurdle, though," Thor continued. "At the end of the two-year preparatory period you'll still have to stand for exams to gain admittance to the standard four-year Academy. If you are accepted you'll then gain your midshipman's rank and then after that it's four more years of training, most of it out in the field with patrol units. At the end of that four years only one out of every six of you will be presented with an ensign stripe at your graduation ceremony.

"And those who don't . . ." He paused for a moment. "Most of you will go back home, where other schools will kill to have a chance at signing you up, because you'll still be one of the best. Even with just a couple of years training here, you'll be able to land non-comm rating with the military. Go back home, graduate from college and you can still come back for officer's training and earn your pilot wings for space. But I suspect all of you want to see it through all the way because a graduate from here stands second to none."

Everyone nodded in agreement.

"And some of you," he said softly, "will never go

home. Our training is real, it's on the line, aboard space stations, research centers, peace-keeping on distant outposts and with solar system defense. Some of you will make mistakes, and some of you will wind up killing yourselves: it's that simple. The bottom line is that nearly ten percent of our students are killed in accidents, or are disabled and discharged with disabilities."

He stopped for a moment, to let his words sink in. Justin already knew those odds. Only last week three second-year cadets and an instructor had been killed when their training shuttle smacked into a golf ball-size piece of rock that just so happened to hit them at nearly forty thousand miles an hour. It was an extremely rare occurrence, running into the odd bit of space debris, but it still happened nevertheless, and four people were dead.

Thor nodded up towards a far wall. Each of the white panelled section walls of the meeting room had a simple motto written on them and the first one listed the most basic rule of all, "In Space There Are No Second Chances."

"When we first set this school up we caught a lot of trouble over the fact that every year some of our cadets were killed. Some Earthers wrung their hands, moaned, and said 'oh my, it's far too dangerous to send our children out there.'" As he spoke he raised his voice into a whiny falsetto which drew a couple of chuckles.

He paused for a moment.

"Well, that's a bunch of crap as far as I'm concerned. Sure, space is dangerous, anything worth going for is dangerous. Those of you who are Americans know that from your history, tens of thousands died settling your frontier. The same thing for you Russians who settled Siberia and you folks from Polynesia who explored the Pacific in canoes. A thousand years ago my Viking ancestors thought nothing of sailing into the unknown and thousands of them never returned. Life is risk. We are heading into the new frontier and it'll cost lives, lots of them, and there's no turning back. Look up, just look up for a moment though, and you'll see why, because out there is the destiny of the human race, to explore the stars — and you will be the leaders in the greatest adventure in history. That is why it is worth the risk, because my friends, we are going for the stars and we'll explore the entire universe."

He paused again and the light in the room dimmed so that the stars above shone forth in all their glory. Justin suddenly felt his pulse start to quicken.

"I don't like it when we lose people in training, one death in my book is far too many as is. But we've made it tough and totally realistic here for a reason," he said softly.

"You see, there are no second chances in space. Make a mistake and you're dead. We want to make sure that you make no mistakes. Here at the Academy, if you mess up, you'll be dropped and sent home, or you might kill yourself, but that will be it. We'll mourn you, we'll bury you or ship you home if we can find the pieces, and then we go back to work. But if you should one day graduate, you'll be responsible for the men and women in your unit or aboard your ship. In turn you and your command might be responsible for the lives of thousands, hundreds of thousands, perhaps even for the well-being of every citizen in this entire solar system, and we can't afford any mistakes when you have that kind of power. That's what we're training you for, to be the best of the best and to help lead humankind to the stars."

He looked around the group as if memorizing each of their faces.

"In the year I was born, back in 1997, we really weren't doing all that much with space, even though we had first walked on the Moon. . . ." He hesitated and finally pointed at Pradeep. "In what year?"

"1969, sir, the Americans Armstrong and Aldrin."

"Good.

"Back then, a lot of people foolishly thought that space wasn't worth it. They used to say, 'why waste money up there, instead of back here where the problems are?' "

Justin and the other cadets chuckled at that famous old saw which was now seen to be as foolish as people saying that man was never intended to fly or that the world was flat.

"And then came the years of trouble, overpopulation, mass starvation, new and frightening diseases and the limited nuclear wars. A lot of people started to believe that humankind was finished, until some leaders with brains finally realized that going into space was the answer to all of those problems. I've seen a lot of progress in my lifetime. Weather control was a big one. Next came the return to the Moon, the colonization of Mars, the asteroid belt, the moons of Jupiter and Saturn. The space-based military which we're part of helped to at least enforce an uneasy peace down on Earth. We've built power stations to beam pollution-free electricity back to Earth, we've built the skyhook towers cutting the cost of getting into space to as cheap as a trip across town, and pretty soon, if all goes as planned, we'll leap to the stars.

"Damn, I'm proud of what we've done," he said, smacking his left hand into his right palm, his eyes beaming. "New drugs developed in zero gravity have helped cure unknown diseases that scared us all when I was a kid growing up in Norway. We've even managed to bring a form of peace to the entire world through the United Space Military Command, which orbiting above Earth can stop aggression and terrorism before it starts. Space-based communications has helped with the peace as well, bringing the world together. Just look at all of you right now. When I was not much younger than you, nations still fought wars with each other. Oh, we still have our differences. I still don't like the fact that the Lithuanians beat Norway in Ice Hockey at the Olympics last year."

"Lithuania forever," came a lone voice from the back of the room and the group laughed, Thor with them.

"You'll be the leaders who take us from the 21st into the 22nd century. The new skyhook towers we've built are even starting to move heavy industries that pollute up into orbit, where they can dump their waste till the end of time without hurting anyone or anything. Earth is returning to the garden spot it once was and I see a day when it will be almost a park, sort of like those history museums where people live the way our ancestors did hundreds of years ago.

"Space isn't for everyone. But I think you'll all live to see the day when there are more people living beyond Earth, than down on it. I might even live to see that too, what with all we've learned about how it's easy to live to be a hundred and twenty or more once you get away from gravity and other such things. We've even got an instructor at this Academy, Professor McCain, who teaches space history, who was born in 1982 and she doesn't look a day over fifty."

Again there was a polite chuckle from the group.

"We've done a lot in my years, and there'll be a lot more to do in yours. Terraforming of Mars and Venus and ten thousand other projects are now on the drawing boards."

He lowered his head.

"And then there's the Tracs. We've met only three of their ships and all three meetings have been hostile. Perhaps this war is a mistake on their part, perhaps not. The one ship we destroyed, we're still working on."

Justin was taken by Thorsson's choice of the word "We" rather than "I." It was already legendary how, when the third Trac ship appeared eight years ago, Thorsson, in a single-seater Mark III, went out to meet the ship with a squadron of twenty other ships. He was the only one to survive, and it was his missile that had destroyed the mysterious invader from another solar system.

It was believed the Tracs came from somewhere in towards the galactic core. Who they were and their reason for visiting Earth's solar system was a mystery. Their first ship had appeared back in 2059, nearly fifteen years ago. Whoever was aboard had refused any communication, destroyed several of the Mars colonial cities and then left. A second ship appeared six years later and did similar damage to half a dozen colonies in the Jupiter and Saturn region.

The third ship was destroyed by a direct hit by Thorsson, and for the last eight years research teams had been painstakingly retrieving the often microscopic bits of wreckage scattered out beyond Saturn. Several thousand researchers were now working full-time putting the mysterious ship back together again, with other teams scouring the empty reaches of space, retrieving tiny bits of debris that had floated millions of miles from where the ship had been destroyed. The job was compared to looking for a handful of needles tossed out of an airplane across the entire Sahara desert.

The Tracs had the secret of how to manage transfer jump points. It was all rather strange science fiction type stuff to Justin, and a lot of folks still claimed it was theory, but there was evidence that the Tracs did not travel at faster than light speed. Rather they had found a means of somehow bending space, going through what were called "transfer jump points," and an instant later arriving dozens of light years away.

If the destroyed ship could ever be fully restored and examined, perhaps they might learn the secret of leaping out across the entire universe. The challenge was reassembling the pieces once they were found, since no one had the slightest idea of what a

Trac even looked like, let alone what fitted where inside their spaceships. Every year, half a dozen of the top cadets at the school were offered the chance to spend part of a semester working at the secret base where the remains of the Trac ship were stored. It was an assignment Justin hoped he could some-day grab.

"Sir, what's your theory about why the Tracs have shown up?"

Justin looked back at Madison, who had raised the question and then at Thor, caught off guard by the sudden question from the crowd.

"You know that any public discussion of the Tracs is forbidden and a violation of the Space Defense Security Act."

Madison nodded and smiled.

"That's why I'm asking you face-to-face, sir. It's a question I've always wanted to hear you answer and I guess here was my chance to grab it."

Justin looked over at Madison, amazed at her calm self-assuredness. He would never have dreamed of interrupting Thorsson, let alone ask a question about a topic wrapped up with such security measures.

Thor smiled.

"Okay, cadet, I admire your guts for asking me. The reason we forbid any open communication is that we suspect that the Tracs have monitored our radio and video transmissions. That's why we have to keep silent. We don't want them to know that we are even trying to reassemble one of their ships."

Justin smiled. The reassembling of the Trac ship was an open secret, even though no information about it could be transmitted. A small part of the ship had wound up in his mother's lab at Purdue University for analysis and she had received permission for him to take a peek at it. It was nothing more than a small section of a wing, nothing all that exciting-looking but still mysterious and even somewhat scary.

"My gut feeling is that they might have a colony fifty-odd light years out from here. At the turn of the century we were finally starting to get serious about going into space, but the information took fifty years at light speed for our transmission to get to where the Tracs were. So they sent some ships out to slow us down."

"What do you think will happen?" Madison asked.

"I suspect that their losing a ship shook them up a bit. It's been nearly eight years though. I think eventually they'll come back, maybe to fight, in order to keep space for themselves, maybe not. For all we know the ships we met might just be pirates or raiders and not even representative of the true government of whomever these people are. At least that's what I'd like to hope for.

"Satisfied, cadet?"

"A bit, sir," she replied with a winning smile.

"I take it you want to work on the Trac program."

"With translation of those book fragments we found, sir. I've got a pet theory it might have some connection with ancient Martian."

"I've heard that theory, cadet, and there might be something to it. Survive this first year at the Academy, work up a proposal that will show me that you can contribute something to the program and I'll see that you get assigned to the project next summer."

"Great!" Smith said with a grin, her voice going almost squeaky with excitement.

Thorsson smiled and looked back at the rest of the audience.

"That's what all of you've signed on for — the greatest adventure in the history of humankind — the exploration of space."

He paused for a moment, as if he was not sure if he should continue or not.

"There's one final thing I wish to mention here today," he finally said, his voice pitched low.

"Here it comes," Matt whispered.

"This Academy is under the command of the United Nations. It was established as a training school for cadets who would eventually serve either aboard United Nations ships, United Military Command or Solar System Defense. When you took your oath of enlistment, that is whom you made it to."

There was a nervous stirring in the room.

"To a bunch of hidebound bureaucrats," Matt mumbled coldly.

"What was that, cadet?"

Startled, Justin looked up and saw that Thor was staring straight at Matt.

Matt stood silently, looking up at Thor.

"I said, sir," Matt announced, his voice clear, filled with the drawl of a deep spacer, "that I made my oath to a bunch of bureaucrats. They don't understand us, they don't understand the colonies and they don't understand space."

An angry mutter swept through the room. Justin

looked around nervously, realizing that he was standing right next to his friend, and that every single person in the room was staring straight at them.

He saw a number of people around him start to edge away, not wanting to be associated in any way whatsoever with Matt when the lightning bolt came down from on high and took him out of the Academy.

Though he barely knew Matt, he would not abandon him and he stood his ground, even if he wasn't sure himself how he felt about what Matt was saying. He noticed as well that a scattering of cadets actually started to edge towards Matt, as if ready to stand beside him in support.

"What's your name, cadet?" Thor asked, and the hall went silent.

"Cadet Matt Everett, solar sailor off the *Corona Wind* and citizen of no nation but my own."

He said the words evenly, not showing any defiance, but not willing to back down either.

Thor stared at him.

"You've got guts, Cadet Everett. I like that in a cadet. I'll only ask you the same question I ask of all my cadets: as long as you are part of this team, will you live up to your oath?"

"I gave it and I'll live by it," Matt replied.

He paused for a moment.

"Until those on Earth force a break, sir, and then we'll all be choosing sides. But until that day, sir, I live by what I promise."

An angry murmur erupted from a number of cadets, while others now openly moved to step alongside Matt. Justin looked around, still not sure of where he himself should stand, and he turned his gaze up to the podium where Thorsson stood.

"Cadets, attenshun!"

Thorsson's voice boomed across the room, startling Justin, who snapped rigid, almost losing his balance and popping off the floor.

Thorsson waited for a long moment.

"I know there are some here who will call Cadet Everett a traitor for what he just said." Several voices echoed agreement and Justin saw that Tanya was one of them.

"I want silence and I'll not ask for it again!" Thorsson roared and the room fell quiet.

"Now hear this loud and clear, people. I will allow Cadet Everett this one chance to speak his piece. I offered him the chance to do so, and he had the guts to take it. I have no intention of punishing him for that. But I want to make this clear to all of you. We are a military branch dedicated to serving all people in this system from Earthers who never step foot off the planet, right out to the furthest miner and even the cultists and isolationists. All of them are under our protection and if need be we will die serving them whether they thank us for it or not.

"Mr. Everett has voiced what might be the greatest political crisis that has faced our species since the nuclear terrorists of the early 21st century, maybe even more crucial than the outside threat of the Tracs. It is the question of whether mankind will stay united as a political force or whether it will split apart in a Civil War between those who live on Earth and those who are going to the stars.

"That, people, is not the question we devote ourselves to here. You are free citizens, you have the right to think your own thoughts, even to debate them in your off duty time. But let me make it clear that it will not interfere with your duty to the service and to this Academy. If it does, I don't give a damn what side you are on, you are out of here.

"Do I make myself clear, people?"

The room was as silent as space.

Thorsson stared straight at Matt.

"Do I make myself clear, Mr. Everett?"

"Yes, sir, and thank you, sir, for letting me have my say."

Thorsson nodded and then looked back out at the group.

"Good luck to all of you. Dismissed."

The call for attention echoed through the room as Thorsson left the podium and with an easy stride started for the exit, walking down the length of the room. He drew alongside Justin, paused and then came over and extended his hand. Justin took it, surprised at the firmness of the grip.

"You've grown a bit since I last saw you, Justin. How's that grandfather of yours?"

"Fine, sir. He told me to send his regards."

"You've most likely heard the stories about him and me a hundred times already. But let me tell you, without your grandpa that expedition to Mars would have been wiped out. I was proud to serve with him."

He hesitated as if wanting to say more, and then with a friendly nod continued on.

Justin was amazed that Thor had even recognized

him, though the man's ability to remember names and faces was something of legend in itself.

Matt stood alongside Justin and hesitantly extended his hand.

"I didn't mean to cause any trouble, sir."

Thor took Matt's hand in reply.

"Don't ever underestimate the ability of an old man to hear comments from the crowd. It had to be discussed, cadet, and you gave me the opportunity to do it. Just honor your oath, son, that's all I'm asking, and your thoughts are your own."

"And, sir, what are your thoughts on it?" Matt asked, and Justin looked over at his friend in surprise, ready to kick him for putting his foot right into the fire again.

"My thoughts are my own, cadet."

Thor smiled, looked around at the group and then turned away heading for the main corridor, a cluster of staff stepping out from the back of the room to join him. Justin looked over at Brian and saw the admiration in the senior cadet's eyes. Brian looked over at him and there seemed to be a brief second of understanding, as if they were two friends sharing a nod of agreement over a common point of acceptance and then the cadet's eyes grew hard again.

"All right, scrubs, let's get you squared away in," Brian snapped. "Now move it!"

The squad fell into a double line, Brian badgering them all the way, and they followed the crowd back out into the main corridor. They finally edged their way up to an elevator and Brian shooed the group in.

"Make sure your shoes are fastened to the floor and hang on to your stomachs.

"Dormitory deck C," Brian announced and the elevator dropped out from under them.

Justin reached out and grabbed hold of Pradeep who started to shoot up towards the ceiling as the elevator fell, with more than one in the group groaning.

And then, ever so gradually, Justin felt gravity returning. It was so faint at first as to be barely noticeable.

"Where's the gravity coming from?" one of the scrubs asked, and Brian rolled his eyes.

"You get all the way to the Academy and you don't know how artificial gravity works?" he asked with disdain.

The scrub at the back of the elevator wilted under his gaze.

"The Academy ship is a rotating cylinder that's turning on its long axis. The docking bay we entered through and the domed auditorium line up right at the very center. The cylinder is spinning at one revolution every three and a half minutes. Because of the coriolis effect, if you are standing inside a spinning cylinder, the angular momentum of the spin actually creates an artificial gravity. It's just like those amusement park rides that spin you around and you wind up getting pinned to the outside wall of the ride even when they drop the floor out from under you. In the very center of the ship where the angular momentum is almost nonexistent we have nearly a zero gravity. Get to the middle deck sections, there's a greater angular momentum and we're up to a quarter gravity. Out at the furthest deck it's at half gravity. The pylons which extend out another hundred and fifty meters are for the exercise rooms which are at a little over one standard Earth gravity."

He paused for a second and then added disdainfully, "Every scrub should already know that."

"Hey, we're new here," Matt retorted, "so just take it easy on her."

Brian looked over at Matt and glared.

"I didn't ask for your opinion, scrub."

"I know you didn't."

Brian smiled coldly.

"Damn it, Everett, first you take on the old man, and he lets you live. But by heavens, boy, take me on and you're dead."

Justin could see that Matt was sizing Brian up and there was a cold light in Brian's eyes, as if daring him to try.

A smile finally flickered across Matt's face.

"You're the boss, Mr. Seay," he finally replied.

"You're the sailor, aren't you?"

"Yeah."

"That's 'sir' to you, scrub, until this summer is over."

"Yes, sir," and Justin was surprised that there was a tone of respect in his voice.

"Used to zero gravity, aren't you?"

"That's where I've been living, sir, when our ship wasn't on spin for artificial gravity."

"I'll see you in the flying court after chow and we'll see how good a spacer you really are."

He paused and looked around at his group.

"In fact, all of you report to deck A, court 21 at 1930 hours tonight."

"Suits me fine, sir," Matt replied, puffing his slender frame up as if expecting a fight at any second.

Brian ignored him and looked away.

"What's the flying court?" Justin asked in a whisper.

"Damned if I know," Matt replied.

The gravity started to increase and Justin looked over to a small meter on the elevator's control panel. It edged up past one-third Earth gravity.

"Dorm level C, let's move it, scrubs."

The door popped open unto a long corridor and written on a support beam over the corridor was a sign — "Scrub Alley."

The group moved out of the elevator with long bounding strides.

Justin looked back at Matt whose features were flushed, and he seemed to be moving heavily.

"I forgot how tough gravity is; the bearings in our centrifugal spin were getting old and we couldn't push it up past one-sixth," Matt gasped.

"It's only one-third Earth, the same as Mars," Justin replied, feeling as light as a feather and a lot better now that there was a definite up and down once again.

"Bell, Everett, Singh, room one, get in, get it squared away and be ready for chow in an hour."

Brian continued down the hallway, assigning rooms without even looking back. Justin, followed by his two roomies, went into their new home.

It reminded him of any typical dorm room back

on Earth: three beds set up in two bunks, with the lower bunk of the second bed converted into a holo display field, nearly six feet long and two feet deep. Three desks were at the back wall, portable notebook computers atop each desk. At a fourth desk was a standard computer terminal and a flat two-dimensional screen. Three closets lined the opposite wall with a small bathroom to one side.

Justin went over to the main computer desk and grinned.

"Say, we've got the latest computer equipment here. Fifty thousand giga core memory and a full holo field besides. This stuff is great!"

Pradeep settled in at the desk and looked back up at his two roommates.

"Let's check it out," he said and turned back to the computer's flat visual screen.

"Computer, display exterior of Academy Ship on the room's holo projector."

"User name please," the computer replied.

"Singh, Pradeep."

"Voice check confirmed, Cadet Singh," the computer replied. "Must advise though, Cadet Singh, that you are expected to make your bed, change into your class C uniform, which will be delivered shortly, and be prepared for dinner in one hour."

"Ah, come on," Justin cut in, "just a quick look to see what you can do."

"Is that Cadet Bell?"

"Of course you know it is, computer."

"The same advice stands for you as well," the computer replied.

"You're starting to sound like my mother," Pradeep replied. "Just get on with the demo."

"It's your problem then, not mine if you get demerits," the computer replied, a note of sarcasm drifting into its voice.

The holographic projection field beneath the bunk bed snapped to life.

"Damn, that's great," Matt shouted. "The holograph projector on *Corona*'s only a foot across."

"According to regulation 23–4A all cadets are to refrain from profanity," the computer snapped.

"Come on, you're not going to squeal on him, are you?" Justin asked.

"You know it is forbidden by law for a computer to report on the actions of humans, unless duly authorized by a sworn court order investigating felony criminal activities. That rule applies aboard this ship," the computer replied.

"Fine then," Justin replied, "just as long as we understand each other here. By the way, do you have a name?"

"Whatever name you want," the computer replied. "As long as it's not obscene," it quickly added. "Most of the cadets call me Uncle."

"All right, then, Uncle it is."

"Say, check out this projection," Matt said and Justin turned away from the flat screen to look.

Inside the holo projection field floated a three-dimensional image of the Academy ship, its resolution so fine that it appeared to be real. It was by far the best holo projection Justin had ever seen, beating even the latest systems at the University back home.

"This is great," Pradeep sighed, sitting down on the floor and suddenly pushing his hand into the model. His hand went right through the image, giving him the appearance of being almost godlike, as if reaching out to grab the ship.

"My resolution is two thousand lines per centimeter," Uncle said. "Screen projection alone requires over ten giga of memory space."

"Uncle," Justin asked, "take us into our room, via the docking port."

The image shifted, like a movie played at high speed. The ship turned, the aft end of the cylinder expanding. They appeared to go right through the side of the ship and then raced down a corridor, going into a turbo lift, and then dropped. A smaller side screen at the same time presented a map, tracing their route, until finally the image froze with an exact replica of their room floating before them.

"You have discovered one of my functions," Uncle said. "If you are not sure of where to go at any time, simply ask me and I will provide directions and, if need be, a hard copy map. There are over one hundred kilometers of corridors and forty three hundred and twenty one rooms aboard ship so it's rather easy to get lost at times. For example, this is the way to the dining hall for chow."

Uncle flashed the three-dimensional map on the screen, showing that the meal hall was a simple walk of several hundred meters down the corridor.

"Might I add, gentlemen, that you are expected there in 51 minutes. If you are late, I am certain that

Senior Cadet Seay will have your hides for his supper. I am shutting off now."

"Say, Uncle, do you have any good space combat simulators on board?"

"Some you haven't even seen before, including the latest Turbo Interceptor Three which I was just loaded with twenty-eight days ago," Uncle replied, sounding almost bored. "Now get to work," and the image of the ship disappeared.

"Boy, he can be really snotty," Pradeep said.

"I heard that," a voice whispered and Justin could not help but laugh at Pradeep's discomfort.

"So who sleeps where?" Pradeep asked.

"Coin toss," Justin replied and he pulled out a shiny half-dollar, the back of which commemorated mankind's first landing on the Moon, a good-luck piece that was an old family heirloom, the coin minted all the way back in the last century.

"Each of us flips at the same time, odd man gets first choice."

"What is this?" Matt asked, and laughing, Pradeep explained the old Earth custom of tossing the coin.

Justin loaned a coin to Matt and together they tossed at the same time. All three coins went straight up to the ceiling, where they seemed to hang. Matt watched, fascinated as gravity started to bring the coins back down at a leisurely fall of just a meter a second. Due to the effect created by the rotating ship, the coins didn't appear to fall exactly straight, but rather seemed to curve slightly, finally dropping nearly a meter away from the three cadets. The coins hit the floor, bounced back up and rolled around the room until at last they settled.

"Heads!" Pradeep announced.

"Heads for me too," Justin replied.

"Well, me buckos, I've got first choice, and it's the bottom bunk opposite the screen."

Pradeep and Justin flipped again with Justin calling a same match and he wound up winning the upper bunk across from the screen, while Pradeep drew the third slot of the bunk above the holo projector area.

The three set to making their beds and were interrupted by a knock on the door.

Opening the door up Matt felt a sudden tug of nostalgia for home. A service bot was in the hallway, pulling a cart loaded down with baggage.

The bot rolled its electronic eye up and looked at Matt.

"Cadet Everett, I presume?"

"How are you, bot?"

"I have your baggage, cadets. Inside each package you will find your uniforms already made to your size, and all other necessary personal gear. Dress for dinner is class C coveralls."

Matt called his roommates and together they unloaded their gear from the pull cart.

"Have a nice day," the bot chirped and continued down the hallway.

Matt picked up his bag.

"Darn, didn't realize it was this heavy," and Justin chuckled, feeling the exact opposite.

Unpacking their gear in their closets the three returned to making their beds. Finished at last, Justin could not suppress the temptation and he leaped straight up, soaring almost up to the ceiling, and then came back down to land on his upper bunk. Matt crawled into his bunk and lay down with a sigh.

"Ah, that's a load off me feet."

Justin closed his eyes for a moment and felt as if he was almost floating.

"Get off that bed right now!"

Justin opened his eyes, already knowing who was in the room.

Brian was staring straight at him.

"We was just taking a snooze," Matt drawled.

"Scrubs are only allowed to lie down in bed from 2200 hours till 0600!" Brian snapped.

"Hey, no one told us the rules," Matt replied.

"Get down this instant!"

Justin, moving too quickly for the one-third gravity, hit the ceiling before finally coming back down. Matt, however, simply rolled off, forgetting for a moment that he was no longer living in one-sixth gravity. He slowly spun over and smacked down on the floor headfirst, where Brian looked down at him coldly.

Reaching down, Brian tore the sheets off Matt's bed, and reached up to do the same to Justin's.

"Remake them, get into your class Cs, and be ready for chow in twelve minutes!" And he stormed out of the room.

"Something tells me I'm not going to like that guy," Matt said coldly, standing up and rubbing his head.

✧ Chapter III ✧

The switching around through gravities to get to the galley was not helping Justin when it came to digesting his first meal aboard the Academy ship. The food was standard for an orbital colony unit. Beef was extremely rare, for that matter so were most meats, except for chicken and rabbit, though the soybean substitutes were so good as to fool almost everybody. There were, however, plenty of fresh greens and dinner the first night was a vegetable stir fry, all the food grown aboard ship.

After dinner several second-year cadets took Justin's squad on a tour of the ship, going through the classroom and lecture hall area located in the one-half gravity section which was down on the lower decks, right next to the outer hull. From there the tour boarded a turbo lift which dropped down an extended pylon out to the one-point-three gravity area where the exercise and close combat training rooms were located. Justin found that even he was starting to sweat a bit from the strain of the heavier gravity, while Matt, who was used to the one-sixth artificial aboard his old ship, was positively dripping.

"All cadets are required to put in at least one hour a day in this area," an upperclassman announced, and Matt groaned with despair at the announcement.

"You'll be trained in hand-to-hand combat in all environments, from vacuum zero g, up to three g if you ever need to handle a situation while a ship is on thrust and you suddenly have a problem, like the terrorist incident aboard the patrol ship heading to the New Harmony colony last year."

Justin looked over at Matt, since what the cadet called a terrorist incident was viewed by the outworlders and separatists as the heroic stopping of a U.N. ship that was going out to subdue the radical separatist colony of New Harmony, which had announced its total secession from the U.N. colonial government. Matt let it pass without comment and, after a quick examination of the exercise and training rooms, the group took the turbo back up to the main part of the ship.

From there they went on a quick walk through the Academy's food production center, where fresh vegetables were grown, exposed to sunlight behind diamond-polymer windows. This section also served to recycle the ship's air, the plants taking out the carbon dioxide and replacing it with oxygen.

Growing up on a farm, Justin thought he'd feel

somewhat at home in this section but it was high tech beyond anything he had ever seen. No soil was used, the plants were grown in vast hydroponic water tanks. Stacked up in racks inside the fifteen-meter-high room, a dozen layers of soybeans, lettuce, tomatoes, sorghum and rice were growing one row atop another, exposed to sunlight twenty hours a day, with a dozen harvests a year. Several dozen acres worth of growing tanks produced five times as much food as his mother's four-hundred-and-eighty-acre farm back in Indiana.

The group then boarded another turbo up into the primary control center of the Academy. The group edged quietly through the main bridge where the technical staff monitored everything aboard the large cylinder floating in high lunar orbit. All other objects in orbit were closely monitored as were the thousands of tiny items of debris which had accumulated over the last seventy years, ranging from nuts and bolts, to lost cameras, titanium beams, food packets, a few baseballs, and on the more morbid side half a dozen bodies which had yet to be picked up from a transport explosion the year before. Closely watched as well were the incoming unknowns, which ranged from objects the size of grains of sand, up to a scattering of car-size boulders which if they should ever hit the Academy, or the more than three hundred other inhabited units in lunar orbit, would certainly ruin somebody's day.

An array of monitors were set as well to close observation of the sun, and were hooked in turn into the solar storm alert network. There was enough shielding wrapped around the kilometer-long cylinder to protect the inhabitants from a solar flare up to class three in intensity, but anything beyond that would require the evacuation of the outer hull areas and a class five, which hit roughly once every seven years, would necessitate everyone heading for the lead-lined storm shelters located along the B deck area. It reminded Justin of the old tornado and bomb shelter dug in alongside the house, which his great grandfather had built during what was now called The Time of Troubles in the early 21st century.

Other control systems monitored air purity and recycling in each of the more than four thousand rooms and hundred kilometers of corridors throughout the ship while yet other systems followed the flow of water, wastes, energy and ongoing maintenance. Most of the repair work was automated with hundreds of service bots, but more than a hundred noncommissioned personnel worked full-time to keep everything running. The ship's master control system even monitored the location of every person aboard since, if several thousand should decide to congregate in one spot, the delicate balance required for maintaining the spin which created artificial gravity would be thrown off. Therefore several hundred tons of water ballast was constantly being shifted back and forth by the computer, compensating for the movements of everyone on board.

One of the more crucial systems, which the tour was not even allowed to enter into, since it was a secured area, was the master system for maintaining pressure integrity, the door into the computer room being guarded by an armed marine. If the ship should ever suffer a serious hulling, the system would kick in, slamming down airtight doors and blocking off the rupture. It was, even aboard the Academy ship, a constant concern. Since the advent of the larger colonial units along the lines of the O'Neill Cylinder, of which the Academy was only of medium size, it had become possible for one individual, either demented or motivated by some grievance, to snuff out an entire colony by seizing control of the pressure integrity computer, blowing the secondary backups and then breaching the hull. The worst such incident, caused by a crazed postal worker, four years back, had killed nearly thirty thousand. It was yet another reason for the existence of the military in space, to protect colonies from such attacks.

The tour finished up and the squad headed for A deck, the zero-gravity section in the center of the ship. Following Tanya, the group got thoroughly lost, and an argument started to break out until Justin stopped at a hallway computer terminal to ask Uncle for directions.

Justin wished he could somehow hold on to his stomach as the elevator gravity meter gradually ticked back to zero. He looked over at Matt who sighed with relief and broke into a grin.

"Ah, back home again," he laughed as the door opened and they floated out into the huge open space which was located in the exact center of the ship.

The circular corridor was packed with hundreds of scrubs who floated around aimlessly, most of them holding on to hand railings, while others moved with slow deliberate steps using their zero-gravity sticky boots.

"There you are. I said 1930 hours and it's five minutes after."

Brian Seay looked over at the group with a sardonic grin, half a dozen other senior cadets around him.

"Hey, is that straight-shooter?" one of them, a tall slender girl with an Irish accent, quipped.

Brian's features reddened.

"Great shot, cadet. I'd have paid good money to see it!" the Irish girl laughed, her features breaking into an open smile.

"Yeah, Sharon, I heard two of your new scrubs did the same to you," Brian snapped in reply.

"But not in the face, Brian, definitely not in the face."

"So what's this little zero-gravity game?" Justin asked, and the other seniors started to laugh again.

"Let's go," Brian said and he pushed off down the corridor, the seniors following the group, floating effortlessly along.

The wide circular corridor echoed with shouts, laughter and more than one groan from a scrub. Listening in on snatches of conversation Justin picked up that this was the favorite gathering place of the Academy cadets in the off hours period from 1930 through 2200 hours, at least when the studies weren't too hard. The corridor ran down the entire length of the ship and was lined with recreation rooms, and training facilities for life in zero gravity.

Justin looked over at Sharon, who smiled at him.

"Brian seems to have it in for you and your loud-mouthed friend," she said quietly.

"Yeah, we didn't want it this way."

"Tell your friend there to mind his talk. There's a lot of separatist sympathy in the corps," she said softly, "but a lot of us still see Earth as home and are loyal to it."

"Us?" Justin asked.

"Myself, yes. Ireland's my home. For me the colonies exist for the ninety-eight percent of the human population still down there," and she gestured vaguely off, as if she could somehow sense where Earth was outside the walls of the ship.

"If the separatists break away and form their own governments, they could cut us off from the resources that we need from off planet in order to keep the show going. Earth would go into chaos if the colonies had their way.

"Where do you stand on it, by the way?" she asked.

"Frankly, I'm not even sure," Justin replied.

Sharon smiled as if he was an innocent child.

"You'll be choosing sides soon enough."

"Where do you think Thorsson stands?" Justin asked.

Sharon laughed.

"He'll never say, though my gut feeling is that he's with the deep spacers."

"Think that's why he let Matt off the hook today?"

"Like hell," she snapped. "Thorsson plays it fair right down the middle. If anyone causes trouble, from either side, they're out of here. I've seen more than one get the boot for starting up a fight over the question, and you'd better tell your friend that, 'cause the word is out about him and there's more than one Earther who would love to get a piece of him."

Surprised, Matt looked over at her and she smiled again, the hard edge in her voice gone.

"Look, scrub, a word to the wise. You and your buddy should stick to the books. You'll have more than enough time to worry politics later. And what the hell, the Tracs might come back at any time, kick all our butts back into the Stone Age and then who will care?"

"If Mr. Seay doesn't get me first," Justin said quietly.

Sharon laughed.

"Well, scrub, I guess all seniors sort of have it in for scrubs at the start. Just grit your teeth and bear it out. It's tradition, and it's also to see what you're made of. Just hang tough and you'll get through it all right."

She flashed a friendly smile.

"Thanks."

"You'll do all right. I've heard about you before. You're Jason Bell's son, aren't you, the kid who got the Medal of Honor appointment?"

"Yeah, that's me," Justin said quietly.

"It's a heavy load, Justin. I know, I've been there."

"You?"

"Sure. Hey you're not the only one here with a Medal of Honor appointment. There're fifteen of us at the Academy counting you," Sharon said, her voice friendly.

"I'm sorry, I didn't know."

"It's all right. My father got his medal dying the month before I was born. I never even knew him. I felt like everyone was looking at me at first, judging me against my father. But it turned out all right. I think you'll like it here."

"I hope so," Justin replied quietly, finding it difficult to talk to someone who was floating alongside him, while he clumsily moved along in his zero-g boots.

"Wait until you see Deck A when the fall semester starts," Sharon said with a smile. "For the summer there's only you scrubs and the upperclassmen advisors. Nearly everyone else is off on their summer research projects but come September close to four thousand cadets return for course work before heading back out on their field assignments at mid-year. The place feels empty right now without them. I just got back yesterday to work with a squad of scrubs. For the spring semester I was working on the Mars archaeology sites providing security and rescue support for a dig."

"There's a girl in our group, Madison Smith, who'd love to talk to you about that one," Justin said.

"Tell her to look me up, I got some great holo photos of some new inscriptions they've just uncovered. They're estimated to be nearly fifteen million years old, from the last dynasty period. Only a couple of researchers have seen them so far."

"She'll love it."

Sharon nodded to a group of scrubs waiting just ahead.

"There's my group. Just hang in there like I said and by September you'll be handling zero g and everything else like a pro."

She stopped before the scrubs who were waiting by a door and at the sight of them she immediately launched into a steady stream of taunts and curses. The change caught Justin off guard and he pushed on down the corridor, following Brian.

Sections of the corridor were made of clear plastic, giving Justin the feeling that he was floating inside a tube, similar to the one his pet hamsters used to run through back at home. He passed over a large open room directly below. A game of what looked to be zero-gravity soccer was being fought out, the players bouncing off the walls, floating after the ball, using small hand-held maneuvering units that shot jets of compressed air so they could move around.

In the next room he caught a brief glimpse of a group practicing gymnastics and from yet another room he could barely hear the strains of classical music, a group of cadets performing a zero-gravity ballet, tumbling through the air, an audience of about ten cadets watching through clear Plexiglas windows.

He stopped for a moment to watch. It was something he never admitted to his friends at school, that he actually liked classical music. The music was one of his favorites, "The Ride of the Valkyries," by Wagner and even though it wasn't ballet music, it seemed to really fit out here in space. Strobe lights flashed in the room and jets of smoke shot out from wall vents. The dancers were in white costumes so that one second they looked like red demons flying through smoke and the next second they appeared to hover like blue angels.

Down in the bottom of the room dancers dressed

like ancient Viking warriors appeared to fight and as they died the Valkyries swooped down and took them to the top of the room, rising up on a rainbow created by a prism that projected a shaft of light into the room.

The performance put a chill down his spine. He caught a glimpse of Thorsson, grinning with delight, watching the show from a window on the other side of the room. He wanted to linger and watch the rest of the show but his group was moving on. He lifted off the floor and pushed himself along by holding on to a handrail in order to catch up. He noticed from the corner of his eye that Tanya had stopped to watch as well and as he floated towards her she quickly pushed off and caught up with the group.

In the next room he caught a quick glimpse of a dance going on, this time to the thumping wail of more modern music, the dancers floating and gyrating around the room. No one seemed to have a partner, everyone was just moving to the music and obviously having a grand time doing it.

The corridor echoed with laughter and shouts, filling up with yet more cadets in their off hour, the stripes on their sleeves showing them to be of all rankings from second-year prep straight through final year cadets, with a mixture of academy instructors and officers sprinkled in. It was easy to see who were veterans, and who were not. The scrubs kept bouncing off the corridor walls, getting in other people's way, a few of them still looking rather green even though they had been wearing their anti-sickness patches for over two days now.

Brian stopped at a doorway and turned back to face the group.

"All right, scrubs, the name of the sport is falcon fighting. Pick up your wings inside."

He punched the door open and they floated into a small anteroom. The walls were lined with folded wings and Justin looked around eagerly. Falcon fighting had just been declared an Olympic Sport in last year's third space sports Olympiad, and the winners of both the silver and gold were cadets. For that matter half of all medals won in the games went to cadets. It suddenly dawned on Justin and he looked over at Brian, his momentary dislike forgotten, and saw the small silver and blue bar pinned over his left breast pocket.

"Now I know where I've seen you before. You won the Silver medal for solo combat in last year's games."

"Yeah, that's me," Brian said quietly, and then ignored him, obviously not wishing to discuss the issue any further.

"Each of you take down a set of red wings," Brian said, "one size fits all, just put them on. The same with the helmets."

Heart racing, Justin first strapped a helmet on and then pulled a set of red wings off the wall, where they were held on by velcro. Each wing was like a small fan, the slats folding in on each other when closed, and expanding out into curved lifting surfaces when opened. He slowly opened them up, while staying firmly anchored to the floor with his sticky-bottomed shoes. On the bottom side of each wing was a long cylinder and he slipped his arms into the cylinders so that the wings rested on his back and shoulders. At the tail end of the wings was a belt and he clumsily reached around behind himself and snapped the belt around his waist, pulling the wings down tight against his back.

"Hit the button at the end of the cylinders and it will adjust to your size, giving you a tight fit. If you do it right the wings will almost feel like they're part of your body," Brian said.

Justin followed his instructions and the cylinder inflated, feeling like the cuff of a blood pressure gauge that was hooked up from his shoulders right down to his wrists.

Brian, looking over at him, nodded and motioned for him to head to the next door.

"Wait for me on the other side," Brian said.

Justin went up to the door, punched the open button and stepped through — out into an open room where the floor was twenty meters straight down.

He felt his stomach knot up for a moment as he floated out and looked around. The room was another cylinder, nearly fifty meters long and twenty across.

Nervously he spread his arms out and then pulled them back down to his side. The wings on his back opened like a bird's and then snapped shut again. He felt a small burst of speed and he slipped forward. He tried it again and his speed increased. He opened his left arm out, keeping his right arm at his side, and he spun over onto his back. He continued to roll until he did the same motion again, this time with his right arm, and the rolling stopped.

"Hey, everybody, I'm a bird!"

He looked back and saw Madison leaping out through the door, laughing with delight. She beat her wings several times, and arching her back she started to climb up to the top of the room. Other cadets followed, some acting as clumsy as Justin now felt, others a bit more graceful, especially Tanya who came through the doorway and immediately pulled a spiraling loop. Even though she was obviously showing off, Justin could not help but look at her admiringly. He found it hard to reconcile the fact that she was extremely attractive with her nasty remarks to him. But as she floated past him, her dark hair streaming out behind her, he felt a little tug in his heart.

"She sure is a show-off."

Justin looked down and saw Matt coming up by his side, extending his wings to break his forward movement, and Justin quickly nodded an agreement.

"So, Earthling, what'ya think of flying?" Matt asked with a grin.

"Awesome!" Justin laughed, and he started into a steady flapping, picking up speed.

"Hey, watch out for the wall!" Matt cried.

So intent was he on looking around the room, and watching the others, that Justin didn't even notice what was coming up until he smacked straight into the padded wall and for an instant saw stars. He rebounded backwards, turning a somersault, and winced when he heard Tanya's derisive laugh. Embarrassed, he looked over at Matt who floated up beside him, laughing as well.

"I used to do this inside an abandoned ore tanker

on Ceres that they had pumped full of air. It was a hundred meters across and three hundred meters long. Boy, you could build up some speed inside of that thing. This is a bit tighter, though. The other thing you've got to remember is that at the top of the room, which is located along the center axis of the ship, it's zero gravity, but if you get down at the outer edge, it's a bit further out from the center of the ship and there is a light touch of gravity down there. I guess it's not much more than one-twentieth of a g but it will still affect how you fly."

"All right, people, gather round."

Following Matt, Justin made his way back to the small landing perch by the door where Brian stood waiting, a set of blue wings tucked under his arm.

"Each of you take a ribbon and hook it around your ankle. Make sure the sensor strip on the end is hooked up so that your computer will register that you are active and in the game."

He tossed a bright red streamer, several meters long and ten centimeters wide, to each person in the group. Justin grabbed one, took the velcro end of the streamer and hooked it around his right ankle. He made sure the thin metal strip Brian had mentioned was hooked together and as he did so, three beeps sounded in his headset, letting him know that the computer had registered that he was now activated for the game.

Brian held up a blue streamer and then looked around at the group floating before him.

"The rules of the game are simple. We're going to have a light game of falcon fighting, using basic rules.

It's like old style airplane to airplane dogfighting. In the Olympics we do it in one-sixth gravity, Moon standard, since the sport was invented there. Here in zero gravity it's a bit safer.

"I'll stand off against all of you for this first game. You try to yank the streamer off my ankle, I'll try to get yours. Once your streamer's been pulled you are dead and out of the game.

"Watch out for the walls, they're padded but you can still break an arm." He hesitated and looked over at Justin. "Or your head if you don't pay attention."

Tanya and several of the others laughed and Justin felt himself blushing again.

"There's a computer monitor attached to your wings. Once your streamer has been yanked off your computer will set off a high-pitched tone in your headset letting you know you're dead. It will continue to sound until you go into the end zones," and he pointed to the far ends of the court, where an interlocking web of laser beams intersected in a grid pattern, marking off the last three meters of either side as neutral corners.

"A flashing light will flash on the back of your wings as well to mark you as dead. If you attempt to make a kill after you are dead, you'll receive a mild electric shock when you touch another player's streamer. In the heat of the game you might forget yourself so the computer does that to make sure you understand that you're out of it. It also keeps you honest. If you yank the streamer anyhow you are in deep trouble, so pay attention to when you've been eliminated.

"Contact against another person in the basic game,

either on your side or your opponent's, is forbidden. If your computer judges that you are at fault you are then out of the game. The more advanced games allow contact but I don't think you're ready for that yet so we'll keep it simple for starters.

"Any questions?"

"Yeah, just one," Matt drawled.

"Sir," Brian said coldly.

"Just one, sir."

"And that is?"

"What do we get if we beat you, sir?"

Brian grinned.

"You won't."

"But what if we do, sir?"

"I'll make all your beds for three days straight if that'll make you happy."

The group cheered.

"But if I win, you scrubs better shape up into the best damn squad in this summer session, and I mean the best in rules, discipline, and course work, or I'll truly make your lives miserable, is that understood?"

The group was now silent.

"You all head down to the far end zone and I'll take the other side. When the buzzer sounds you have five seconds to clear the end zone. If, at any-time after that, you drift into the end zone, the lasers will trigger your computer and you are out of the game. Make sure your faceplates are down and your helmets are secure. Now move it!"

Matt weaved his way down to the far side of the playing field and crossed through the laser beam grid. He floated to the very end of the court, braking gently, and then stuck his foot out so that the sticky bottom adhered to the wall. The rest of his section joined him so that there were twenty-one scrubs looking around at each other nervously.

"Any of you guys play this before?" Madison asked.

"Yeah, I have," Matt said quietly.

"I've won dozens of matches, I'll captain the team," Tanya interjected.

"Oh, really?" Madison replied.

"Yes, really," Tanya said coldly. "Remember, I lived on the Moon where the game's a lot tougher in gravity."

"Get ready," Brian's voice echoed down from the other side of the playing field.

"Form into groups of three, we'll do it by roommates. When he approaches, go into a spiraling circle, cover each other's tail, that way when he goes for one of you the person behind you can knock him off. My group will go straight up first, the other six groups form a clockwise spiral behind me."

"Thanks for the advice," Matt said quietly.

"It's not advice," Tanya retorted. "It's an order and it's the way to win."

"Yes, sir, Leonov, sir," Matt quipped.

A high-pitched buzzer sounded, and confused, Justin looked around, not sure of what it meant.

"Go!" Tanya shouted. "Follow me!"

She lifted off, going straight in and not looking back.

"Stick close to me," Matt shouted and he broke to the left, Pradeep tucked in close behind him.

Justin beat his wings, his sticky shoes holding him

down for several seconds until he broke free and clumsily cleared the laser grid into the playing field. He looked around in confusion and heard a number of beepers snap off, Pradeep and two other cadets all shouting angrily at each other, for the collisions which caused them to be disqualified from the game. Back in the end zone several more players were flopping around, never even clearing the end zone, their lights flashing on their backs, signalling that they had not made it out in five seconds and were already out of the game.

Where's Brian? Justin wondered, and then he heard another shout. Looking over his shoulder he saw a flash of blue wings, back down from where they had started. The senior cadet was already circling back up, skimming the end zone, four red streamers in his hand.

Half the group was already dead and they weren't even thirty seconds into the game.

"Yo, matie!"

Justin looked around and saw Matt up at the other end of the room where Brian had started, waving for him to join up. Justin beat his wings, arching his back, and started to climb.

"To your left, Justin!"

Justin looked over and saw Brian circling in for the kill. He fought down a sense of panic, pulled in his left arm and started to beat furiously with his right. He spiraled over, pulling a tight corkscrew turn and Brian shot past below him, just missing his red streamer by inches.

Out of the corner of his eye Justin saw Matt diving

down, almost catching Brian's streamer in turn. Laughing, Brian rolled over, pulling a somersault and where his legs had been he was now waiting with outstretched hand. He yanked Matt's streamer off.

It had only taken a matter of seconds and even as he watched he saw Brian turning to come up after him. Justin started to fly hard and an instant later he felt a tug on his leg — he was out of the game.

Glumly, he moved up to end zone, where Tanya and the others were already waiting.

"If you'd listened to me we would have beat him," Tanya snapped peevishly.

"Ah, shut up," Matt replied.

"Don't tell me to shut up," and Tanya's features went bright red.

"Rather than arguing couldn't we figure out how to beat this guy?" Justin interjected.

"Who asked you?" Tanya retorted. "I already told you how to beat him."

"He's not giving us enough time to plan," Justin said softly. "We don't have time for anything elaborate, we've got to figure out something simple."

Justin could not help but suspect that this casual game was in some ways a test, allowing Brian to observe the group under stress to see if they would pull together or not in their first day at the Academy.

Another shout of dismay echoed from the playing field and the group looked back to see four more of their comrades succumb to Brian's graceful swooping turns. Finally Madison was the only one left flying, the other players floating dejectedly inside the end zone.

"She weighs too much, she's too clumsy," Tanya snapped.

"Well, she sure as the devil lived longer than you did," Matt replied sharply.

Brian broke away from an attack, swooped across the room, turning with precision so that he missed the opposite wall by inches. Arcing back over, he came straight at Madison who was attempting to follow him and he snap rolled in a ninety degree turn as if winging over into another dive. Madison turned to follow him. With a quick flick of his wings Brian shot back up, skimming over Madison's back and a second later her red streamer was in his hand.

A groan of disappointment went up from the group.

Brian circled back around Madison.

"Good game, kid," and she grinned happily as he tossed her streamer back.

"Thought I had you for a second," she replied with mock seriousness. "I'm lucky I lived as long as I did."

"Another game?" Brian cried, and the group, shouting their approval as Brian swooped into the end zone, dropped the captured streamers and then started back to the far side of the court.

"Nice try, Madison," Justin said, coming up beside her.

Breathing heavily she looked over at him and smiled.

"He just got around to me last, that's all," she said quietly.

Justin smiled at her shy modesty. Except for Matt she was obviously the most skilled flyer in the squad.

"Now remember, stick together by threes," Tanya shouted.

Justin rolled his eyes.

"She's actually right," Madison said quietly. "It's just we haven't worked together as a team yet and we don't have the time to practice."

The group settled down in the end zone and waited for the computer to signal the start of the next game.

"All right, everyone," Justin said quietly, "there's no time for arguing. Tanya's right. Get with your roommates. When the buzzer sounds, lift off slowly, avoid hitting each other and let him come to us."

Tanya looked over at Justin.

"Glad you finally realized," she said.

"Chill out, Tanya," Justin replied, "we're on the same side."

"Oh, really, straight-shooter?" and again she gave him that mischievous grin.

He couldn't decide at the moment if he was really starting to hate her or not.

The buzzer sounded.

"Move slowly now," Madison said, "come on people, no collisions."

The group lifted off from the end zone, only one of them failing to get through the laser grid within the five-second time limit.

Brian came down fast, shouting a bloodcurdling scream. He shot between two of the groups, reaching out with both hands as he passed. Two red streamers were snapped off, the two groups closing in on him. Several buzzers clicked on as the two sections collided with each other. Laughing, Brian pulled up and away, making another kill and Justin had to chuckle as he heard Tanya's angry curse at being knocked out. In the confusion the groups fell apart, turning into a confused swirling mass.

"Come on, scrubs, get with it!" Brian shouted, "you're making it too easy on me."

Within a couple of minutes Matt and Justin were the only two left.

"Stick to me like glue," Matt whispered, and he moved over to a wall while Brian floated just beyond their reach.

"All right, scrubs, it's just you and me," Brian said quietly.

"Stay close to the wall, move down very slowly so your streamer floats up behind you," Matt whispered.

Justin did as his friend suggested.

Brian swept down past them and arced back out. He pulled straight at them, breaking at the last second and turning down. Matt shook his head for Justin to stay put.

Brian came to a stop in the middle of the chamber and floated in front of the two.

"The best defense won't bring a win," Brian said, "it's offense that takes the game."

"Just watching," Matt said quietly, "trying to figure out your style."

A thin smile creased Brian's features.

He dodged forward, landing right next to Matt and almost swept up Matt's streamer. Matt broke free from the wall. Brian pushed off after him. Justin leaped out as well, straining to grab Brian's streamer in turn, but Brian was too fast. Brian pulled away from the two and started back down the court.

"All right, let's get him," Matt shouted, and the two started off in pursuit. Matt's skill at the game quickly became evident as he stayed close to Brian's tail, while Justin struggled to keep up. Reaching the end of the court Brian arced up and over, Matt following. Justin turned as well, just barely missing the end zone. They raced back down the court, their speed building up, and Justin doggedly followed in pursuit. They swept past the end zone where their teammates watched, cheering them on. Brian swept down and then pulled straight back up, cutting behind Justin with a lightninglike strike, taking his streamer. Seconds later he nailed Matt as well.

The three drifted to a stop in the center of the court.

"Standard tactic," Brian said easily, while Justin hovered before him, panting for breath. "If you're outnumbered, let them chase you. Your opponents' blood will get up, they won't stick together, and then you simply pick them off. The trick, of course, is to be able to fly faster than those chasing you."

He paused for a second and looked at Matt.

"You show promise, kid. Practice and you might make the varsity."

Justin looked at Brian as the senior tossed him his streamer. He was expecting some sort of positive comment for hanging in to the end of the game but Brian said nothing to him and turned away to start back down the court for another game.

"Mr. Seay."

Brian looked back up to the entry door where

Senior Cadet O'Malley floated, a set of blue wings tucked under her arm.

"Care to pit your squad against mine?"

Brian smiled and looked back at his squad.

"All right, people, we're facing off against first squad Company A, Sharon O'Malley's group of scrubs."

A happy shout went up from the players as they hooked their streamers back on. Justin looked up at the platform and recognized the senior cadet as the one who had been friendly to him in the corridor. She gave him a cheery wink and then turned back to her scrubs, shouting out commands.

Brian flew up to the perch and landed, going inside to change his wings. A group of scrubs, wearing blue wings, started to float out into the playing field.

"I'd like to have finished another game with him," Matt said quietly. "I think I've got him figured out."

"Hey, he did win the Silver Medal last year," Justin replied.

"Yeah, but that was last year. Three years from now who knows?" Matt said with a smile.

Justin moved down to the red end of the playing field and looked up to where the blue team was forming. Most of them flew as clumsily as he did, while their senior cadet fluttered around them, giving last-minute advice.

"Hey, Sharon!"

Brian stood in the entry doorway, a set of red wings now on his back.

"How about a class two playing field with limited contact?"

Sharon hesitated and looked at her cadets.

"Hell, Brian, most of them have only had wings on for less than an hour."

"They've got to learn sometime. Remember the scrub company championship is only seven weeks off."

Justin looked over at Matt.

"The big game," Matt said quietly, "the entire scrub regiment, all eight companies play off against each other the week before finals. I hear most of the seniors bet their entire summer's pay on the game and heaven help the companies that lose."

Sharon hovered with her group and hesitated for a second.

"All right, but only class two and just light contact."

Brian disappeared from view.

"This is going to be great," Madison announced.

Justin looked around, suddenly hearing what sounded like rushing air. The walls of the playing field started to distort, sections of it inflating outward, other sections pulling further away, and within seconds the flat round interior of the playing field was transformed into a jumble of dozens of rectangles five to seven meters high, so that the entire inside surface of the game court was transformed into a maze of valleys and hills.

Brian came back out from the perch and flew down to where his team waited.

"All right, red team, gather round and listen up, we've only got a couple of seconds.

"You might think that weaving through the valleys created by the blocks is the trick but it isn't. We've got to control the open space in the center of the field. Once we've got that, we can track down anyone hiding in the valleys. Choose a partner, and stay close. When we start, move as a group to the center, don't get pulled down into the valleys. Fancy maneuvering is out, slash in hard, get above and behind your opponent and yank their streamer. Then keep on going; if you get caught up in a swirling dogfight, unless you really know what you're doing, you'll get caught. The rules allow light contact, but if your computer judges a use of excessive force you're out of the game."

He looked up to where the blue team was gathered.

"Ready, Sharon?"

"Ready."

The start buzzer kicked off.

"Go!"

With an exuberant shout Brian lifted straight up, his group following him. The blue team broke into two halves, moving to either side. Brian continued straight up through the center, watching as the two sections of blue swung outward.

"Straight to the top!" Brian shouted.

They continued on through and Justin realized the soundness of the move. If they had decided to dive on one section the other would have closed in on them from behind. They weren't skilled enough yet to maneuver as a coordinated team. The group reached the top of the field and Brian arced back over, now skimming down along one wall, staying just above the jumble of inflated blocks sticking out from the wall. The two blue teams had both turned, and Sharon was shouting for them to rejoin in the center.

"Break through on the left," Brian cried.

Justin, thoroughly confused in the zero-gravity environment, wasn't sure which direction was left or right, since he was now flying sideways in relationship to Brian but he followed his lead anyhow as they cut up and struck into the rear of one of the blue sections.

Beepers started to kick off, yellow lights flashing on the backs of wings, and within seconds four players were down, with Pradeep the only casualty so far for the red team. Justin, in the middle of the pack, wasn't even sure what happened. All he saw for a brief instant was a leg and a blue streamer and he grabbed hold, tugging it loose.

"Confirmed strike," his computer whispered in his ear and, grinning, he let the streamer go and continued on as Brian dove straight down to where they had started. Justin looked over his shoulder and saw all of blue team in pursuit. Brian started to curve out, following the slope of the field, skimming just above the blocks, and then he dove into a valley and swung around the base of a block, reversing direction.

Justin tried to keep up, and slapped into the side of a hill so hard that he thought he had broken a wing. He spun off to one side and saw a blue player closing in on him. A red wing snapped past and he saw Madison streaking back upwards, dropping the blue player's streamer.

Recovering from the spin, Justin looked around. Most of his team was halfway back up the side of the field, casualties turning to head back to the end zones, where cheering sections were urging their teammates on.

Justin started off in pursuit, beating his wings, pulling a quick spin to check that no one was above him. He felt vulnerable out in the middle of the court without any escort. The battle had broken down into a series of chases through the checkerboard-like field of peaks and valleys. Picking his target, Justin dove straight down, lined up and pounced a blue player, her streamer fluttering behind her. He yanked it clear, almost smacking into a wall as he pulled back out. The blue player looked up at him and flashed a downcast but still friendly smile.

"Never even saw you," she shouted, her green eyes flashing, and Justin found himself swallowing hard, almost feeling a quick sense of guilt for knocking her out of the game.

"Ah, yeah, ah I guess that's how it goes," he muttered and he dropped her streamer. He felt a hand brush against his leg and startled, he looked back to see a blue player struggling to grab his streamer, even as he floated downward. Justin pulled his legs in with a jerk, flapped his wings, and somersaulted over. Not even quite realizing how he did it he nailed his third player, dropped the streamer and continued on.

The court was nearly empty and as he looked to his end zone, to his astonishment, he saw Brian floating with the group.

Across the court he saw Matt, and Tanya, and

above he saw only two blue players left, but one of them was Sharon.

The two blues moved up to the top of the field and Justin quickly moved over to join his two comrades.

"All right, now what?" Justin asked, still breathing hard.

"Go straight in," Tanya replied.

"Not that easy," Matt replied, looking up warily at Sharon. "She took out Brian and three others."

"Sacrifice," Justin said quickly. "I'm the least experienced of the three of us. I'll move ahead of you two, try to get in her way, and if she goes for me you two make the kill."

"Here they come," Tanya said.

"Follow me then," Justin replied and he started straight up at her.

He spared a quick look back and saw his two teammates closing in behind him.

He threw all his strength into flying, beating his wings, feeling his speed increase with each stroke. Everything else was forgotten for a brief moment and he felt a strange sense of joy as he flew like a hawk, rising up into the heavens. Sharon came straight down. At the last second he cut straight out in front of her. She dived past, curving inward, reaching out to snatch his streamer. He quickly jerked his legs in, pulling the one maneuver he had already mastered, turning head over heels. Even as he did so the other blue player came past and reaching out, Justin took his opponent's streamer with a sharp pull. A shout went up from the crowd and Justin turned over hard. Everything seemed to blur.

He wasn't sure if he saw a blue wing ahead or not but he reached out anyhow and grabbed hold, pulling hard.

He felt another streamer pull loose and a bedlam of cheers and groans echoed in the playing field.

Confused, he looked around even as he started to turn back up, not sure if the game was still on. He saw Sharon turning away, the blue streamer behind her gone, beside her Matt and Tanya.

The other players started to fly back out onto the field and he braked to a hover.

"Hell of a game, straight-shooter."

Justin looked back and saw Madison coming up beside him.

"What happened?"

"I'll tell you what happened," Tanya snapped, coming up beside him. "So much for your sacrifice move. You tucked your legs in, she diverted from you and nailed Matt and me. Thanks a lot."

"Hey, our team won, didn't we?" Matt interjected. "It doesn't matter who makes the kill as long as we win. It was a great maneuver."

"Frankly, I'm not even sure what I did," Justin whispered, hovering up by his friend's side.

"Don't tell anyone," Matt said with a grin.

"Hey, straight-shooter, where'd you learn that trick?" Sharon asked, coming up to float by Justin.

"I just sort of did it," Justin replied, somewhat embarrassed by all the attention.

"Keep it up and I'll see you at the Olympics," she said with a grin and reaching out, she shook his hand.

"Hell, you're the one who won the gold in the singles competition."

"The same," she replied. "Hey, Brian, we've got competition here with straight-shooter. That's a good name for him. He might save our money for us in the big game."

Brian floated up beside Justin and looked at him appraisingly.

"Maybe, just maybe, if he survives being a scrub first."

Again, Justin wasn't sure if Brian had looked at him with approval or disdain. The senior cadet turned and started back to the perch.

"Twenty-one hundred hours, head back to your rooms, scrubs. Tomorrow morning comes at 0600 and with it your first day of classes, now move it."

"You know, I can't figure that guy out," Matt said. "I'm not sure if he hates us, likes us, or just doesn't care."

"He's a tough one to figure, that's for sure," Madison interjected, floating up to join the two as they started back to the perch.

"Say, Madison, do you know who that green-eyed girl is?" Justin asked, nodding towards the crowd of blue players.

"Thanks, Justin, I thought you were interested in me," she replied. For a second he felt embarrassed and then realized that she was grinning.

"She's from the Moon. Sue Mannheim, that's all I know."

"And she's already got a boyfriend back home," Tanya interjected as she floated by.

"Thanks for the input there, Miss Expert," Matt replied. Tanya looked back, laughed, stuck out her tongue and then continued on.

There're a lot of people here I can't figure out if I like or not, Justin thought to himself.

❖   ❖   ❖

The first few days at the Academy were something of a blur to Justin. The day started at 0600, with inspection of rooms at 0630, with breakfast till 0700. From there they headed to the exercise pylons for a rough hour-long workout which was just PT for starters but promised to turn into the basics of hand-to-hand combat by the end of the summer. Justin never could figure out why they did the PT after breakfast, since he found that he darn near lost his meal from the exertion and that when it was finished he was near to starving. After a quick shower they headed back into the main part of the ship for classes which started at 0830. There were no excuses for being late, other than being dead.

The academic day started with the History of Space Exploration, which for Justin was a breeze. Professor McCain was the oldest member of the faculty, born the year after the first shuttle was launched, and was still spry at ninety-two thanks to having spent the last forty years living in space. Her classes were made even more interesting by the simple fact that she had witnessed darn near everything that had happened since the late 20th century and even impressed Tanya by having once met her famous great-grandfather.

Next came Procedures and Rules of the United

Space Service, run by Professor Hazler, an owl-eyed stickler for details. For Justin it was one of the most boring classes he had ever been forced to sit through, requiring, first off, the memorization of the 21 General Orders of the Service. The first night after class Brian had come into their room just prior to lights out and demanded that Justin, Pradeep and Matt recite the first five from heart. Needless to say, they all flubbed it, and wound up scrubbing their bathroom with toothbrushes until 0100. The only consolation was that the following morning Justin discovered that everyone in his squad had suffered from the same visit, and even Tanya had toiled halfway through the night on her hands and knees, toothbrush in hand.

After lunch came the true nightmare of the day—Introduction to Astro-Navigation, the washout course that every scrub had been warned was the true killer of scrub summer. What made it even worse was the fact that anything less than a B average at the end of the semester resulted in dismissal from the Academy.

On the very first day, without any preliminary introduction or friendly chat, Professor Xing immediately launched into a rapid-fire lecture on the basic principles of launch mechanics from Earth, topped off with a quiz that not one in ten passed. She ran the course with the full assumption that every cadet had already passed Calculus, Physics, Astronomy, and had a good smattering of Engineering in his background. There was not an ounce of sympathy in her and, within minutes after class was dismissed, she had already earned a number of nicknames, the mildest of which was "The Terminator."

After Astro-Navigation came the class that most of the cadets looked forward to — "Basic Orientation for Cadets." The course covered a wide range of topics, starting with a series of in-depth walking tours of the Academy ship, which included crawling down access chutes, learning all the ins and outs of what made an orbital unit work, and emergency procedures. The course would then progress to EVA orientation, manned orbital maneuvering units, and culminate with a two-day field trip to the Moon.

With the end of classes at 1600 came another hour of PT in the exercise pylons or running kilometer-long footraces down the length of the ship, inspection, dinner, a mandatory ninety-minute recreational period and finally, some time to study before lights out at 2230. The lights out, however, was rarely observed, and Justin found himself up till at least midnight, sometimes to one in the morning studying, unless Seay had found some nasty little chore to divert them with.

Astro was a breeze for Matt and Pradeep, and Justin found himself feeling more than a bit envious when the two of them would take the time to fool around with Uncle, exploring the computer library for the fun of it, or worse yet having some friends in to talk. Worst of all though was when the discussions of politics started.

"You Earthers just don't seem to get it," Matt opened, when Tanya, Madison, and half a dozen cadets from B squad crammed into the room for the first Saturday night session. One of them was Sue Mannheim, and that alone drew his attention away from study.

Justin closed his computer notebook shut with a dramatic flourish, the others in the room looking over at him.

"Oh, that got the attention of the bookworm," Tanya quipped.

"No, it's just impossible to study with you people here," Justin replied sharply.

"Relax, bucko, all that studying will make you go blind," Matt said, leaning back comfortably in his bunk.

"It might come easy for you, Matt, you've lived with this stuff all your life," Justin retorted a bit angrily.

"Some folks will never get it at all," Tanya announced.

"Hey, Tanya, just shut up," Matt interjected. "Not all of us are such gifted geniuses like you."

Tanya looked quickly around the room for support and saw that none was about to be offered.

"Well anyhow," she replied, looking back at Matt, "I'm sick of hearing, 'you Earthers this, you Earthers that.' The problem with you damn colonials is you think you're so high and mighty, just because you live full-time out in space. Earth is still the center of this little system, and the purpose of the colonies is to insure the survival of the planet, not the other way around."

"In other words, we're the servants of Earth and thank you so much, master, for letting us continue to exist," Matt replied.

"You wouldn't even be out there on that junk scow of yours if it hadn't been for trillions of dollars spent on Earth," Tanya pressed.

Matt bristled at the mere mention of his beloved sail ship as a junk scow, and Justin could see that the argument was going to take a turn away from where he wanted it to go. The issue of the separatists had never really troubled him before, though he knew that his father and grandfather both supported it, while his mother was dead set against them. Now was the chance to get the straight view from Matt and Sue.

"Why did we spend the trillions in the first place?" Justin interjected before Matt could jump down Tanya's throat over the insult.

The group laughed as if his question was so foolish as to not even be worthy of a reply.

"No, damn it, I'm serious. Just why did we spend the money in the first place?"

"Are you for real?" Tanya asked.

"Yes, damn it, I'm for real," Justin snapped back. "Let's take this question from the beginning."

"What is this, a discussion of the Socratic method of inquiry or the separatists?"

"Justin's got a point, Tanya, so leave it be," Madison interjected.

"All right, then," Tanya announced sarcastically, "just why did we spend the trillions to get into space?"

"Instinct," Madison replied. "An early 20th century Russian theorist once said that Earth is the cradle and we cannot remain in it forever. We did it because it was there."

"Garbage," Pradeep announced. "We were strangling to death on Earth. By the early 21st century we'd reached the limit of the planet to support us. Hell, you remember the history of the wars. Pakistan and my country blew off half a dozen cities with nukes in a struggle over the province of Kashmir. The same thing happened in the Middle East, in Africa, and the nuclear terrorists, all their ideology aside, were fighting for land and resources. Space became the only answer, the only place we could expand. We get eighty percent of our energy from orbit, most of our polluting industries are moving off planet now, and a lot of mineral resources are getting shipped in from space. It also means we could get our surplus populations moved off planet as well."

"That surplus population argument is off the mark," Justin replied. "Just over a hundred million people have gone off planet in the last eighty years, half of them only in the last ten since the skyhook tower went on line."

"With the skyhooks," Nagama, a cadet from B squad interjected, "it's finally going to happen though. Almost anyone can afford a ticket now. They say we might see a billion people leave in the next twenty years."

"And where the hell are they going to go?" Tanya sniffed. "They'll die like flies."

"Space is big enough," Matt replied. "If they're tough enough and lucky enough they'll survive. Thousands die every year as is, that's part of what a frontier is — risk. Besides, they'll become separatists too once they get out. More recruits for the cause."

"Even if I leave Earth, I'm still a Russian," Tanya said.

"Ah, there we have it," Matt announced. "You didn't call yourself an Earther, even a member of the United Nations. You're still a Russian."

"That's not what I meant."

"Then why did you say Russian?"

"Because Saint Petersburg is my home. It's where my mother and father were born. It'll always be home, and it is down on Earth."

"Space is my home, not Earth," Matt replied quietly.

"Your family still came from Earth though," Sue finally interjected. "I was born on the Moon, but I'm still German."

"Your kids might not feel that way though," Matt replied. "Look, according to the government down there, I'm an American citizen. Why? Because my father happened to be born on American soil. Now, according to the government and the United Nations taxation laws, my father, my uncle, and even I have to pay taxes to the United Nations, half of which then goes to America."

"It's only fair though," Sue replied. "All the governments of Earth, and especially the United States and Russia, spent one hell of a lot of money over the last hundred years to put us into space."

"Yeah, I know," Matt replied, "trillions for the good of all mankind. Bull. They did it for their own good, to save their hides when the rest of the world was eager to knock them over, and always looking at the bottom line of finally turning a profit."

"Well, they did save the world," Justin said.

"Sure they did and I thank them for it. If we hadn't gone into space we would have turned Earth to a cinder by now. Hell, there's still a chance we might wind up doing it. It's still overpopulated at five billion, and though the U.N. has its orbital military command, there's still some nukes kicking around down there in the hands of individual governments. And frankly, I don't see why the colonials still have to define themselves as being part of it."

"Don't you have any love for America?" Justin asked, his voice serious.

Matt looked at him, taken a bit aback by the question.

"Sure I do. It's where my family came from."

"Then why are you turning your back on it?" Sue asked.

Matt shook his head.

"Justin, you're from Indiana, right?"

"Yeah."

"Where did your family come from before then?"

Justin had to sit back for a second and think about that.

"Ireland and Scotland, I think."

"Do you pay taxes to those two countries?"

"Of course not."

"That's not the point," Nagama said. "America's been an independent country for over three hundred years."

"My point exactly," Matt replied sharply. "And they got their independence by fighting against a mother country that set it up first as a colony, then mismanaged it, and taxed it unfairly."

He paused for a second.

"And we'll do the same."

"You're talking treason," Tanya said quietly. "You're talking about a separatist revolution."

"In America we call them patriots," Justin said quietly.

"You mean you support him in this?" Tanya asked.

"I'm still not sure, it's a complex issue. The colonization of space might be like the colonization of America, but then again it's different. The early colonies were chartered under individual nations, until the United Nations colonial chartering act of 2049."

"Cramming for Space History, are we?" Madison said with a smile.

"I already knew that. My grandfather was living on Mars when it went through and I'll tell you he wasn't happy about it."

Justin smiled at the thought of his grandfather. Wasn't happy about it was an understatement. A guaranteed way to get a good round of obscenities was to even mention the treaty within hearing distance of grandpa. He had been fully behind the idea of Mars going independent and being incorporated into the U.N. as a free nation, rather than as a colonial protectorate with the ruinous taxation that resulted.

"The U.N. act was a declaration of war against us," Matt announced.

"That's not true," Sue replied. "The United States, Russia, Germany and a lot of other countries and corporations spent half a trillion dollars getting Mars up and running. They're entitled to some kind of return."

"Then let it be through free trade, and not this damn one-third space-to-Earth import tariff."

"What the hell can we get from Mars anyhow?" Tanya replied. "Sand?"

"It's a major port, terraforming is really starting to take hold, it's loaded with rare metals and if given a fair shake it'll continue to grow. As is, it's crippled and I think that's what the U.N. wants."

"Let's get back to the American example for a second," Justin said. "Matt does have a point there and I want to follow up with it."

"Go on then," Madison replied.

"You're talking about a historical trend here. England made America not with the intent of launching a new country, but rather out of a dream of Empire. It gave them resources they needed. In the beginning the colonists saw themselves as loyal to England, until it was felt that England was violating their rights as citizens. To their way of thinking they weren't traitors, rather it was England who had betrayed them."

"I don't see how Earth or the U.N. has betrayed the colonists," Sue quickly replied. "We didn't hear you squawking when the flow of resources up to get things started was a hundred times more than what was coming back."

"I'll agree to that," Matt replied. "It was the same with England for America, or Spain for South America. Damn near everything needed had to come from the motherland. It's the same with a mother and child in a way. In the beginning the child depends on its mother for its very life; it can't even eat without being helped. But there comes a day when the child grows up and at that point is it fair for the mother to ask it to be its slave?"

"That's not a fair example," Sue replied.

"Yes it is. The child didn't ask to be born, but it was. There'll always be an affection there, but there comes a time when the child has to lead its own life, and there'll come a time when the mother grows old and finally dies but the child lives on after her. He'll look back on her with love, but he isn't expected to die with her."

"Are you saying Earth is dying?" Justin asked.

"No, I hope not. I hope it's always there though at times I doubt it will be. But I am saying that we have something happening here. The human race is starting to split apart. I was born in space, and I'll die in space. I guess I'll step foot on Earth finally, now that I'm with the Academy, but my home is out here. Who do I hold allegiance to? My ship, I guess the asteroid colonies, other sailors like myself; and no damn petty bureaucrat from Earth is going to tell me how to live, when to pay taxes, how to run my ship, or when I've been good or bad."

"You're talking anarchy then," Sue interjected.

"No, I'm talking freedom. Listen, America's not a place, it's an ideal in here," and he pointed to his heart. "It's a dream, a belief that the individual is more important than anything else. That no one group is more important than another. It's a dream that unites people, that government is there to serve the people rather than the other way around. It's a belief that the government exists to protect the people from outside threat, to insure that everyone has a chance, but that whether a person makes it or breaks it is up to him, and him alone. You saw what happened in America when they lost sight of that back at the turn of the century. That's what their second revolution was all about, when the people finally rose up, threw out the bums running their government and the pressure groups that kept them in power and wrote their second constitution. They didn't want their government to be big daddy, mama, or anything else. They finally remembered that the best kind of government is the one that does the least and simply leaves people alone. And I'm telling you right now that the U.N. government is turning into big daddy or big brother like in the Orwell novel. It thinks it knows best when in fact it doesn't know a damn thing about living in space, or how best to govern us.

"America is that dream and I'm saying that we in space have just as much right to our revolution as the Americans have had to their two."

"So what the hell are you doing in the Academy then if you hate Earth so much?" Tanya asked coldly.

"Learning, dear Tanya, learning," Matt said with a grin. "Someday the colonists are going to need leaders, and I plan to be one of them."

That provoked a round of chuckles and Madison made a big show of standing up, saluting Matt and then bowing down low before him.

"Matt, what you're talking about is still anarchy," Sue replied. "You know how wild it is out on some of those asteroid bases. It's like the old American West, with only a couple of Space Service officers like we'll be to keep the peace."

"Hey, I'm not saying we don't want any government at all," Matt replied. "I'm just saying we can do a damn sight better job of it than the U.N. Any society needs rules, all I'm saying is let us make our own rules and stop draining us dry with taxes, and crippling us with rules that some vacuum-head government official, who ain't never been further off Earth that the top of his office building, dreams up in his sleep."

"And what about the Tracs?" Justin finally asked.

There was a moment of silence to that one.

"What did America do when England was threatened by Hitler?" Matt finally replied. "It'll be the same with us. We don't hate Earth, hell some of my best friends are Earthers," and he looked over at Justin with a grin.

"So you would fight, is that it?" Sue asked.

"Of course."

"And run to Earth for weapons, protection and the skill to stop the Tracs," Tanya sniffed.

"Maybe so, but we'd all be in the same boat if they come back looking for trouble."

"Let's just hope we figure out how their ship works in time," Justin said, and there were nods of agreement.

"Let me just ask all of you this," Matt interjected. "Let's say we do figure out how their translight system works and we leap out to the stars. Do you honestly think then that colonists on Alpha Centuri, or around Wolf's Star will still view Earth as home, will follow its laws and pay its taxes?

"I'm telling you this separatist movement is only

the beginning. Once we get translight, it's gonna be so long Earth, hello universe, and I plan to be one of the first to go. This solar system's getting too crowded as is. Earth is the past, where I'm going is the future."

"You're going to be giving me a hundred pushups, mister, if you can't recite General Order number fourteen really fast."

Startled, the group looked up to see Brian and Sharon standing in the corridor.

Surprised, Justin wondered just how long they had been listening in on the conversation. With mixed company in the room they were required to keep the door open. According to regulations what was said in one's own room, as long as it was not insulting to a superior officer or treason, was fair game. As far as he could tell, Matt had not come right out and announced any intention to join in an armed rebellion but he wondered how Brian would interpret it.

Matt rattled off number fourteen at lightning speed finishing up with a drawled, "and report all such occurrences to my superior officer, sir!"

Brian stood silently, hands on his hips.

"You really buy that separatist line, don't you, scrub?"

"It's my right to free thought, sir," Matt replied.

"Just don't let it interfere with your work, mister, or to your oath to the Academy 'cause if you make a black mark on my squad, Loud Mouth, you'll be answering straight to me."

"I wouldn't dream of damaging your record, sir, or hurting the squad," Matt replied, and Justin wasn't sure if Matt was being sarcastic or not.

"I'm loyal to the Academy," Matt added a second later, and Justin could hear the sincerity in Matt's voice.

Brian nodded ever so imperceptibly.

"All right, scrubs, lights out in fifteen and keep it quiet down in here," Brian snapped, obviously disappointed that he hadn't nailed Matt.

The two continued down the hall, the crowd in the room now silent.

"You're going to get your butt in the wringer one of these days, Matt," Nagama said, standing up to leave the rest of the visitors joining him.

"Fully expect it, Nagama," Matt replied with a smile.

✧ Chapter IV ✧

The morning alarm cut through his dreams, bringing Justin to a half awake state. It had been so pleasant, he was back on Sugar Creek, floating downstream in a kayak, the covered bridge at Deer's Mill drifting into view around the bend in the river, its faded red clapboard siding reflecting in the rippling water. It was his favorite part of the river, with Shades Park just ahead after a swift line of rapids, the sandstone cliffs lining the river pockmarked with hundreds of tiny caves where swallows made their nests, and darted over the river.

Kayaking had been his favorite sport on Earth. You competed against yourself, when you were in the mood to compete, and at other times you just drifted along, soaking in the countryside, watching the birds fly overhead, and listening to the sounds of the river and the turkey calls echoing out of the dark forest that lined the creek.

The only problem was that Brian Seay was flying above him like a bothersome horsefly and no matter how hard he tried he just couldn't swat him. And then Tanya flew in to join Brian in tormenting him. The rapids were straight ahead and he kept trying to concentrate on them, to keep from rolling the kayak, but the two just wouldn't leave him alone, and the sight of Tanya just made him somehow angry.

The alarm echoed away and there was a moment of silence, except for the throaty snore of Matt in the bunk down below.

Justin groaned softly and pulled his pillow over his head to block the sound out. Today was midterm exams day. It was hard to believe that four weeks had already passed and as the cold reality of what today represented started to sink in Justin felt a knot tightening up his stomach.

He had started to almost feel comfortable with the Academy. The discipline was tough, but he found he could handle it. The biggest pains were Astro-Navigation and Brian Seay, and he wasn't sure at any given moment which of the two was on top. Brian, though, was still not as bad as some of the guys who used to harass and mock him at school. Surprisingly, he found that the tough treatment in school on Earth had actually prepared him for the harassment dished out by upperclassmen towards the scrubs. More than one cadet, who was used to being part of the "in" crowd in high school on Earth, could not handle the mocking, yelling and sarcasm of their squad commanders. In the third company two cadets were expelled on the same day when they cracked and took a swing at their squad leaders. The only real pleasure for the two out of the whole incident was that one of them had connected, leaving the senior with a serious black eye. As for the scrub who connected, the senior was justified in his "self defense response," and the scrub was now in a fiberglass cast for a broken wrist.

There had been several other scuffles as well, the rest between separatists and Earthers, fights flaring up when late night dorm room discussion got a little too out of hand. If the fights came to the attention of upperclassmen, as it did in two cases, all involved had been expelled by Thorsson with no hope of appeal. Matt had almost landed in one himself, when he claimed to overhear another scrub announcing that all separatists were "traitors who should be fed to the Tracs when they showed up again." Justin found that he was almost as strong as Matt when he dragged him away before blows could be exchanged.

The alarm kept on beeping and he finally surrendered and sat up.

"All right, Uncle, turn the damn thing off, we're up," Justin groaned.

"You're so cheerful in the morning," Uncle quipped, the alarm still ringing.

"Turn it off, Uncle," Pradeep yelled.

"Not until I hear from Cadet Everett."

"Ah, shut up, Uncle," Matt snarled.

"So friendly, the three of you," and the alarm shut off.

Justin sat up and groaned, rubbing the back of his neck, which was still sore from last night's game.

Though he was by no means a master at falcon fighting, he could at least hold his own and he spent every spare minute away from studies practicing. It was a sport which required some strength, but more importantly required an ability to think in three dimensions; and he found that it sort of came naturally to him. The games had become more elaborate, with dozens of variations, his favorite one being when the room was darkened to twilight and strobe lights were fired off at random. Though Matt could still trounce him in a one-on-one, he found that he was learning. In squad-level games, they formed a three-person section with Madison and usually managed to be the last survivors and credited with the most kills.

The entire school was getting psyched up for the big game at the end of the semester and heavy bets, though illegal, were already being wagered, with most of the odds going in favor of B company, thanks to a particularly aggressive scrub from France, Collin Bugniazet, who had emerged as a natural-born leader in the game. Company B had booked up every spare minute it could get in the large 100-meter court and under a strict security blanket was practicing its game strategy.

As for a team leader in Company A, a cadet in the fifth squad, Bob Jenkins from Mars, appeared to be the natural choice, though Tanya had made a rather loud protest over his selection in company elections with Matt winning the second in command slot. Brian was proving to be an excellent coach in company level tactics and excitement was building for the big match.

Not making it as the company leader, Tanya drifted to the sidelines and took orders along with the rest, deciding instead to focus her main attention on zero-gravity ballet. Though Justin hated to admit it, he had even sneaked in once to watch her perform and came away rather impressed. He wasn't sure if it was her gracefulness with the ballet, or how pretty she looked when floating across the room, her black hair billowing out around her. The mere thought of her actually being attractive gave him the cold chills and her taunts and sarcasm reinforced his dislike. If there was any girl he found interesting it was Sue Mannheim in Sharon's squad, but he couldn't find any real way to talk with her. Whenever she was nearby he felt a lump as big as baseball growing in his throat and he simply couldn't speak.

Stretching in bed Justin fought down the temptation to roll over and get another ten minutes of sleep. There was no time for that today, and at the mere thought of why he was getting up early, a knot formed in his stomach. Today was the mid-term exam in Astro-Navigation.

Nearly a dozen cadets were already out of the course, flunking the four weekly quizzes. All he had been able to pull was a D average, and that just barely. Over a hundred and fifty cadets in the summer session were already gone for other reasons. Some were just plain homesick or found they simply didn't like it. Others messed up on discipline or couldn't adjust to the constant changes in gravity aboard an orbiting ship, something that still bothered him at times. Several cadets flipped out when they went on their first space walk and resigned as soon as they got back inside the Academy. It was the classwork, however, that was the big killer and Justin feared that, the way it was all going, his name would turn out to be on the casualty list once the summer was over.

"Gentlemen, it is 0500," Uncle announced in his disgustingly cheerful morning voice. If there was one thing Justin really hated at five AM, it was the sound of someone being cheerful, even if it was only a computer.

"Ah, shut up, Uncle."

"I'm just doing my job," Uncle retorted. "You asked to get up an hour early to study for your Astro exam, and I'm just doing my part. Now get out of bed!"

All of them groaned in chorus.

"Check this maneuver out," Matt announced as he swung up out of his bunk and floated gracefully down to the floor, turning a double flip on the way down. Hitting the floor he pushed off, vaulted back up several feet, and then came down with a final backwards somersault. He extended his hands like a circus performer expecting applause after landing and looked up at Justin.

Shaking his head, Justin kicked the blankets back, grabbed hold of the sides of his bed and pushed. Floating up, he hit the ceiling with his feet, kicked, turned head over heels, and came down to land on the balls of his feet, then springing back up did two more flips, landed and extended his hands to imitate Matt.

"5.8 for Matt, 5.5 for Justin," Pradeep said, rubbing his eyes.

The two looked expectantly at Uncle's monitor.

"Matt's performance, though brilliantly executed, showed a certain repetitiveness in style, the same maneuver having been executed three days out of the last five," Uncle said drily, "while Justin demonstrated an imaginative grasp of the finer techniques of acrobatics in light gravity environment. Therefore Justin gets a 5.6 and Matt a mere 5.4."

"You've been bribing the judges again," Matt cried.

"But of course," Justin said with a smile.

"Hey, it's space walk day, guys," Matt said, looking around at his roommates. "You're gonna love it."

"Yeah, sure, but first the Astro exam," Justin said softly, as he headed to the bathroom to grab a shower.

Stepping into the stall he set the one-minute water timer and turned the shower on. The water floated out in the light gravity, filling the compartment with mist. He turned the water off, and soaped up, then turned it on to rinse back off.

Space walk.

He knew he should be excited. Orientation had finally finished up with the detailed tour of the Academy, so that he could almost recite in his sleep every emergency procedure in the book and knew just about every corridor and accessway by heart. Now they were about to move outside. It was, after all, what being in space was all about, not just to hang around inside a station, but to actually suit up and get out there. His afternoon class of the last four weeks had been leading up to this moment. But first the exam.

Drying off, he came back out of the bathroom, quickly made his bed and then put on his uniform, the standard class C whites of loose coveralls and canvas shoes. He checked himself in the mirror to make sure they were spotless. White uniforms were a pain to keep clean but he realized that was part of the discipline of being a scrub. He realized he was starting to become a bit self-conscious as well of the fact that except for the Academy insignia on his lapels there wasn't a single stripe, pip, or award on his uniform. Brian made it a point of telling them that the Academy didn't waste time on rank for scrubs — that way they didn't have to tear anything off when they got kicked out.

He settled into a chair next to Uncle's holo screen; Pradeep was already hard at work, studying a projection of an aerobraking reentry to Mars.

Matt left his chair to grab a shower and Justin tried to follow Uncle's description of what was on the screen.

"Remember, aerobraking is a way of slowing down a spacecraft by using a planet's upper atmosphere as a brake, the air providing the friction to slow the ship down, without having to use precious fuel. It is a standard procedure for interplanetary spacecraft approaching Venus, Earth, Mars, Jupiter, Saturn and their moons, Uranus and Neptune.

"The first set of variables in the formula are based upon the gravity of the planet, the density of the atmosphere, the depth into the atmosphere that the spacecraft goes and the duration of transit inside the atmosphere. The second set of variables relate to the spacecraft's aerodynamic design, whether its shape is altered by inflatable bags to increase surface area for friction, its mass, and angle of attack in relationship to the planet. And the big final variable is the velocity of the spacecraft at the beginning of the maneuver and the desired velocity at the end of the aerobraking maneuver, along with the desired orbital inclination. This can be expressed in the following formula."

Justin sat back, rubbing the sleep from his eyes, watching as the formula with all its As, Bs, Xs and subsets hovered before him, noting down each of the variables on his portable touch pad.

"Justin, I'll set a problem up for you," Uncle said. "You are approaching Mars at 7.31 kilometers per second aboard a standard Lockheed and Gagarin Mark 17 transplanetary shuttle. The shuttle is fully loaded and weighs 5,402 tons, and is supposed to obtain standard orbit at one hundred and fifty-two kilometers above the surface. Here is your angle of approach to the planet's surface and intended orbit, now calculate and punch in an aerobraking maneuver to make that orbit. I'll keep it simple and won't toss in a total failure of your primary thruster controls, a trick I suspect Commander Xing will throw at you. We'll also leave out any trick stuff like an upper atmosphere dust storm."

"Gee, thanks, Uncle, you're a real friend," Justin groaned.

Coming out of the shower, Matt looked over Justin's shoulder as he struggled with the formula, working it into his hand-held unit, and Pradeep got up to use the shower.

"With all the backups we've got on board," Justin groaned, "I still don't see where we'll ever use this stuff."

"My uncle once had to decelerate our ship by aerobraking when we'd lost all sails and primary computers," Matt said proudly. "He did it with an old-fashioned calculator and paper, and got it within four point three kilometers an hour, and this was in Jupiter orbit no less with over a dozen moons to screw up your gravitational effects."

Justin was tempted to reply that Matt's ship was a third-class solar sailor ready for the junk heap, but knew he'd get a black eye the way a guy in fifth squad had if he dared to really and truly insult his friend's home.

Pradeep came out of the shower, dressed, and sat down by Justin, immediately falling into the problem Uncle was displaying on the screen.

Justin, with a mumbled curse, was forced to dump out his entire problem and start again from scratch. Basic Astro-Navigation had seemed to be such a snap back home. He'd flown hundreds of simulator runs on the school's computers, but this was different. Back home even a D was still a pass but out here the Academy required a B in all math-related courses in order to be moved up to the next section.

"All right, Uncle, here it is," Justin finally announced and he held up his hand unit, pointed it at Uncle and clicked the transmit button.

"Let me show you what you've got," Uncle replied.

By his tone Justin instantly knew that he had screwed it. Uncle projected an image of Mars and traced a trajectory line in, complete to a high-resolution image of a spacecraft. It looked like it was going perfectly, the ship entering the atmosphere, deploying its aerobrake bags to increase atmospheric drag, a plume of red ionized gas streaming behind it. The ship coasted in, dipping down into the upper atmosphere of the planet, the surface of Mars rolling by underneath. Uncle suddenly threw in the additional touch of presenting a view from the cockpit, the image so realistic that it instantly made Justin feel like he was really there. Everything was going perfectly and then straight ahead he saw disaster.

"Damn it!" Justin cried, and he braced himself for the impact as his ship slammed straight into the side of Mons Olympus, the highest mountain on Mars.

The special effects were rather spectacular, with the ship disappearing in a fireball of smoke and debris.

"Say, no fair! You said no trick questions," Justin snapped. "You never told me the angle of approach would take us right into the highest mountain on Mars."

Matt laughed, turning away from Justin to hide his grin of amusement, and Pradeep lowered his head to hide his grin.

"Justin, you should know by now that aerobraking maneuvers on Mars will take you down lower than Mars's highest mountain. It's a one in ten thousand chance, but you know the old saying: 'Triple check everything, and always plan for the worst.'"

"I don't think I'd be violating testing security by telling you that Professor Xing will throw at least one curveball in her test questions. She loves to trip scrubs up, especially the overconfident ones like a certain solar sailor in this room."

"Who, me?" Matt asked in surprise.

"Yes, you, Matt Everett," Uncle replied, imitating Matt's voice.

"You must remember that aerobraking maneuvers are strictly forbidden if they come within two hundred kilometers of any potential obstacle, such as a skyhook tower, or within fifteen thousand meters of a planet's surface, or over any populated areas on Mars," Uncle said.

"Now let's do it again."

"This time no curveballs," Justin asked.

"Just a straight-in approach," Uncle replied, and the computer fed the three a new problem.

Pradeep, as usual for the trio, finished first, followed quickly by Matt, with Justin dragging in third. Uncle played the results back, Justin groaning when Uncle showed him that he had miscalculated the angle of approach and the ship had skipped off the top of the atmosphere like a flat rock ricochetting across a lake.

"Room inspection in ten minutes," Uncle finally announced.

"Oh damn!"

The three jumped and scrambled to make their beds, store away their clothes and clean up the bathroom.

The door popped open just as they finished. They lined up by the door, standing at attention as Brian walked in.

"Room one, Squad Two, Company A ready for inspection, sir," the three chorused in unison.

Wordlessly, Brian walked around the room, looking under the beds, peeking into the closets and then stepping into the bathroom.

He came back out a moment later and Justin could tell by his look that they had been nailed again.

"The wall of the shower stall is dripping wet. Who took bathroom cleanup this morning?"

Justin and Matt looked sidelong at Pradeep. Since he was the last one in the shower it was his job to clean it up and wipe the walls down. The old code still applied, however, and before Pradeep could speak Justin blurted out, "We all did, sir."

"Then all three of you have a little toothbrush cleaning job tonight," Brian replied. "Immediately after recreation report to my quarters. I have a bathroom that needs a good going over and I'll supply the toothbrushes."

He walked out of the room and slammed the door shut.

"I'm sorry, guys," Pradeep moaned.

"It's all right, Pra," Matt said, trying to force a grin. "Hell, he would have nailed us on something or other, the rotten creep."

"Come on, we'll get screwed if we're late for breakfast and PT," Justin said, grabbing up his notebook computer. "Let's go."

They headed for the door, the three grabbing their computer notebooks and stuffing them into the regulation shoulder carry bag.

"Good luck on your exams," Uncle called and

Justin looked back at the monitor and smiled. The darn thing almost sounded like his mother.

"Yeah, thanks, I'm gonna need it."

Rather dejected, he followed his two friends down the corridor to the dining hall. The morning fare today was at least a little better than usual: real eggs rather than powdered, toast and synthetic soybean bacon which tasted just as crisp as the genuine article.

Following breakfast they formed up with the rest of their squad for roll and then double-timed down half a kilometer of corridor to the turbo which dropped down to the exercise pylons. Waiting for them as they came into the room was Chief Petty Officer Kevin Malady and he looked at them with a cold sardonic grin.

"Oh no, it's Malady this morning, now we're in for it," Matt whispered and Justin could only gulp and nod. They had already heard stories from the other squads about the first session with Malady and no one was looking forward to their turn.

Malady was an old fleet hand, with enough service stripes on his dress A sleeve to go from his elbow down to his wrist. His beet-red face was battered and scarred from what legend had was at least a thousand barroom brawls fought in every dive from beyond the asteroid belt to the sleazy taverns around the old rocket lifting stations back on Earth. And his specialty in teaching was also his favorite sport, brawling in any shape or form imaginable, in any gravity where spacers went, from vacuum to full pressure.

"Ah, my bright young lads and lasses," he growled as they came through the door after changing into their exercise clothes of T-shirts and shorts. The group came stiffly to attention and nervously stared straight ahead as he stalked down the line.

He did not try any punches on any of them as he walked a quick inspection of the line, which showed that either he was in a rare good mood or had worse planned.

"Let's start with fifty," he snapped, and the group went down on the floor and groaned out fifty pushups, with Malady coming over and putting his foot on the small of Justin's back and bearing down as Justin strained through the last ten.

"All right, now, pay attention," Malady announced, pushing off Justin's back with his full weight, as if Justin was a doormat, and motioned for the group to form a circle around him.

"Mr. Garcia, your senior cadet PT instructor's informed me that you aren't such a bad lot, though most of you look so weak and sickly it makes me want to puke at the sight of you. Thor must really be scraping the bottom of the barrel if you're what he's letting in these days. But he's the boss and if he gives me garbage to work with, I'll work with garbage.

"Mr. Garcia claims he's run you through basic hand-to-hand disarmed fighting in standard pylon gravity, and you've even had some sessions in half g and zero g."

Justin winced at the memory of the zero-g training session and instinctively wanted to rub the still-blackened eye he had picked up from Garcia after bouncing off a wall and spinning straight back into an extended fist.

"Today though, we're going to have a little fun, and that's why Thor has let me loose on you."

Malady grinned and, unsnapping a sheath strapped to his right thigh, he pulled out a full-bladed bowie knife and held it lightly in his hand.

"They used to call this an Arkansas toothpick once upon a time. What with possession of firearms aboard orbital units being considered a capital crime in some areas, this little beauty has become the preferred weapon of choice with some folks. It's designed to slide into your gut real easy like," and as he spoke he lunged forward with it as if driving it into an imaginary foe, "and then you rip upwards as you pull it back out," and he finished the job, a thin smile creasing his battered face.

The group was silent, looking at each other nervously.

"Listen, children, the service ain't all nice clean neat uniforms, shiny ships and all that officer and gentlemen crap they feed you. You walk into a remote mining camp, alone, and tell folks you're the law and they damn well better believe you. For that matter you damn well better believe yourself, or some young hotshot miner, or back lane jockey will come after you quick with one of these," and he held the knife back up, "and you're either going to be dead or he's going to be dead. My job is to make sure your worthless hides aren't ripped open, thus spoiling the good image of the service. You might not be worth a pinch of owl dung, but the uniform that covers your miserable carcasses is, and I'm supposed to make sure it doesn't get bled on.

"Have any of you ever seen one of these used before, and I don't mean in some damn holo movie."

"I have, sir," Matt drawled quietly.

"Ah, the sailor, the damn separatist, I've heard about you," Malady snapped, looking coldly at Justin.

Matt remained quiet.

"Where you seen it, sonny boy?"

"My uncle got in a fight once." Matt hesitated for a second. "He won, the other guy's fingers got sewed back on, but his hand looks kind of funny now."

A flicker of a smile creased Malady's slit of a mouth.

He reversed the blade in his hand and tossed the knife to Matt who gingerly caught it.

"Well, sonny boy, let's see if you can match your uncle."

"What do you mean?"

"Come at me, boy, try and cut me up."

Matt grinned sheepishly.

"Sir, I don't think I want to . . ."

"Damn it, I told you to come at me!"

"Sir, I don't want to hurt you."

Malady laughed coldly.

"Just like a sailor. All talk but no guts. Talks big like all the other lousy scum-eating separatists, but that's it," Malady laughed, turning his back on Matt.

He looked back over his shoulder at Matt who stood silent.

"A cheap little coward, just like the rest of them. I bet his old man and his mama were . . ."

"Shut up," Matt snarled coldly.

"Oh, shut up is it," Malady laughed. "Like I was

saying, I bet your old man, the pox-eaten sniveling worm, and your mama were . . ."

With an angry cry Matt leaped forward, knife held low. For an instant Justin thought Matt was truly going in for the kill.

It was all over within a second. Malady stepped sideways, catching Matt's hand at the wrist, pulling him down and turning his hand to break his hold. The knife went skidding to the floor. Malady caught Matt's foot with his own and flipped him over. With a snakelike ease Malady scooped the knife up, pinning Matt to the floor with a knee to the chest, and brought the blade up to his throat.

"Don't move, son," Malady said quietly.

Matt looked up at him red-faced and Justin felt a cold rage when he saw tears of humiliation and anger in Matt's eyes.

"It's all right, son, it's all right," Malady said quietly. "No harm done."

"You bastard," Matt snarled. "My parents are dead."

"I know," Malady said almost gently. "I knew your mother and your father, they were my friends."

He withdrew the knife and stood back up, helping Matt to his feet.

Matt heaved a sigh, struggling for control.

"You come from a proud family, Matt Everett, your old man once helped to save my neck during a little unpleasantry out at Ceres Station. He was an honorable person, and so was your mother. I said what I did for a reason."

Matt looked up at him coldly.

"What reason?"

"So that someday, when you're out there, and someone does say something against you, your family, or the service, you'll know how to take care of yourself.

"Now, are you all right?"

Matt nodded, suddenly ashamed at the tears that streaked his cheeks.

"It's all right, laddie, now go back with the others," and Malady patted him on the shoulder in a fatherly way.

Matt stepped back alongside Justin, who wanted to say something but knew it was best not to. He knew a little about what had happened to Matt's family and knew as well that Malady had picked the one pressure point which would cause Matt to explode.

"I did it for a reason," Malady said coldly, looking around at the group. "Out there," and he waved vaguely to the walls, "out there sooner or later you're going to meet someone, or some group that will want to take you on. The mere sight of the uniform will be enough.

"Mr. Everett had every right to defend his family honor but he made one key mistake," and Malady paused, "he got mad.

"That's the first rule in this service, never, never let your emotions take control. Whether you're piloting a ship going down, or your suit's been breached, or you're in a bar and things go ugly, never let your fear, your anger, or your hatred take hold. If you're going to die, do it coolly and with guts, that's the fleet tradition. Do it coolly and do it with style. I know because enough of my friends in this damn service have died and they died doing it right."

He paused for a brief second and looked straight at Justin and Justin realized that Malady had known his father. Malady gave him a quick nod of recognition and then looked back to the rest of the group.

"My job is to teach you that. To teach you to keep your cool, and by keeping your cool you'll learn how to survive. Before I'm done with you six years from now I'll have personally beaten the living daylights out of each and every one of you, man and woman and by heavens, you'll leave me either dead or officers and there's no in-between. Now do we understand each other?"

The group stood silent.

"Damn you all, answer me."

"Yes sir!" the group chorused.

"Good."

Malady turned to Justin and tossed him the knife.

"Now it's your turn, Bell, let's see what you can do."

✧   ✧   ✧

Cursing softly Justin rubbed his swollen right wrist as he tried to concentrate on the history class. The wrist was most likely sprained, his knife lunge at Malady ending just as ignominiously as Matt's. He looked to the back of the room as Madison came in. She gave him a friendly smile and sat down a bit gingerly and he wondered how many stitches she had taken in her leg to sew up the cut she had received from slipping and falling on the knife during a wrestling match with Malady.

History class seemed to drift by, and being in the back of the room he was tempted to switch his computer over to a quick review for the afternoon test, but knew better, since McCain, like most teachers, would occasionally switch into a student's system to see if he was on the proper channel or was doing something else instead. Getting caught was an automatic failure for the day. If someone attempted such an action during a test, by somehow hacking his computer to bypass standard testing security, it was an automatic expulsion from school.

The lesson was familiar territory for him anyhow, a review of the treaties that established the United Nations and Colonies Space Commission back in 2031, which created the first unified space program for mankind. He mentally tried to work out aerobraking maneuvers throughout the class.

By lunchtime he was a nervous wreck, and looking around at the other people in his section he knew they were wrecks too. Companies D through G had already taken their Astro exams in the morning, and though most of them looked relieved he saw more than one who was visibly upset. Rumors were already circulating that more than thirty students had scored so poorly that even if they aced the rest of the session they would still get no better than a C. Those students were going home aboard the evening shuttle. One of the students, right in the middle of lunch, broke down in tears, got up and ran out of the mess hall. No one laughed at him, there was just a sad quiet in the room.

The end of lunch bell sounded and, picking up his

computer which he had been hunched over during the meal, Justin started down the hallway, going past a group from Company E.

"You'll be sorrryyyy!" one of them chortled.

Justin said nothing, barely noticing a quick flash of a smile from Sue who was walking beside him.

"Luck to you, Justin," she said and he glumly nodded a thanks, not even interested at the moment in trying to pick up a conversation with her.

He filed into the lecture hall with the scrubs from his company and Company B and stood by his assigned seat. The bell rang and Commander Xing came into the room and stopped in front of the holo screen.

"Be seated," she snapped and the group settled in.

"My benighted scrubs. Today is your midterm exam for the summer semester. I have heard loud lamentations and wailings in the corridors and hallways. Uncle has even informed me that hundreds of you were begging him for help at all hours of last night, and that he holds little hope for some of you."

Justin wilted in his chair.

"Security laws prevent me from asking Uncle just who the late-night crammers were, though from your sleepless faces I can figure out who you are.

"I know I've picked up the nickname of the Terminator in this class," and she stopped and looked around the room for a long moment, the room as silent as a tomb. "I have that name for a reason," she finally continued.

Justin had a quick fantasy of watching Xing getting

trapped with the infamous Yolinder expedition which crash-landed on Pluto's moon Charon half a dozen years ago. The party had gone cannibal by the end, and he suspected that if Xing had been with the group she'd have been the chief headhunter.

"Plug your computers into the main system for security check and let's get this little ordeal over with," Xing announced.

Justin waited while Xing's main computer checked to make sure that the only files in the students' computers were the standard class files that contained data that they were allowed to carry into the exam.

The security check went without a problem and with a bit of a flourish Xing punched a key on her own computer which instantly uploaded the exam into the students' systems.

Ten problems appeared on Justin's screen, some of them made up of two or three parts. Justin took a deep breath and then hunched over his computer to start. The first problem was a fairly easy computation of a comet's orbital path and the inserting of a remote sensor into the comet. Next were five fairly tough questions regarding launching from and orbiting the Moon and Earth with a variety of different spacecraft and then came the crushers: four questions regarding orbital insertions of spacecraft traveling on interplanetary routes. At least Xing had taken pity on them and not thrown in any questions set on Jupiter or Saturn, where the moons and ring made calculations infinitely complex, but they were killers nevertheless, each question looking for several different points.

To Justin's amazement, one student, her features bright red, suddenly stood up, looked at Xing, shrugged her shoulders and stormed out of the room.

"Scratch one scrub," Xing said quietly.

The questions seemed to swarm in front of Justin and he fought with a rising sense of panic. He had heard of cases of astro-navigators who suddenly were forced to punch in such calculations with only minutes to spare after a loss of primary navigation computers, but such events were unheard of now and usually were the stuff of Grade B holo dramas that played on the tube at three in the morning. But even though he was in a quiet classroom, except for the occasional groans and sighs, he felt, nevertheless, as if his life was on the line.

He sat back up for a moment to stretch and saw the clock on the far wall, only twenty minutes left! Pradeep, down at the front of the room, was staring at the ceiling, hands clasped behind his head. An A most likely and already finished, Justin thought enviously.

Justin cracked his knuckles and winced from the pain in his right wrist. He stared at his computer screen which was filled with the formula for the second of the orbital insertion problems. It didn't seem to be adding up right!

He looked back at the clock, only fifteen minutes left!

He jumped into the next problem, hoping he'd get at least part of the last one correct. This one seemed straightforward enough, an aerobraking maneuver into Venus. He accessed the open testing file on Venus's atmospheric density and gravity, plugged it into the formula and started to work.

A bell echoed in the room.

"One minute left," Xing announced and a groan rose up from the group.

Justin furiously punched the keys, trying to put the rest of the formula together, rushing to get the file data on the ship's mass and aerodynamic design.

Another bell sounded and his computer locked up.

Sighing, he sat back in his chair, trying to refrain from nervously biting his fingernails, an action which was viewed by Academy officers as behavior unbecoming a cadet.

The seconds passed and the room filled with tension as the class waited for the main computer to grade their tests.

The results flashed onto Justin's screen. All around him he could hear the reactions: sighs, groans, relieved laughter, an occasional triumphant whoop. He closed his eyes and then opened them again.

Sixty-four.

He shook his head, feeling numb. He had managed to squeak into a D by four lousy points. He did a quick calculation. He'd need to get well over a ninety on the final if he was to have any hope of surviving.

"Settle down, people," Xing snapped, and the room went silent.

She looked down at her screen and then back at the class.

"Cadets Agira, Daniels, Effingham, Goveri, Linstrom, Manchester, Mancini, Petrovski, and Ying, report to the commandant's office at 1700 hours today. You are excused from your next class. The rest of you are dismissed."

Justin stood up and looked around the room. Nine of his fellow students had scored so low that there was no hope of their surviving the rest of the class. They were going home. He saw one of them walking out of the room, his features pale, friends on either side of him, arms around him, offering condolences.

Just what the hell am I doing in this place, Justin suddenly thought angrily. *I'll never cut it, I'll never cut it, it's just too damned hard!*

In a definite bad mood, Justin wandered out of the classroom. Matt came up to join him.

"How'd it go, buddy?" Matt asked.

Justin shook his head.

"Sixty-four. I'm cooked, Matt. I need a ninety-six for the final to squeak by with a B. I'm outta here. Besides, who needs the damn place anyhow."

Matt grabbed hold of him by the shoulders and turned him around.

"Look, buddy, you start thinking like that and you really are cooked. We've got four weeks to get you ready for this and by God, I'll kill you if you aren't."

Justin tried to force a smile but couldn't. He found, to his own shame, that he was darn near at the point of tears. It was curious, when he came to the Academy only four weeks ago he wasn't even sure if he wanted it. In fact by the end of the first day, if there had been any way whatsoever to gracefully bail out of it he would have. He still wasn't sure if he really wanted it. If it hadn't have been for the Astro exam, his first EVA coming up next would have had him scared half to death.

Damn, why did my old man have to go and be a hero and get killed doing it? he wondered coldly. Even as he thought the question he felt ashamed, wondering what his father and grandfather would say. And yet he felt some anger nevertheless. Space had taken his father away from him, even while he was still alive. Justin could remember, at best, a half dozen times when his father had actually been with him, taken him someplace or simply been around when he needed him. Most of the time he was a flickering image on a commlink, or a vidmail beamed in from halfway across the system. And then he went and got killed, leaving the burden of expectations behind.

"I don't see how I can pull it together now," Justin said, feeling bitter at everything and angry with himself.

"Hey, buddy, what the hell do you think you have friends for?"

Justin looked up at him.

"Look, I never really had any friends when I was on *Corona*. Just faces on a screen, voices on a commlink, my Uncle and bot. That was it. I ain't about to let myself lose one now. Starting tonight, we begin the big cram. Uncle will help us out."

"You forget we have a date with our all so friendly senior cadet at 2200."

"Oh yeah, him. Well, once we get done, we'll throw in a little extra time, get up a half hour early every morning. Hell, you're a whiz at this history stuff, you can give me a hand in turn."

Justin forced a smile. He felt it was useless, but Matt's infectious smile couldn't be ignored.

"All right, deal."

"Come on, it's EVA time, let's move it."

They pushed their way into the stream of cadets heading for the far end of the ship, jogging down the kilometer-length corridor then took a lift up to deck level A, the zero-gravity corridor that ran the length of the axis of the ship. The squads broke up into their separate groups each heading to an EVA prep chamber. Justin followed his companions along with the members of first squad of A company into the room where their instructor, First Lieutenant Vanderberg, was waiting for them.

"All right, squads A and B, everyone here?"

The group nodded excitedly and Vanderberg led them into the suiting up room. Hanging on the wall was a row of standard class C space suits. Justin had already been through the routine half a dozen times before in practice sessions. But this one was different, this one was for real.

He floated over to the suit assigned to him, turned it around on its rack and unzipped the front.

"Remember, people, take your time, this is not an emergency suit up," Vanderberg warned.

Turning around, Justin reached around behind himself and grabbed hold of hand bars placed to either side of the suit. He then rose up and pushed both feet down into the suit. He felt his feet slip into the boots, which were locked in place to the floor. Letting go of the hand bars he stuck his arms into the suit, sliding his fingers into the gloves which were part of the unit, then reached over and zipped the inner, then the outer, layer shut. Next he attached the suit's utility belt and punching a button on his chest monitor he felt the suit gradually contract around him until it was a snug fit.

Justin looked around the room and saw that everyone else was just about done. Vanderberg went over to his own suit and within seconds was inside of it.

"All right, easy enough, all of you are doing really fine. Now, let's go over things one last time. Do a thorough buddy check after you put on your helmets and get your backpacks on."

The charged-up backpacks were mounted along a far wall. Using the sticky-bottom boots rather than floating, Justin made his way over to the wall, turned, and slipped his arms through the backpack harness. Reaching around, he clipped the power cord and air line into their attachments just below his left shoulder. He fumbled with it for a moment, and Vanderberg came over to help, a friendly smile on his face.

"It takes some getting used to. Just relax, Justin, this isn't an emergency time test today."

Justin felt the lines click in and a small LCD readout on his chest went to green. Finally he reached up, took down a helmet and slipped it over his head, snapping the four buckles down. He punched the first button on his control panel attached to his left forearm and felt a rush of cool air float into his helmet. He watched the row of LCDs inside his helmet. They blinked green three times then went steady, indicating that there were no leaks in his suit and all systems were functioning correctly. He double-checked the outside display on his arm which was a row of steady green lights as well.

"Justin?"

He turned and looked over at Matt.

"Ready for check."

Matt recited off Justin's checklist and Justin did the same in reply. Next they both made a visual exam of each other's suits, checking the seals, connections and backpack.

"All right, people, check off with me when I call your names," Vanderberg announced, and waiting his turn Justin called out A-OK and gave a positive check on Matt's suit as well.

"Now listen up, people. We've gone through the routine before. It'll be just like in the zero-g room aboard ship that we tried out yesterday, the only difference being that this time you'll be outside.

"Remember, if you should suddenly feel the need to hit the bathroom, you can do so, the suit will handle it, but then again you'll have to clean it yourself when we get back inside," and there was a round of groans over that bit of information.

"Next, stick close to your buddy at all times, it's your job to keep an eye on him. Things can happen fast out there. There might not even be time to call for help and it's a buddy's job to be on top of the situation. You've gone through emergency patching drill, the patches are in your left thigh pocket. If you should start to get vertigo just look at your buddy, focus on his faceplate and don't look out. If you start to get sick, try to hold it. Remember, if you let go, and your filter gets jammed up, you'll suffocate. It's not a nice way to end your day.

"Now, let's stick close together and stay inside the red circled area. Remember, there'll be some other classes out there. Don't mingle up with them, stick with your squad. If you should start to wander outward down the side of the ship, centrifugal force will create artificial gravity out there just the same as inside the ship. If you pop off and get flung clear, it'll mean we have to send a tug out to get you. That's expensive and I can tell you I won't be amused with you."

He paused for a second.

"Let's go look at space!"

Leading the way, Vanderberg went through the first of the double airlock doors, the rest of the group following. Up until this moment Justin had been too focused on his problems with Astro-Navigation to really worry about what was coming up. He suddenly realized that his heart was starting to pound and his knees felt decidedly weak. Turning his head slightly, he looked at the radio transmit light, blinked twice and then stared straight at Matt. A laser mounted in his helmet, and focused on his eye, picked up the movement and switched his radio to a private link with his partner.

"Say, Matt."

"Hey, Just, how's it goin'?"

"Ahh, kind of a bit shaky here."

Matt laughed.

"It's okay. I've done it hundreds of times. You'll love it."

"Yeah, sure."

He felt like such a wimp. A total one hundred percent jerk. Chances were he was going to get washed out in four weeks anyhow, and now he wasn't even sure if he'd be able to step through the airlock door.

He heard a klaxon sound.

"Stand clear of inner airlock door," a computerized voice announced and looking over his shoulder he saw the double seal slide shut behind him.

Around him, in spite of the bulk of the suit, he heard excited chatter from his comrades, with Tanya, somehow able to look nonchalant even in a space suit and zero gravity, lounging against a wall.

"Depressurization initiating now," the soft feminine voice of the computer announced and a flashing yellow strobe over the outer door started to blink.

Justin looked around, breathing hard, half expecting that he would see something.

The effect took hold gradually. He felt his suit start to bulge out slightly and then noticed that the sound of talking around him started to drift away into silence.

The flashing strobe went to solid red and then snapped to green.

"Final check," Vanderberg announced through the squad comm line.

Justin looked down at his LCD readout on his arm, and then cross-checked it against the small heads-up display projected against the upper right side of his faceplate.

Justin called off that all systems were green, helping Matt to double-check one last time.

"All right, people, here we go."

Vanderberg leaned over and hit a button next to the door.

It slid open.

Directly ahead were the star-strewn heavens and Justin took a deep breath, fighting down the panic. Vanderberg went out first, attaching a small ladder to the side of the open door. There was really no up and down here and Justin found it disconcerting to approach the door, then rotate ninety degrees, grab hold of the ladder and climb out sideways.

He slowly climbed up, following Matt, not looking up. A hand reached out to steady him and he stepped out onto the side of the Academy.

"Clear the ladder area, Justin," Vanderberg said, motioning for him to step away, "and remember to stay inside the red line area."

Still not sure of himself, he walked cautiously, making sure one sticky boot was firmly attached to the side of the ship before lifting the other foot and stepping forward.

"Hey, old man, how're ya doing? You walk like you were a hundred years old. Stand up straight and take a look."

Justin looked up and saw Matt standing in front of him, waving, and directly behind him was the crescent Earth.

"My God," Justin whispered.

The Earth appeared to be floating directly above Matt's right shoulder, a thin sliver of the coast of Asia and the western Pacific clearly visible. He stared at it with open mouth amazement, watching as it drifted behind Matt, disappearing for a moment and then reappearing over his left shoulder.

He looked up and saw the crescent moon straight overhead, far larger than Earth.

The vast bulk of the side of the Academy ship stretched out around him like a giant plate three hundred meters across, the edge of the cylinder-shaped ship a clear cut line of white etched against the blackness of space.

As the ship slowly turned on its long axis, a glaring orb of white hot light came into view, and the polarization on Justin's face plate darkened it, blocking out the light so that he could look straight at the sun without squinting.

He stood awe-struck at the sight of the Moon with the Earth beyond it, and finally the sun glowing hot above them. He barely noticed Matt's happy boastful chatter. Justin turned away from the sun, walking cautiously, Matt following alongside. As they moved away from the center axis point of the ship and headed outward Justin became aware of an ever-so-faint pulling outwards. It gave him a momentary sensation that he was hanging on the side of a vast building and at any second he'd start to slide down the side and spin off into space. Rather than panic him, or trigger a sense of vertigo, he found it to be absolutely delightful.

"On the red line, buddy, no further," Matt called and Justin looked down to see the broad red strip, which marked the point beyond which centrifugal force would make it difficult to remain standing upright.

He leaned backwards slightly, extended his arms wide and looked up.

Space was spread out before him, and as the side of the ship momentarily blocked the sun, plunging them into darkness, he felt as if he was floating through the universe, the stars so close he could reach out and cup them in his hands.

He started to laugh, to laugh with pure joy, all his cares, his fears dropping away from him into the night. He could hear Matt's laughter echoing in his headset. There was no need to explain to his friend, or Matt to him, what they were laughing about, for both knew the thoughts of the other.

They were intoxicated with the joy, the limitless freedom, the universe spread out before them. Justin Bell, at that moment, realized he never again would call Earth home, not when he had eternity laid out before him.

✦ Chapter V ✦

Justin Bell moved his hands ever so slightly to keep himself from turning over. He was alone in the auditorium, floating in the middle of the room where the cadets had first met Thor upon arrival at the Academy over five weeks ago. It had become one of his favorite spots aboard ship, a place to be alone. Here, in the conference room, it was usually empty this time of the evening and he'd slip in for fifteen or twenty minutes before going out to join his friends to practice for the big playoff in another two weeks.

He sighed quietly, relaxing as he floated in the middle of the room, trying to ignore the pain radiating from nearly every muscle in his body. The afternoon PT session had been an all-out one hour run, ten kilometers flat out up and down the corridors of the ship while wearing light EVA gear, with Malady,

Garcia and the other instructors screaming and shouting at them all the way, ready to apply a liberal dosage of foot to backside on anyone who lagged. At the end of the run the company came up minus one more scrub who collapsed a kilometer from the finish and when she came around stripped out of the EVA, and went down to Thorsson's office for a 1023, a one way ticket back to Earth.

As he flexed his aching legs Justin still found it to be amazing that he had even finished the dreaded run while wearing forty pounds of EVA suit, which even in the half gravity was bulky and murder to run in. In the last kilometer he had staggered as if in a dream, with Matt half pulling him along and Malady right up alongside him, shouting imprecations and taunts every meter of the way.

He closed his eyes for a moment. Though not overly religious, he felt somehow as if this place was sort of like a cathedral, a cathedral floating through the heavens.

He liked this spot since the first day at the Academy, and ever since the space walk he found it impossible to stay away. Something had clicked inside when he had seen the heavens as they were truly meant to be seen — from space. There had been only one more space walk since, this time using ropes and hand thrusters, the group going out several hundred meters from the ship. He just couldn't get enough of simply looking and the auditorium was the next best thing.

When he had gone out with a hand thruster to the end of the tethering rope it had blown him away to turn and look back, watching as the ship slowly turned on its long axis, eclipsing the sun and then Earth. Tomorrow they were going out on their first free flight, using MMBPs, Manned Maneuvering Back Packs. He couldn't wait.

He sighed, waving his hands slightly to steady himself and to keep from turning over. Why zero g had ever bothered him was now something of a wonder. It seemed like the most natural condition one could ever be in, far better than gravity, even the low level one-third gravity of the dorm area.

It was a wonder, so unlike lying in an Indiana field in autumn. Back home he thought he had really seen stars before, thousands of them. Across the dark sky he would follow the tracks of the orbital stations, or the pearl-like string of solar power plants which crossed the heavens, their fifty-square-kilometer panels soaking up the sunlight, beaming hundreds of gigawatts of energy down to an Earth that always needed yet more energy.

Out here, however, it was infinitely more splendid. The station was pointed straight at Earth, the sun behind the Academy as they drifted in orbit around the far side of the Moon. The blue-green orb seemed to glow with its own internal light, beyond it the Milky Way shone dimly, barely visible due to the reflected glare of the planet. It was high noon over Europe, the western United States just coming into dawn.

He could see home, Indiana and the Midwest clearly visible under a cloudless sky. It'd most likely be around six in the morning down there right now.

The sun just breaking above the trees, the golden light slanting across the high fields of corn. He realized that he still missed it, it was, after all, home. He missed the sounds, especially the birds, singing their morning greetings to the sun. He could almost picture Lady, his old retriever, lying on the porch, soaking up the first touch of warmth, the grass of the front lawn glistening with dew. He missed it, but not with the heartbreaking pain that had still gripped him only a week ago. He found he could actually smile fondly now with the memories of dawn and of thunderstorms darkening the evening sky. There was no aching sense of loss when he remembered the soft murmur of Sugar Creek or even the memory of the first flakes of winter drifting down out of a leaden sky.

They were part of him, and yet they already seemed distant. Instead was the haunting sight of what was before him and all that was beyond it. He now knew what it was like to float, godlike, above the world and somehow sense the power of the infinite. He found he could dream the dreams of eternity, drifting through the Rings of Saturn, watching lightning dance across the face of Jupiter, standing in the deserts of Mars and witnessing the coming of a cold dawn, the sand swirling about him in the thin high air. To lose such dreams now was beyond what he felt he could bear.

Occasionally he'd ask Uncle to play some music that seemed to fit, usually old classical pieces like Holst's "Planets" or Demby's "Novus Magnificat," or one of the more modern space composers like Juan or Ostoric. He wasn't in a mood though for that kind of music now. The sense that he might lose all of this troubled him too much. Tonight, he wanted the music to fit his sense of depression and he had asked Uncle to play some good somber Wagner while he floated.

It was a place to be alone, to forget. No longer were there the worries of home, the mocking comments of those he went to school with, who teased him about his skinniness, his gangly height, or the cowlick of hair that would never stay in place, though with the crew cut of a cadet that at least was no longer a problem.

Here as well he could forget about the perpetual taunts of Tanya, who seemed to take a delight in making every moment miserable, the constant egging of Senior Cadet Seay, or even the pushing of Uncle, who at every free moment kept suggesting that he do some additional studying for Astro-Navigation.

Astro-Navigation. It was a nightmare, the source now of all his worries. What had once been so much fun, the plotting out of orbits, the playing of simulator games, was now a constant nightmare, even invading his dreams, with the damnable Xing the tyrant destroying his life. And destroying it she seemed to be doing so efficiently. She seemed to make it a habit of picking on him when it came to a question that he wasn't prepared for, her pale features crinkling up with disdain when he missed the answer, her sarcastic voice telling him that he obviously had not studied hard enough.

If it wasn't for the fact that studying was forbidden

during the recreational period he'd be down in his room right now.

At the moment he felt downright miserable, as if he had spent his entire life scaling a mountain. He had finally taken a break and looking out saw the wonder of all that was possible. Yet when he looked straight up he fully realized that the roughest section ahead was impossible to climb. He had heard older cadets refer to it as "the hump," the point when you felt so desperate you simply knew you couldn't go on. They'd chuckle about it, claiming that nearly every semester had "the hump," when it seemed as if the whole universe was crashing down. The difference was, though, that for himself this hump, the very first one, was going to knock him off and send him straight back to Earth.

It was never going to work, never. But now what? Go home? He could just imagine that, starting the fall back at home, in high school again. He could picture John Ellington and his buddies standing in the hallway, "Hey space cadet, couldn't cut it up there, could you?" and then taking delight in administering a good working over.

And of the Bell half of the family, Grandpa Bell would most likely disown him. It might even get picked up by the media, he thought coldly, imagining the headlines: "Jason Bell's Son Flunks Out of the Academy, Greeted with Derision Back Home." There was only one person who he knew would rejoice over his failure, and that would be his mother, who would be thrilled that her "baby" was back home. The mere thought of that was a bit comforting, but at the same time filled him with a certain embarrassment.

"Damn it, I'm sixteen," he thought. "I can't go back to being her baby anymore, it'll kill me."

He couldn't even quit and just take off. It would take another year of the Academy before he'd even get his high school equivalency degree. Not even a junk cargo ship would sign him on as a hand and the U.N. or American territorial defense forces would kick him out of the recruiting sergeant's door.

He felt a heaviness in his gut, as if he wanted to cry, a luxury he would never allow himself but which he wanted to do nevertheless. It looked impossible. There was no way out, the mere thought of trying to score a ninety-six on the final seemed impossible. Even Pradeep and Tanya, who ate up the course, had passed the midterm with grades in the low nineties and they seemed to be absolute geniuses, something he was convinced he was definitely not.

The sky forward started to turn darker, as the Earth drifted out of view. The somber cords of Wagner's "Gotterdammerung" reached a crescendo, and then drifted away.

"Cadet Bell?"

Startled, Justin looked around and saw another figure floating on the far side of the room. He felt embarrassed, not sure how to act or what to say.

Thor Thorsson started to drift towards him.

Instantly he came to attention and tried to bring himself up vertically in relationship to Thor, who looked over at him and smiled.

"Relax, cadet, mind if I join you?"

Justin gulped nervously.

"Yes, sir. I mean no, sir. I mean . . ."

"It's all right, I guess I startled you," Thorsson said and with a gentle motion of his hands the Academy commander floated over to Justin and stopped. He closed his eyes for a second.

"I thought I heard Wagner playing out in the corridor so I followed it in here. I didn't know you were a fan of classical music; that's not too common with fellows your age."

"Well sort of, sir. My grandpa got me interested in it. He says that classical music somehow seems to sound even better when you're in space. I found out he was right."

Thorsson closed his eyes and nodded.

"Your granddad had a great collection of music which he brought along to Mars. He's the one that got me interested in classical music. Wagner's music fits space in a way, dealing as it does with old Norse legends about the Gods in Valhalla. But you're listening to "Gotterdammerung," rather depressing stuff at times, isn't it? Personally, I like the "Ride of the Valkyries" myself. It's great stuff to play when you're throttling up a Mark III attack ship and punching through six g, the roar of the engines rattling through the cabin."

Justin wasn't sure how to answer, and decided it was best not to.

"Uncle, let's cheer this place up a bit, put on Holst's 'Planets,' the last part of the recording, the movement called 'Neptune.' "

"As you wish, sir," Uncle replied, and Justin noticed

that the computer's voice was all so respectful.

The music started and Thor smiled.

"Actually, I like *Peer Gynt* a lot. The family claims Grieg, the composer, was an ancestor, but I don't believe it."

He turned slightly to float on his back, looking up at the sky.

"You found my favorite place aboard ship, Cadet Bell. When I need to be alone for a while I like to come up here and float, the same as you do. With the right music playing you can almost feel like you're drifting straight out into the universe."

"I'm sorry if I intruded, sir," Justin said nervously, and he started to turn looking for some sort of handhold to pull himself back down to the floor.

"At ease, cadet, at ease. It was I who intruded on you. After all, you were here first, not I."

A bit surprised, Justin looked over at Thor.

"Just relax for a minute and let the music take you up out there."

Justin turned to look straight back up. The Milky Way was straight overhead now, turning slowly as the ship pivoted on its long axis. Justin looked at it with wonder, never having truly seen it like this before. It was magnificent. And the music seemed to help carry him out. The piece was gentle, soft, the choir singing a wordless chant which made him feel as if he was floating straight up into the stars. Ever so gradually the music drifted away into silence.

Justin heard a sigh and he turned his head to look over at Thorsson.

"I've been out in space for fifty years," Thorsson said softly, "and it's yet to lose its wonder."

"I can see why, sir," Justin replied.

"It's funny that I find you here, Justin. It's kind of rare to find cadets floating in this room, especially during the recreation period. Not interested in a good round of falcon fighting? I hear the money's running heavy on B company. I thought you people would be practicing tonight."

"Company practice doesn't start for another forty minutes, sir. I just wanted to come in here first, to watch space, to float and think."

"To think about what, son?"

"Just things, sir," Justin replied quietly.

Thor smiled.

"You know your father and I were good friends. I guess that's why I couldn't help calling you 'son.' You know, I don't have any children of my own. Never did marry. The children of my friends sort of filled in, I guess."

He smiled.

"And don't ever quote me on this, Justin, but I sort of feel that every cadet in this Academy is a bit like a child of mine as well. Don't tell anyone though, but there's sort of a special interest in you."

Justin smiled at the confidence and Thorsson's friendly manner.

"Your father was a good man, Justin. One of the best. I knew him for twenty years. I knew your mother too, she was a wonderful woman, a good scientist. She's doing well, I hope. Last time I chatted with her, she was teaching at Purdue University."

"She's fine, sir."

He didn't want to add that the admiration was not mutual. His mom blamed Thorsson for the loss of her husband and blamed him now for luring her only child away to space. The mention of Thorsson's name would not bring a very happy response on her part.

"I can see a lot of your father in you, Justin," Thor said quietly, "and I knew him better than most."

Justin wanted to say something but couldn't. It was hard to imagine anyone seeing something in him that was like his father. His father was a hero, while as for himself? His father was a ghost, a name that he carried, nothing more, and worst now, an image to live up to, a living up to that he knew he was failing.

"I remember the first time I met your father, that's when I was still a flight instructor and the Academy was still Earthside."

Thor smiled.

"And anything related to math almost killed him. He came into my office once and announced he was dropping out."

"Really?" and Justin could not keep the questioning tone out of his voice.

"And do you want to know something else?"

"What, sir?"

"He was a lousy pilot as well."

Thor chuckled at Justin's surprised look.

"First time he went up to the Moon he was sick the entire way. Screwed his approaches, it was almost comical."

Justin tried to force a smile, suddenly wondering

if Thor was telling the truth, or simply trying to encourage him.

The smile on Thor's face disappeared, replaced by an almost pained expression.

"You know something, Justin, I can still remember the moment when word came in that your dad died rescuing the passengers on the *Condor*. At that moment all I could think of was the day he wanted to quit and I talked him out of it. It was a horrible moment when my aide told me that he was dead. All I could think of was the fact that if I hadn't encouraged your father he would still be alive. He'd be Earthside for sure, most likely even teaching at Purdue the same as your mother, rather than . . ."

Thorsson fell silent for a moment, looking back out in space.

They had buried his father out in space, a thought that still troubled Justin at times, when he realized that his father, what was left of him, was floating somewhere out there, drifting for all eternity.

"And five hundred people aboard the *Condor* would be dead in exchange, because without your dad they never would have made it," Thor finally said.

"A lot of good people have been lost out there but a hell of lot has been done as well. We've even saved our planet in the process but the price, as usual for such things, has been high.

"What I finally came to realize about your dad, and about all the others, is that they were volunteers. They wanted to be out here, to be at the edge of the frontier. Your father lived and died being what he wanted to be, a deep spacer, an explorer, a pilot, a man living on the frontier."

Thor looked over at Justin, his features now grave.

"It's a hell of legacy to live up to, Justin and sometimes we get tagged with a job we really don't want. I'm going to ask you something now, strictly between you and me, and I promise you that when I leave this room I'll forget the answer. I'll never discuss it with anyone, and it won't affect any decisions I have to make regarding you. I just want you to be honest."

"Sure, sir, I'll be straight with you, sir," Justin said quietly.

"Justin, are you doing this, I mean, going to the Academy because you really want to, or because you feel you have to because of your family name?"

Justin sighed and closed his eyes.

The room was silent, as silent as space itself, and he looked back up at the stars which went on into the eternity of night.

If Thor had asked him this question on the first day, even just a week ago, he knew how he would have answered. There was, even then, a hell of a lot of him that wanted this, but underneath it all was the driving force that it was expected, this path in his life picked out in the instant his father was killed.

That had always hung over him, that no matter how uncoordinated, how gangly, how disorganized he might be, a precious slot into the Academy was waiting for him. He knew that was one of the real reasons why the guys at school down on Earth gave him such a rotten time. He had an Academy slot for free, without even having to try, made worse by the fact that he looked and acted like the least likely candidate around.

Did he want it now? There was no doubt of it, ever since he had stepped out of the Academy ship into open space he knew he was hooked forever. To lose it would be a nightmare.

"In the beginning, sir, I guess I was pushed into it. But now, now that I'm out here," and he gestured to the darkness and the light overhead, "I can't give it up."

Thor smiled.

"What I was hoping you'd say," Thor replied. "It shows you're honest. So it got to you then."

Justin smiled and nodded.

"When?"

Justin told him about the two space walks and a grin creased Thorsson's wrinkled face.

"Same for me. First time I went up was to Space Station America, aboard an old class B shuttle. I was scared to death. And then I went out on my first EVA. They just about had to drag me back in. I spent my next four years Earthside, busting my butt to get on the Mars expedition and every minute I was down there, I kept dreaming of being back up here. Even when I was asleep, it haunted me."

"I wonder what it is that does it, sir?" Justin asked.

Thorsson smiled again.

"It's something in our heart, our souls. I remember when I was six, maybe seven. My mother was a professor of Scandinavian Literature and she was invited to be a guest lecturer at a college in the states. Somehow she wrangled a ticket to go watch the launching of the last of the old class one American shuttles."

Justin almost wanted to stop him right there and go into technical details. The class ones had stopped flying in the first decade of the 21st century; but he didn't say anything, since there was such a strange, wonderful distant look in Thorsson's eyes. Justin felt as if he could look into them and somehow see the awesome power of an old vertical lift rocket roaring into the heavens, riding on seven million pounds of thrust.

"I know you might be disappointed, but I can barely remember the launch, other than it was loud, so loud I thought that the heavens were being ripped apart. But what I'll never forget were the people around me. There were thousands there, reporters, scientists, special guests like my mother. I remember looking up at my mother and she was crying."

He paused for a moment, and Justin realized that there had been a bit of a choke in Thorsson's voice.

"I looked from her to the others. All the adults standing around me were looking up, watching as that glorious ship rode upwards on a throne of fire, the Earth shaking beneath her, the thunder rippling across the sky. Yet I, six-year-old me, wasn't watching it. Instead I was looking at the people, their faces turned upwards, shining with the reflected light, lips moving as if they were praying, the sound of their voices washed away; and all of them with tears in their eyes.

"I had never seen adults behave like that before and it frightened me, and yet it awed me as well.

And then I turned and looked heavenward. I didn't know why, maybe because they were crying, but as I looked upwards and felt the power, the tears came to my eyes as well."

He paused for a moment, and Justin was surprised to see a bright misty shimmer in the old man's eyes.

"I remember as the thunder rolled away, when at last the ship was merely a glowing dot, far away, I remember asking my mother why everyone was crying.

"She looked down at me, tears in her eyes, 'because we're seeing the future,' she whispered."

"I think, Justin, that was the moment when I knew I would go into space someday. I think it is something that lurks deep in our souls. An old psychologist of the early 20th century used to refer to it as the 'collective unconscious.' I think space touches that collective unconscious. It's an instinct that compels us to go, no matter what the risk."

"Then why are some people afraid of it?" Justin asked, thinking back to his own fears.

"A lot because they've never touched it, or allowed themselves to touch it. Why was it that some people felt this compulsion to go and watch the early space launches, while millions of others couldn't have cared less? Why is it that you and I listen to Holst and feel a chill run down our backs when we look up, while others stay deaf to what some called the music of the spheres?"

Justin found he couldn't answer and he looked at Thorsson, unable to reply.

"I think space, like any frontier, only draws a few.

My own ancestors, they launched their ships into unknown seas, going where no one from Europe had dared to venture before. To be certain, most of them went simply to plunder. But I think there were some, a chosen few who went for something far different, to reach out and go beyond the known limits, to be the first to tread on new lands, to see new seas, the world as limitless to them as the universe now is to us.

"Others followed, but there will always be someone who will go first, called by a different voice. It was those kind of people who stood with me that day when we watched the shuttle fly, tears in our eyes, seeing all the possible futures ahead. As for the others, they will always stay behind."

Justin thought of Matt. He had been slightly in awe of him at first, surprised that one who had traveled so far would pick him as a friend. He could see from the moment they had first met that there was that distant look, a certain feel to his presence. He felt the same about Thorsson, and he suspected that if he went to the outer reaches of the solar system it would be the same with all whom he met.

"How do you feel about the separatist movement, sir?"

He was surprised that he had even asked the question, and wished he could somehow withdraw it. The man before him, after all, was the official head of the Academy, a part of the United Nations space program and a member of the Space Affairs Commission, which had to deal directly with the ever increasing political and potential military threat.

Thorsson laughed softly and shook his head.

"If you were a reporter I'd give my standard line that as a member of the United Nations Space Affairs Commission I fully obey the orders of my superiors."

He paused for an instant.

"And I do obey those orders, the same way I expect you and every cadet on this ship to obey mine, instantly and without hesitation."

Justin swallowed hard, expecting a good chewing out.

"At ease, Justin, at ease. It's a fair question and I'll take it. I'll answer it because I know and have flown with three generations of Bells. This might sound strange, son, but I expect this to be between you and me."

Justin nodded, a bit awestruck.

"Oh, I'm not going to say anything treasonous. If I felt that way I would have resigned my commission by now. It's just that my personal feelings are my own and not to be shared with most of the people I serve with."

"You have my word on that, sir," Justin replied.

"Good, and your word is all the assurance I need."

Justin felt his features flush, amazed that someone as exalted as Thorsson would treat him thus.

"I think we're looking at a natural process of history. It could almost be defined in biological terms. Parents bring a child into the universe and raise it with certain dreams and expectations. No matter what a parent might say about wanting a child to grow into whatever it wants, down deep they still work hard and hope for certain paths. There comes a time when the child leaves, the same way you did, not five weeks ago. I can imagine how your mother felt, but she knew there was no stopping what would be."

Justin found it painful to recall the moment when he said good-bye and walked out the door, his grandfather waiting to take him down to the airport. She couldn't even bring herself to go with him. He knew she dreaded what he was doing, and he knew as well that even if he had wanted to, at that moment he couldn't turn back.

"It is the same with nations and peoples. Colonies are never started for the same altruistic reasons that most children are created and born. They are not created as an act of love, but of necessity. They are created as a means of gaining resources, expanding power, or as a place to flee, to find refugee from the mother country. It is what started the colonies of Phoenicia, Greece, my own ancestors, the English, Spanish, and the other European powers. The colony might serve the purpose intended for a year, a decade, even a century or two, but eventually there will come a day of self-awareness. A day when those who live in the colony look around and see themselves no longer as a part of the motherland, but rather as somehow different.

"It has to happen, it is as inevitable and unstoppable as the planets swinging forever in their orbits. The land they live on is different and that changes the people. The village yeomen of England came to the shores of America, and for a generation or two they built their small towns the same as they remembered back home, close to the shore and to England, what they thought of and feared as wilderness hedging them in. Your small New England village still has that charm, the look of England even after four hundred years. But then there came a day when the sons, the granddaughters of those colonists crossed over the next mountain and saw that the land was limitless, stretching, to their eyes, forever. It was no longer something to be afraid of, it was to be embraced. The small bounds of their village, the thinking of an island people was gone from their souls. They were no longer English — at that moment, they were Americans.

"What came after that moment was inevitable. For their government at home still thought of them as colonists, and that word has a certain connotation. It carries with it the sense, on the part of the mother country, that those who are colonists are somehow second best. They are not cosmopolitan enough, they don't understand the true complexities of government and of power. Their speech is becoming different, their ideas strange, they have to be reined in and controlled. The English even went so far as to pass a law forbidding settlers to go over the Appalachian mountains to the rich lands beyond."

"To Indiana," Justin said, remembering how he used to look across the fields and imagine how they once were, when Tecumseh and his fellow Indians lived but ten miles north, or when a young Lincoln settled with his family just over the border in Illinois.

"The law, in a way, was only fair for the Native population. After all it was their land first and the English didn't want any more conflicts with them.

But what they were trying to stop was an inevitable process and to the colonists the law was absurd, passed by a government thousands of miles away, for the land was there and had to be taken.

"Yes, the Indians suffered, were robbed of what was theirs, but history in its coldest sense sheds no tears when one society is supplanted by another that is innately stronger. Sure there are some historians who wring their hands and whine about how unfair certain things are. But ask them to figure out a different way, how to prevent the stronger from supplanting those who cannot keep up and they'll mumble and turn away. They are apologists for those who lose, and I daresay if it had been the other way around, they would be singing the praises of the winner. It might not be fair, but it is a process that can never be stopped. It is the same process that saw the power of Europe shift to this new America, and now finds it leaping out to the stars."

"And the Tracs, could it be the same with them?"

Thorsson nodded.

"It's a race that I'm truly afraid of, Justin. If they are stronger than us, they know what history shows. Either they must reach an accommodation with us, destroy us, or in the end be destroyed by us in turn. I'd like to think we can reach an agreement, but not even space is limitless. They might see us as a child who could one day grow into something far more dangerous. Their actions so far have not indicated any friendliness. They might want to strangle us in our cradle before we grow any more. I think the three raids were scouting missions, and once it sinks in that we are close to reassembling one of their ships, they'll be back, this time in force.

"What we're seeing with the Tracs is, to my sense of things, simply an extension of what we've seen before. The shifting of power, the confrontation over power and control, and then new things emerging out of it."

"Close to finishing one of their ships?" Justin asked. Thor smiled.

"That's classified information, son, so keep it that way. Prove yourself out over the next year and you might get a slot at the station working on the ship."

Justin grinned with delight.

"Now the separatist movement, we can at least talk about that," Thor said. "There's one more point here to consider."

A bit disappointed that he couldn't find out more about the Tracs, Justin nodded, allowing Thor to turn the conversation away.

"I think there's one key point here that not many people are willing to talk about, and I'll call that the evolutionary factor."

"I've heard grandpa talk about that one," Justin said, "but I never really got the point of it all."

"Well, son, it was your grandfather who first set the thought in my own mind. We talked about it endlessly on that trip out to Mars, back when it used to take six months to get there.

"It's really quite a simple point, but most folks don't want to think about it. Everyone is, and should be, equal in all things in the eyes of the law, and in the common ideal of humanity. But there are differences.

Differences in skills, intelligence, physical ability and how one views existence.

"Space, quite frankly, is creating a new man, what I'll call the second generation of man. It is already happening, it cannot be stopped, and some of those who will be left behind on Earth are frightened by it.

"I remember talking with some of the first of the old cosmonauts and astronauts, who flew during the space race of the 1960s."

"Who?" Justin asked excitedly.

"Greckho, Rusty Schweikert, even Buzz Aldrin, the second man to walk on the Moon. I met him and Schweikert when I was at a ceremony to commemorate the fiftieth anniversary of the first Moon landing."

Thor smiled as Justin looked at him in awe.

"I know, it is kind of strange when I think of it. All that I've seen in this century of space, and yet I actually met someone who took part in it at the very beginning. What I remember the most though was how Schweikert described his first space walk. He said that when he floated out of his Apollo spacecraft and looked down, a new consciousness was born. He called it a paradigm shift. He said that at that moment he saw the absurdity of borders, of dividing Earth apart. From space he saw Earth as it was meant to be seen, as a whole, floating in the vastness of space.

"Nearly everyone who has been out here reports the same thing, the same shift in thinking. It's what helped us to solve some of the problems back at the turn of the century, because for the first time we saw Earth as a whole, not as something divided.

"Your grandfather, when he talked about this, took

it a step further, to its final conclusion. There seems to be a natural selection process going on as far as going into space is concerned. You first have to want to go. Unlike the colonies of old, where people were often shipped there whether they wanted to go or not, those who come up here have to really want it.

"Granted, increasingly there are groups, particularly some of the religious colonies and social experiment colonies that go collectively, but in general it is still individuals who choose to leave. They are therefore adventurous to start with, but more importantly they are in fairly good shape, and even more importantly they tend to be awfully damn smart."

Justin chuckled and shook his head.

"If you saw my Astro exam you might think twice on that."

"I have seen the exam, and I've seen your records and intelligence tests as well, Mr. Bell, and son, whether you realize it yet or not, you've got the makings of a damn good officer in you."

A bit startled, Justin didn't know what to say.

"Anyhow, as I was saying, here we've got the best and the brightest going into space. They tend to marry each other and their children are born, not on Earth but out in the asteroid belt, on Mars, in the orbital colonies, and in the far reaches of the system, out in orbit around Jupiter, Saturn and even beyond that. The children born to these families are born into an entirely new environment unlike any other in the history of mankind.

"The children of these pioneers are being raised in space and already they view Earth differently.

They're being raised in new environments, even different gravities. You look at some of the third generation kids now being born on Mars. They tend to be one hell of a lot smarter than your average Earther. Somehow they don't even quite look the same as those raised on Earth and they sure don't think the same as Earthers.

"Let's use the America example again. When Columbus set sail nearly six hundred years ago, there were a lot of people on the docks to see him off. Some of them most likely cheered, and I'm willing to bet a hell of a lot of them thought him crazy. There was most likely more than one person who whined, 'what the hell are we spending money on this for, when we should be spending it on our cities to kill the rats, clean up the garbage and feed the hungry.' Now no one had a crystal ball that day to see into the future, because if they had they would have seen all that was to come. They would have seen that the voyage starting that day would one day result in an entirely new form of government with a political declaration that all men are created equal. They would have seen the birth of a society that would one day find the cure for the plague, provide haven to tens of millions, and even return to save the Old World from the darkness of Fascism and Communism. I think we're seeing the same thing happening with our going into space. Who knows what it will bring?

"What I'm saying here is that nature is at work, the forces of evolution are coming into play. We have a natural selection to start with, new social systems, new environments, and entirely different views. Call it nature or call it God, but whatever the driving force, it loves to see change, and to see something new fill a niche in the universe that was empty. Give it a hundred more years and the difference will be even more pronounced. What you are witnessing, Justin, and what you are part of, is the birth of the next generation of humankind. An entire new species is coming into being, born from parents of superior ability, born in an entirely new environment, and born to believe that the universe is limitless and there for the taking. On Earth, the view is still one of limits, of being closed in, and even now the best and the brightest are leaving it behind. That birth of a new generation will shake the first generation, those who remain behind, to the core.

"That is what I believe is the real issue. Behind the arguments about taxes, governments, imports and exports, and status of nations and colonies is a far more profound argument: it is the division between the parent and child, the old generation and the new, the next evolutionary step for man, versus what is left behind. And you, son, you will live in the very heart of it and I envy you your youth. Because the changes are only beginning and I would love to be able to stick around another hundred years to find out just what happens next."

Thor stretched out and sighed.

"I think I've gabbed on a bit too long here, Cadet Bell."

Justin looked at him, wide-eyed, unable to speak.

Thor smiled, somersaulted over, and with an easy

grace reached down and grabbed hold of a handrail attached to a wall. He extended a hand to Justin and, a bit nervous, Justin took it. Thor pulled him down and together they touched down on the floor, letting their sticky boots take hold.

"You'll get through scrub summer all right, Justin. I wouldn't say it if I didn't believe it. You're going to have to bust your tail to do it, but I think you've got the stuff to make it.

"Tell me, Justin, did you ever do something really scary, really dangerous?"

Justin laughed softly.

"Coming here about matches that one, sir."

Thor nodded and laughed.

"I remember when I went to Mars, I really wasn't much older than you. It was back in the early days, the trip out took six months, not the two weeks we have today. The ship was downright dangerous, no backups, no other ship to come and pull your hide out if something went wrong. I used to have a knot in my gut when I was doing a watch alone. Couldn't keep my eyes off the instruments for a second, always afraid something would fry off, the way the first attempted Mars expedition did when an oxygen cylinder blew and they all died before reaching the planet.

"Well, Justin, we made it, and a year later I came back to Earth, hailed as a hero. Of course then, after it was all over, I looked back on it and said it was great, a wonderful exciting time. But down deep I knew differently. The key thing was that I didn't let my fears kill me, even though I thought they would.

"I'll tell you something in confidence, Justin, and it's a secret."

He smiled and Justin nodded in reply.

"It's a secret, sir."

"Good then. I'm still scared at times, Justin. It should be a motto I think: stay scared and stay alive."

"Then why do you do it, sir?"

"Because, son, it's in the mastering of our fears that we prove something to ourselves. I had a great-grandfather who fought in the resistance against the Nazis in the Second World War. I used to listen to his stories when I was a little boy and thought he was the bravest man I ever knew. But I think I know differently now.

"I know he was scared to death most of the time. But the key thing was that he kept on going for what he believed was right. The same way your father did."

He paused for a moment.

"The same way I'm sure you will. And as you look back on it all, you'll realize that there were times that were scary but by heavens you wouldn't have missed them for anything. You'll find yourself to be part of the greatest adventure in history and will be proud to be part of it."

"But, sir, I feel so out of place here," Justin suddenly blurted out.

Thor smiled in reply.

"Don't you think I know that?" Thor replied. "Listen, son, that's why I want you to stick it out."

"Why's that?"

Thor laughed.

"Because you aren't quite like some of the other

cadets. The physical stuff — we don't need muscle-bound giants out here in space. I think you've even seen some cadets here with what would be called disabilities back on Earth. Zero gravity requires different things when it comes to strength and coordination. I think that since you are a bit different you might even turn out to be better than most in the long run. I know you have the stuff mentally as well," and he smiled, "in spite of that problem you're having with Astro-Navigation. It'll teach you guts as well, Justin."

Justin looked away, ashamed. Guts, his father had it, but as he looked into himself he was afraid he simply did not. Damn near everything scared him, from the guys at school who picked on him to the silent vacuum of space.

"Justin, heroes like your dad were simple ordinary men and women. Nothing special, but circumstances suddenly put them into a situation where they had to think clearly, calmly, and be willing to risk all, or as Chief Petty Officer Malady puts it, 'doing it coolly, with guts and style.' You'd be surprised how many heroes, down deep, can't understand how or why it happened. Can't believe that they actually accomplished what they did. It's just that when the time comes, the training takes hold and you get through."

"And you, sir?"

Thor laughed.

"Most definitely me, Justin, most definitely. And son, you might be surprised to find the same thing happening to you someday. You might actually look back on your time here at the Academy, and perhaps even forget just how really miserable you're feeling, as I suspect you are at this moment."

"How do you know that, sir?"

"I think anyone listening to the final act of Wagner's 'Gotterdammerung,' alone, floating in this room, must be a little bit down."

Justin laughed softly.

"No, seriously, son. I think I know what you're feeling, I've been there plenty of times myself. I'm grateful in a way that I didn't have the additional burden of a family name to prove something with. It's a harder road for you to travel because of that, Justin. But I want you to know something. Your dad, and your grandfather as well, underneath it all, were just ordinary people, with the same fears all the rest of us have. Just remember that, Justin. Your dad was not some statue cast in bronze, like the one of him at the museum at Cape Kennedy. He was someone just like you, and as I look at you, I can almost see him again, a nervous cadet, on the edge of quitting, not realizing all that he might become if he toughed it out."

Justin was unable to reply.

Thor looked at his wristwatch.

"It's past 2000, I've got to catch the late shuttle back to Earth, the usual round of boring meetings to argue about budgets," Thor said. "Justin, when you get to be an old man like me, try to avoid flying a desk, it'll drive you crazy."

Thor extended his hand.

"Take care, son, and remember my door's always open. Out there," and he nodded towards the rest of the ship, "we might have to be a little more formal with each other, but know that I still feel the same."

"Thank you, sir."

"Thank you for being here, Justin, for taking a stab at it. Take care of yourself, son."

They shook hands and Thor headed for the door. He turned and looked back at Justin.

"Uncle, put on some more Holst, 'Jupiter.' It's one of my favorites."

"An excellent choice, sir," Uncle replied.

As he left the room the music started with a dramatic flourish.

Justin turned to look at the stars, the Moon drifting back into view, the music swelling around him, and he smiled.

✧ Chapter VI ✧

"Uncle, sometimes I think you have it in for me," Justin said quietly.

"Why would you ever accuse me of that?" Uncle replied, his tone somewhat peeved.

"You're always throwing me these curveball questions. Before the exam you crashed me into Mons Olympus and Xing didn't throw any tricks like that at all. Now you've got me wading through hypothetical orbital mechanics for star systems a hundred light years away. We'll never even get that far in my lifetime."

"What makes you think that?"

Justin hesitated. He had to keep reminding himself that he was, after all, only talking to a computer. With the advent of the 988 series, there was serious debate as to whether the machine was truly self-aware. Because if it was, then machines at last had

179

reached the ability to fully replicate the emotional range of humans. He had even asked Uncle if he was indeed self-aware, and if he considered himself to be alive. Uncle had launched into a debate as to what was the definition of life. He had finally hit Uncle with the response that if the ship was destroyed, he as a human believed in a concept of immortality, whereas what would happen to a computer? Uncle's response, that he would simply cease to exist, was disturbing in a way and he dropped the subject.

"It's just that we all know that actual faster-than-light travel is still proven to be impossible, at least for any living creature. Sure, there's that tachyon theory, and the bit about going through wormholes and black holes, but anything living would come out the far side looking like soggy oatmeal."

"The Tracs still managed to get here," Uncle replied.

"Yeah, but that has to do with jump transfer theory and we know even less about that than wormholes and tachyons."

"Which you'll study in your third and fourth years as a midshipman," Uncle said. "Who knows, maybe by then they'll have put that Trac ship back together again and figure out how it works. If so, that class should prove to be a lot of fun."

"God help me when I get there."

"Just take it all one step at a time, but let's get back to this problem."

"What about jump transfer?" Justin asked. "I mean, what do we really know?"

Uncle chuckled softly.

"Justin, you know you have to pass a level three security clearance before we can discuss that."

"Yeah, I know, I'm just curious though."

"So just pass this Astro-Navigation final and survive four more years of this place. You'll get the clearance and I'll fill you in on everything when you're ready."

"And you know it all though, right inside that core memory of yours?"

"I'm supposed to be questioning you, Justin, not the other way around."

A bell sounded out in the corridor.

"Good luck in your afternoon match," Uncle announced.

"Yeah, sure."

"By the way, which way is the money running at the moment?"

A bit surprised, Justin looked back at the computer.

"Gambling's illegal," Justin said quietly.

"Oh come on," Uncle retorted, "every cadet in the school's betting on this match."

"And the instructors and upperclassmen?" Justin asked with a smile.

"You know it is illegal for a machine to report on an illegal activity unless ordered to do so by a superior court pursuant to a class three felony or higher."

"So how would you bet on the game?"

Justin was surprised when Uncle actually started to chuckle.

"What good is gambling and the winning of money

to a computer? Just how would I spend my ill-gotten gains?"

"I don't know, buy more core memory with it. But seriously, your interest must be aroused by the sheer mathematical challenge, a probability study if you will, of the scrub championship game."

"Of course it is. The number of variables involved is staggering in its complexity even for me, but you're reversing the question here. It was I who asked you how the money was running."

"Two to one on B company," Justin announced. "This Bugniazet is a killer in one-to-one games. In a couple of squad against squad fly offs with other units, his unit smashed their opposition. They have nearly two dozen cadets in their company who were raised either on the Moon or in orbital colonies so they've been playing the game for years. The next unit with even half as many non-Earthers is our own."

"So you think they'll win?"

"I said the betting's going their way," Justin replied sharply, "not that they'll win."

"I detect a bit of unit esprit in your voice, Justin Bell."

"Well, so what if I'm proud of the company," Justin replied. "It's a good unit. Jenkins knows what he's doing, and Matt's ready to take command if Jenkins buys it, and frankly I think Matt is even better. We've got a couple of tricks planned as well."

"Good luck then."

"I bet you're saying that to every cadet right now," Justin said, actually feeling a touch of jealousy that Uncle undoubtedly treated every cadet on board ship with equal friendliness.

"Well, you're right," Uncle replied, "but maybe I might mean it a little bit more for some rather than others."

"Come on, Uncle, you're saying you have emotions, sentimental attachments?"

"I'm a machine," Uncle replied, his voice suddenly flat and toneless.

"Cut it out, Uncle."

"If my emotions are mere programming or genuine is hard to say. I might ask the same of you, Justin. Are your actions yours or are they predetermined by an all-knowing deity and your free will is nothing but illusion? Perhaps all of us are doing nothing more than what we are programmed to do."

"Great, we've gone from gambling to philosophy," Justin said, suddenly feeling a bit uneasy with the concept that Uncle had just put forth.

"Just doing my job of making you think," Uncle replied cheerfully.

"Yeah, thanks."

"Uncle doing the blow your mind routine again?"

Justin looked up to see Matt in the doorway.

"Hey, Uncle, don't rattle him with predetermination versus free will, unless it's to say that it's preordained that we win this afternoon's game."

"What will be will be," Uncle replied.

"I wish we could just shut you off sometimes," Matt announced, making a dramatic show of searching for a switch on the frame of the holo projection unit.

"Well, if you want to be that way about it, goodbye!"

"Uncle?"

The room was silent and Matt grinned. Reaching into his pocket he pulled out a sandwich and tossed it over to Justin.

"Skipping lunch and studying is fine, but going into the big game on an empty stomach is crazy."

"Thanks, Matt, dumb of you to do it though," and Justin quickly wolfed the sandwich down.

"No one saw me, old Brian was busy looking at Sharon. I think he's really got it for her."

"But still, if they caught you smuggling food out, it would have been ugly for you."

Matt simply shrugged and smiled.

"That old food restriction stuff is straight out of the 20th century. It's safe to eat anywhere aboard this ship, a few crumbs more or less floating around ain't going to upset the ecosystem."

"Given enough cadets violating the rule and leaving enough uneaten food tucked away in forgotten corners, it might pose a very serious problem."

"Hey, Uncle, I thought you were out of here."

"I'm still doing my job. Taking food into a private room is a violation subject to demerits, punishment detail, and even possible quarters confinement. The rule's there for a purpose."

"You're not going to squeal, are you?" Matt asked with mock horror.

"You know I can't, but I still don't like it."

"Sorry, Uncle."

"I don't detect any sincerity in your voice."

"Because there is none," Matt said with a laugh.

Uncle was silent and Matt finally went up to the holo camera pickup and smiled.

"Hey, no hard feelings."

"Don't start that," Justin interjected, "we might get stuck in another philosophy discussion before we're done, come on, it's game time."

"No hard feelings," Uncle said quietly.

As they started for the door Pradeep came in, reached into his pocket and pulled an apple out which he tossed to Justin.

Justin looked over at the monitor.

"Go on, I won't say anything."

"Thanks, Uncle."

Justin bit into the apple. It was every bit as good as the apples from the family orchard back home. What passed for an orchard up here, however, looked nothing like what he was used to seeing. There were no trees, instead it was nothing more than a genetically engineered root system, buried in a hydroponic tank, with each tiny branch emerging out of the tank bearing an apple every forty-five days. As quickly as it was picked, a bot pollinated a new flower which blossomed within half a dozen days, and then another apple was soon ready.

Finishing the apple, Justin put the core in the bathroom waste bin. Within seconds it would be whisked to the bio recycling center, broken down and used as nutrients to help grow something else.

"Let's hit the game, gentlemen," Justin announced.

"Good luck," Uncle said as they headed for the door.

Shaking his head and laughing, Justin left the room, his two friends following, and they headed for the lift. There was a mob of cadets waiting to go up.

"Come on, let's take the access tunnel," Matt announced and he went over to a side door, opened it and jumped onto the spiral stairs. Taking them three at a time, he started up, with Justin, Pradeep and a number of other cadets tired of waiting for the lift following.

As they ascended towards the center of the ship, gravity lessened, so that they were soon bounding up four, six, and eight steps at a time, until finally their feet barely touched the steps at all. They came out into the main central corridor that ran down the axis of the ship, and floating out the door they pushed off into the stream of cadets who were all heading to the far end, where the matches would take place in playing field number one.

Justin felt like he was in a river of fish, hundreds of white-clad cadets floating in the same direction. It was a far cry from over six weeks before, when this same corridor was crammed with sixteen hundred people, most of them rather miserable and all of them confused, bouncing off walls, and totally lost.

Groups of cadets started to break off from the main flow, heading into the assembly rooms where their companies were forming up, the hallway echoing with taunts, boasts and shouts.

"Here we are," Pradeep announced and they pushed their way into a practice room in which the cadets of A company were gathering.

Justin easily floated through the crowd heading for where his friends in the second squad were gathering in a ball.

"Hey straight-shooter, how long you gonna last?"

"Longer than you, Tanya," Justin said easily, drifting into the group.

"Yeah, you wish."

"I know."

"I doubt it, straight-shooter, unless you simply barf on whoever's after you."

"Thanks, I might try that on you before the day's done," Justin retorted and he made a motion as if he was about to stick his finger down his throat and the group laughed.

"A company, listen up!"

Justin looked back to the entry door into the room where Cadet Jenkins, the company commander for the game, was floating.

"You all know the signals and maneuvers," Jenkins said, "so stick close to your squads and fight as a team. Remember, if I buy it Matt Everett will come on the command circuit. After him command will go down the line in order of squad commanders from number two squad on down. So keep a sharp eye out, listen up, and stick together."

The group was silent.

"Whose butt we gonna kick?" Jenkins shouted.

"The whole damn school's!"

"Well, let's get out there!"

The group swarmed to the door and headed back into the corridor towards the spectator area. Members of E company poured out from another room and the two groups mingled together, spirits in both units high as they chanted their unit letter, pushing and shoving each other as they floated and leaped down the hallway.

The stream finally parted as they reached the far end of the ship where the playing field was located. The playing field for the falcon fighting championship was over a hundred meters long, running lengthwise within the ship, and fifty in diameter. Its primary function was to serve as an internal pressurized docking port, the far side of it opening out into space so that cargo ships could be hauled inside and then unloaded or overhauled under atmospheric conditions. Today the docking entry was sealed off, and protective panels removed around both ends of the bay so that spectators behind the Plexiglas wall could watch the game. Pushing his way in through the crowd, Justin saw that the first elimination match was already under way.

"Who's ahead?" he asked, shouldering his way into a crowd of cadets.

"Which company you with?"

"Company A."

"Well, buddy, I'm with D, and we're gonna kick your butt."

"Hey, look I just want to know who's winning in there so we know who we're playing against once we trounce you."

"B and C, and C is going down quick."

Justin watched the action as the two companies fought it out. They were playing in a class one field, which meant that it was a wide-open court. C was definitely on the losing end of it, and within a matter of minutes the last of them were hunted down and finished off, to hoots of derision from the spectators. B company finished up the slaughter with nearly sixty of its members still alive, flying in tight formations. The victory surprised no one since C company had gone into the game with the disadvantage of having lost nearly a third of its cadets to washouts, quitting or accidents and thus was severely outnumbered. The court was cleared and then E and H companies went out. The game was a slaughter. H had worked its tactics out to perfection, maneuvering in squad size units, each squad supporting the next. The members of E retired from the court to a shower of taunts from the other companies while F and G companies moved out into the court.

"A company, report to playing room blue, D company to room red."

Justin fell in with the flow of cadets leaving the spectator area, both sides trading jibes that were generally good-natured, but in a couple of cases threatened to get rather hot until senior cadets moved in to shepherd them along. For some reason that was a mystery to Justin, the feelings between the members of A and D company were not all that bad, something not at all true with B company which for some reason was viewed with animosity by nearly everyone else in the school.

Going into the suiting up room, Justin went over to where 2nd squad had already formed, and taking down a pair of wings he put them on.

"All right, people," Matt announced, calling his squad around. "Remember what we've learned. Keep your formations tight, cover your wingmen. There'll be only two voices on the command circuit. Jenkins's and mine. So listen up and stay sharp."

A buzzer sounded, signalling that the match between F and G was over and the court was cleared for the next battle.

A door more than a dozen meters across slid open behind them and the hundred and sixty cadets of A company moved through it out into the playing field. A hundred meters away, at the far end of the field, Justin could see the swarm of red wings marking the arrival of D company. He felt his heart start to race with excitement. Sports back on Earth had always been a humiliation for him. In falcon fighting he knew he could at least hold his own; he was fighting on a team he was proud of and more than ever he wanted to win. The number of players floating at the far side was a bit intimidating. What made it worse was that D company had suffered fewer washouts than A company and outnumbered them by nearly twenty players.

A spider web of laser beams snapped on, criss-crossing the field five meters out from the wall, marking the end zone behind which A company would form up.

"X formation!" Jenkins's voice whispered in Justin's headset.

"Second squad on me!" Matt announced, and they formed up, in two standard V formations, one half of the squad slightly above and behind the second half. To Justin's left, first squad was the upper left unit, then third squad the lower left, and fourth the lower right, directly beneath second. Closer into the center were four more squads, with sixth squad below Justin and to the left. Finally in the middle, the apex of the X formation, were two squads organized into one large unit, directly under the command of Jenkins.

"Ten seconds."

The playing field echoed with whistles, shouts and chants, and finally the buzzer sounded.

"Charge!"

Hundreds of pairs of wings started to beat. Justin felt a surge of adrenaline and with a wild yell he started forward. Within seconds the range started to narrow and the red team changed formation from an X into a compact arrow attack, designed to slam straight into the center of A company's line.

The two sides closed in a wild flurry.

"Close the X in on the center," Jenkins announced.

"Down on them, down!" Matt shouted, and with a dramatic wing over, he dived into the melee, the rest of the squad following. It was a mad confusion, and with level two contact allowed there was a lot of pushing and shoving. Justin caught a glimpse of Madison colliding with a red and snatching off her streamer. Madison, laughing with glee, waded through the melee, grabbing hold of another player and getting her in turn before her own streamer was yanked free, setting off a blinking light on Madison's unit.

With a laughing curse, she turned away from the attack, taking her two trophies with her.

The game seemed to turn into a brawl with little semblance of formation remaining. Justin found a red streamer dangling in front of him and he pulled it free, making another kill seconds later. Laughing, he tucked the streamers into his belt and looked around, seeing Matt attempting to shake off three blues. Matt pulled in a tight circle, folded his wings, and somersaulted, his streamer whipping up over his back as he turned over. Reaching out, he snatched the streamer of the first attacker. Justin closed in from behind, and within seconds dispatched the second while Matt took out the third.

"Retreat to circle," Jenkins called.

"Second squad to me!" Matt shouted, pulling up out of the melee.

The blue flyers struggled to break free of the confusion, red team hovering in the middle of the field in a solid swirling mass.

As blue broke off, discipline on the red side broke down, dozens of players rising up in pursuit of the blues. Justin formed up on Matt's side, looking around, seeing most of his squad was still alive, closing in on Matt as he kept shouting out the recall.

"Stagger attack, stagger! First squad, dive!"

Confused, Justin looked around and saw first squad diving back in on the red team, charging straight into the mass of red wings and disappearing, swarmed under. But their ball formation was broken, dozens of them, maneuvering, turning, trying to dispatch the rest of first squad.

"Dive, dive!" Matt roared, and Justin winged over, beating his wings hard and then tucking them in. Within seconds he caught another red and then all around him was confusion. Someone slammed into his back, another red elbowed him in the face, a blow that would have broken his nose without the helmet and faceplate. He grabbed hold of the leg of the red player who elbowed him and snatched another streamer, and then felt a tug on his own leg and the beeper went off in his headset, just as he started to wrap his hands around yet another dangling red streamer. He felt a sharp electric jolt in his hand as his fingers wrapped around the streamer and cursing, he let go.

With a couple of sharp beats of his wings he dived through the bottom of the fight and came out the far side. Dozens of dead players were heading back to their respective sides and looking back, Justin saw that the suicide dives of first and second squad had triggered the desired result. D company had attempted to fight in too big a formation, breaking down into confusion, while A company still had eight squads intact. Even as Justin reached the far end of the court, the eight squads of A company closed in for the kill. Within seconds the mass formation of D completely disintegrated, the game finishing up with the hunting down of the last survivors.

As the last of D company died, a klaxon sounded and the court echoed with wild shouts of triumph. The dead players of A company swarmed out onto the court, shouting, hugging the forty survivors and together they left the court.

Landing in the suiting up room, Justin pulled off his wings, hung them up and held his five red streamers aloft.

"Five kills, straight-shooter. Not bad, but it could have been better."

Justin turned and saw Brian looking at him

appraisingly. Matt came over, trailing seven streamers in his hand, his own streamer still attached to his leg. Brian smiled, said nothing and walked away.

"Boy, doesn't anything make that guy happy?" Justin grumbled.

"Forget about him, let's go watch the game."

They left the room as B company came in to suit up for the second round of eliminations. B won again, taking H company apart in less than five minutes, charging straight across the court at high speed in a single V formation, against H's X formation. Minutes later Justin and A company were back out on the court against F company, taking them apart when F company's leader was killed in the opening skirmish and the second in command failed to take over.

Justin ended the game breathing hard, having made two more kills and this time surviving the match.

A ten-minute break was called to allow A to get its wind back while B suited up for the final match to decide the championship. Hovering at the far end of the court, Jenkins called his team into a circle around him for final orders.

"We're not advancing," Jenkins said. "B company comes straight in aggressively, then folds in its outer sections to pounce the center. Let's give them something to think about this time, so when the klaxon sounds, we advance just beyond the dead area and then wait. Be careful not to back up, 'cause if you let a laser hit you, you're out of the game. Assume a circle formation. If we can spot where their leader is, we swarm him under and take him out. That's B's weakness, they've built their morale on one person. Kill him and we break them apart. Now let's get them!"

With a shout the company broke up and formed for the fight. On the far side of the court B company was formed, chanting "B, B, B." Justin could see the gallery was packed. Nearly everyone aboard the ship was in the spectator area to watch the final championship match.

"Ten seconds."

"Second squad get ready."

The klaxon sounded.

From the far end of the court B company charged forward, wings flapping, advancing fast in an X formation which they quickly shifted to a double-layered V. Tucked in behind Matt, Justin followed him out as they crossed through the crisscross weave of laser lights that marked off the end zone of the field.

"Hold!"

Fluttering his wings, Justin braked and came to a stop, the rest of his squad spreading out slightly. B continued its charge through the midcourt and Justin swallowed hard, his heart pounding as they advanced, still chanting. When they were less than ten meters away the attack started to grind to a stop. Several members of B company, unable to slow their advance, continued straight in. One came straight at Matt, and he quickly nailed him. Another one flew straight through the formation, trying to turn, and cut into the end zone, the lasers triggering his computer, eliminating him from the game. Swearing, he and half a dozen others who broke clean through came to a stop against the far wall, and disgusted, hung against the wall to watch the game.

A standoff now ensued, both sides hovering five to ten meters apart. B company's players started to taunt and yell and Justin looked down towards Jenkins, waiting for a call. With the laser field not five meters behind him Justin didn't like the idea of a general melee breaking out.

The seconds ticked away the tension building. Justin looked back at Matt and then straight ahead. Jenkins slowly flew around his formation, shouting for everyone to hold steady. A flurry of action broke out down at the bottom of the court when a dozen players from each side started to engage, more and yet more moving in. A squad from B company darted in, and Jenkins maneuvered support into the threatened area, half of B's attack force and a dozen A's players wandering into the end zone in the ensuing fight and getting themselves eliminated. Directly ahead a number of B company flyers started to edge closer in. Justin watched as what looked like a squad leader moved slightly forward, stopping not three meters away.

"Come on, you damned coward, one on one, let's do it!" he roared.

Justin looked around and realized that the squad leader was shouting the challenge straight at him.

"Come on, geek, you lousy wimp, what's wrong? You chicken?"

Justin felt his blood start to boil, and he started to edge forward.

"Justin!"

Looking up he saw Matt hovering directly above him.

He tried to calm down, waiting, and at that moment he was startled when Jenkin's voice cut in.

"Charge to the far wall!"

Out of the corner of his eye he saw Jenkins start forward, leading a squad straight into B company.

"Charge!"

With a wild yell Justin started forward, aiming straight at his tormentor, slamming into him. The two grappled for a moment, and then his opponent fell away, he started to dive down after him.

"Justin, stay with me, stay with me!"

Looking ahead he saw Matt, already on the far side of B company, his entire squad following. Justin flapped his wings hard and pushed off, weaving his way through the confusion and out into the clear on the far side. Flying hard, A company stormed down the length of the court, B company setting off in pursuit. Looking over his shoulder Justin saw the cadet who had taunted him furiously closing in.

"Reversal!"

Following Matt, Justin arched his back, winging over, diving, the squad still in formation, skimming B company's end zone. Swinging down to the bottom of the court A company rose back up, moving with a full burst of speed built up in their flight down the length of the field.

They slammed through A company, not stopping. Flyers crashed into each other head-on, striking with such force that both players were eliminated by their computers for hitting with excessive force. The court echoed with loud shouts of joy, anger, excitement and pain.

Laughing, Justin slashed in under two reds, snatching their streamers, and the race continued down the court, B still in pursuit.

Jenkins led his company back and forth three times and as he turned on the third swing through, Justin realized that he was flying faster than he ever had before. It was intoxicating, the wind rushing past him, his wings taut, fluttering with each beat as he darted and weaved, making another kill. Reaching the far end of the court, Justin swept through another turn and saw that B company had broken off pursuit, forming near their own end zone, regrouping. Formation in A company was starting to break apart. As they swept through their turn and started to head straight back he saw a melee down below him with half a dozen members of A company getting swarmed under and then a short piercing whistle sounded in his headset, the signal that Jenkins was out of the game.

"All right, A company, this is Matt, I'm in command now," his friend drawled calmly.

"Twenty meters short of end zone, break, turn and reform in X formation."

Justin tucked in close to protect Matt as the squad and company staggered to a stop and turned, struggling to regain formation. B company came straight on in and within seconds the two sides collided in a wild melee.

Justin moved up to protect Matt, Pradeep and Madison joining him. Matt maneuvered, trying to back out of the fight, to observe what was happening and figure out the next maneuver. Dead players streamed away in every direction, the fight in the center of the court spreading out into individual duels.

"Pull back to their end zone!" Matt roared.

Justin followed him, looking around to see that in the confusion few of the players were able to follow. Madison had disappeared and Pradeep died seconds later when he pushed off two red players closing in on Matt, taking one down, the second nailing him in turn. Justin killed the other one and then moved in directly behind Matt's streamer.

Gaining the edge of the end zone, Matt turned. Less than twenty survivors of A company formed up around him, while out in the middle of the court fifty or more survivors from each side were fighting it out, with a knot of players from B company forming up on their leader.

"Straight on them!" Matt shouted and the group charged. The two groups closed in, circling, yelling. Matt killed another one and closed in on their team leader. He made a slashing pass, missing the streamer by inches. Justin wanted to yell at Matt to think more about command than fighting, but knew it was useless in the confusion. The enemy leader turned and Justin saw that it was the squad leader who had taunted him earlier. The squad leader cut in behind Matt, and with a triumphal shout pulled his streamer loose. There was a brief high-pitched whistle in Justin's headset, signalling that Matt, as his squad commander, was gone.

Justin dived on the enemy squad leader in turn,

but two red players blocked his approach, and even as he killed one of them, the enemy squad leader dodged away, the surviving members of B company forming up around him. With a cold start Justin suddenly realized that it was not a squad leader who had taunted him, it was Bugniazet, B company's commander.

Justin looked around and saw that all semblance of formation was lost and that the surviving individuals of his team were being taken out.

The headset circuit was dead, which could only mean that not only were Jenkins and Matt out of the game, but along with them every other squad commander was dead as well. There was no one left to command.

"A company!" Justin roared, "A company to our end zone!"

Justin pushed his way through the confusion, shouting as loud as he could, and saw that several members of his squad were falling in, picking up his order, shouting.

They retreated down the length of the court, surviving members of A company falling in around him. Gaining the edge of the end zone, he turned, coming to a stop. In midcourt B company was forming back up, while hunting groups of several players each tracked down the few lone players of A company still out in the middle.

Justin looked around at his panting group. There were less than twenty left, and doing a quick count he saw that at least thirty or more members of B company were still alive.

"All right, I'll take command now. Get ready to charge."

Justin looked up to see Tanya moving into the center of the group.

"Like hell, Tanya, they outnumber us nearly two to one."

He looked around quickly, there were only seconds to decide what to do and Tanya came up before him, shouting for a charge.

B company was already formed into a tight ball and starting to advance straight in. The plan formed in that instant.

"We form a front up in a corner, let them charge us and we push them into the end zone."

"Listen, Bell, I've had enough of you," Tanya shouted. "Now get ready to charge!"

"Damn it, Tanya, you're wrong. A company, follow me to the wall!"

Without looking back, Justin started to the nearest wall. He could hear Tanya swearing behind him, her cursing cut short by Madison yelling at her to shut up.

Reaching the wall, Justin turned around. The few survivors of A company were all with him, B company closing in from behind.

"Back up against the wall, get the laser grid directly behind us," and Justin nodded over his shoulder. Less than two meters away was the embedded line of laser emitters marking off the end zone directly behind them.

"If they close, push them into the end zone!"

The group backed up against the wall, with only

seconds to spare as B company closed in. Being at the outer edge of the playing field, and thus further out from the center of the ship, Justin could feel the light gravitational effect holding them against the wall.

B company collided into them, their forward momentum playing into Justin's hands.

He grabbed hold of the nearest red-winged player and, bracing his back against the wall, he pushed him away into the end zone. A mad battle of grabbing, pushing and shoving ensued, Justin laughing with delight as he nailed yet another player. But his own side was losing players as well in the confusion. The two sides thinned out and from the other side of the Plexiglas wall he heard wild shouts as the spectators roared their approval.

Suddenly he felt a shove at his back and he rolled to within inches of the laser grid before beating his wings to come to a stop. Looking over his shoulder, he saw Tanya turning away.

She had tried to push him in. Furious, he turned, ready to grab hold of her, when a red set of wings intervened, grabbing Tanya by the leg and snatching her streamer. Justin looked around and could not see a single remaining blue player and pushed off from the wall, eliminating a red flyer who tried to grab hold of him. Turning, he looked back. There were four reds left and only one other blue, some-one he didn't even know.

All strategy was gone now, it would be a straight fly off.

The four reds leaped forward and within seconds his companion had nailed an opponent, while Justin dropped one in turn, and then his last surviving comrade was gone, hit by the red team's leader.

Justin backed up, turned and started to fly hard. If he engaged two on one, while moving slowly, chances were that at least one of the two would get him.

"Hey, wimp, you gutless piece of chicken crap, you're mine!"

Justin looked over his shoulder and saw the red leader moving forward in hot pursuit. He flew down the length of the court and looking around at the Plexiglas windows, saw that the entire school was watching, all of them screaming their heads off.

Reaching the opposite end zone he winged over, diving straight down for fifty meters then leveling out and heading back down the length of the court. He could still hear the taunts of his opponent and looking back, saw that his pursuer was still behind him, half a dozen meters away, laughing, taunting.

Justin felt his own anger building. It was like being back in middle school again, John Ellington and his all so courageous friends chasing him, taunting, laughing, ganging up on him. Cornered, they'd work him over until he started to cry and they'd jeer about the space cadet, the wimp, and then walk away.

It felt the same now, and he could imagine that all the spectators watching were in fact laughing at him as he fled from his pursuer. He felt his rage building and then a coldness set in. He would use the same strategy Brian had used against Matt and himself.

He ignored the taunts, pulling hard, sweat soaking his back, beading up on his face. His arms started to tremble but still he continued to fly, weaving, dodging, racing down the length of the court, building up speed and yet more speed so that as he turned, he skimmed within inches of the end zone.

The long chase dragged out, the taunts stopping, his two pursuers saving their breath. He arched over at an end zone and saw that Bugniazet was now a good dozen meters ahead of his companion who was starting to lag, coasting for several seconds between each beat of his wings.

Reaching an end zone yet again, Justin started to arc down, hearing the cheers of his company as they hovered just on the other side of the laser web. As he turned he suddenly corkscrewed, swinging not down but to one side and then shot straight back up, cutting in behind his second opponent. A red streamer snapped free and he let it go, barely hearing the roar of approval from his comrades in the end zone.

Justin turned over hard, curling up into a ball, turning end over end. As he went through a spin he saw his opponent closing straight in on him. At the last possible instant he extended his wings wide, breaking the spin. The red player slammed into him, and he felt a hand grabbing around his leg. Justin kicked himself free, the two tumbling across the middle of the court.

Justin extended his wings, swinging around in a sharp turn.

He barely saw the flutter of red, and reaching out he grabbed hold while at the same instant he felt a hand snatching his ankle.

He bunched the red streamer up in his hand and pulled. As if from a great distance away he heard a klaxon sounding and a wild pandemonium erupting. For a second he wasn't even sure if it was he who had been eliminated.

Numbed, panting for breath, he looked down and saw the red streamer flapping in his hand. The red player circled slowly around and came to a stop, looking at him, stunned.

"Damn you."

Startled, he looked at his opponent, who was doubled over slightly, panting for breath.

Justin stared at him, somehow imagining that his opponent was all the people who had ever teased and tormented him wrapped up into one.

The red player continued to pant and then flipped his face mask back up.

"Damn you, I thought I had you."

"Well you didn't," Justin replied, not sure if he was angry at him or not.

A thin smile finally creased his opponent's face.

"That was a good game, a damn good game," he said, and he extended his hand to Justin.

Justin held the red streamer out as if to give it back.

"Keep it, you earned it," and they shook hands.

At that instant a swarm of blue wings closed in around Justin, cheering, yelling, and the red player disappeared.

"Well, bucko, you even outdid me on that one!" Matt cried, pushing his way through the mob to hug him.

Shaking with exhaustion, Justin could barely fly, but there was no need to as the crowd pushed him towards the end zone and into the locker room. The senior cadet in charge of the games was waiting, grinning, and she shook Justin's hand.

"Company A is the official winner of the scrub fly off," she announced and another round of cheering erupted.

Justin saw Tanya floating at the edge of the crowd and he drifted over to her.

"What the hell did you try and do back in there?" he asked.

She looked at him wide-eyed.

"It was an accident, someone pushed into me and I banged into you."

"Yeah, sure."

"Well, don't believe me then," she snapped. Turning, she pushed off and floated away, her long black hair streaming out behind her. He watched her go, not sure if he was really angry with her over the fact that she might have tried to eliminate him, or whether it was because she looked so darn attractive at the moment.

"Bell."

Justin turned and saw Brian Seay.

"Not bad, Bell, not bad. I saw you used the trick that I taught you."

"Thank you, sir."

"You know, if you don't flunk out of here, you just might make being a cadet after all."

"Gee, thanks, sir," Justin said, suddenly feeling rather deflated.

Brian moved away, letting the crowd of admirers close back in around Justin.

Somehow, Justin realized, Brian had just managed to kill some of the fun. Taking his wings off, he started back to his room, cutting the celebration and back-slapping short. Another long night of studying was still ahead.

✦   ✦   ✦

"I hate to confess this, Matt, but I wish we weren't going on this field trip. I'm even thinking of calling myself in sick so I can stay behind."

The two cadets weaved their way down the dorm corridor, heading for the lift to the main docking bay.

"No can do, if they figure you out, you'll flunk Equipment and Station Orientation and then you'll be out anyhow. Hey, what's the matter, Justin, it'll be great."

"Yeah, I know, but the final exams are in five days and Vanderberg won't let me bring my notebook along."

"Say, look, bucko, we're supposed to be learning a couple of other things here beside astro-navigation. Come on, a little hike on the Moon will do you good, put some color back into that pale face of yours."

Taking the lift up into the docking bay section, Justin went through the lock doors into the vast docking bay. Only the day before it had been the scene of his triumph in the fly off, now it was back to serving its main purpose as a hangar and launch bay. Floating up by the forward airlock were five Shepherd class lunar landers, the light utility vehicle for getting small payloads back and forth from lunar orbit down to the surface. Squads of cadets from Company A were already loading aboard their assigned craft and picking out their vehicles, Matt and Justin drifted over to the entry hatch and climbed aboard.

Vanderberg was waiting, checking their names off his list.

"All aboard, let's get this show going," he announced and pulling himself into the pilot's seat, he closed the airlock. Thirty two cadets of first and second squads settled down into their seats, Justin making sure that he got the one directly behind Vanderberg so he could watch him at work.

Across the aisle he noticed that Tanya was craning forward to watch the launch as well. She looked towards him for a second and then made a deliberate show of breaking eye contact and turning away. They had not said a word to each other since the game, she maintaining to her friends that he had falsely accused her and that it had been an accident in the pushing and shoving match in the last minutes of the game.

Vanderberg gently edged his ship up to the inner airlock door, which slid open. Guiding the ship through, he waited while the inner door into the hanger bay closed. Seconds later the outer door slid wide, open space beyond. With a nudge of thrusters he slipped out of the Academy.

Once well clear of the Academy, he turned his ship, lining up for the proper insert for retro fire to drop out of lunar orbit. Justin, fascinated, watched the main computer screen as the ship reached its proper X, Y and Z axis alignments.

"Ten seconds to main engine start," Vanderberg announced and Justin leaned back into his seat, making sure his safety harness was snugged down tight.

The three engines aft flared to life, and with an ever increasing velocity the Shepherd dropped away from the Academy, pushing Justin back into his seat with its two g's of thrust. After weeks aboard the Academy, in its varied g zones, he felt awfully heavy. He settled back, relaxing, trying to work out mentally the math involved in going from lunar orbit to a soft touchdown on the surface. There was no way he could possibly even try to study and realized that it was best simply to give it up for now and enjoy himself. The rumble of the engines was almost soothing, and closing his eyes, he drifted off to sleep.

❖   ❖   ❖

A jolt startled him awake, and sleepily he opened his eyes and looked around.

"Welcome back to the land of the living," Matt announced, and he heard some of his friends chuckling.

He sat up slightly, realizing that the engine was still firing, and raising his hands, he rubbed his eyes.

"Still heading in?"

"You've been in dreamland to be sure. You slept right through the flight. We're coming in to land. You've been out of it for the last four hours."

Surprised, Justin looked around. Four hours? Stretching, he felt relaxed, wishing he could simply close his eyes and go back.

Justin leaned over to look out the small viewport. Down on the surface of the Moon he could see dust kicking up from the retro rockets, the shadow of the lander moving in closer. The dust blasted out and away from the ship, catching the slanting rays of the sun.

A shudder ran through the ship and he looked up at the overhead instructional board as it ran through shut-down procedures.

"All right, scrubs, you can unbuckle."

Justin got up out of his seat, the other scrubs in the ship talking excitedly.

"Been a couple of years since I've stepped foot on a planet any bigger than Ceres," Matt said. "After the Academy, it's good to know we'll have some comfortable one-sixth gravity for a couple of days."

"Can I have your attention?"

Justin looked up and saw Vanderberg, the class instructor, standing in the doorway to the lower deck.

"You all know the procedures. Let's get below, suit up and go over safety review with your partners."

Justin followed the crowd down to the lower deck of the ship. The girls went to the aft changing room while the boys stayed in the forward area. Hanging in racks along the ship's walls were the space suits, and going down the line he stopped at the one with his name above it.

Turning on the suit's computer, he ran a quick diagnostic which came up green on all systems, and then, as he was trained to do, he repeated the procedure once again. He stripped down and changed into the extended EVA undergarments. Satisfied that everything checked out, he opened up the coverall-like suit, climbed into it and zipped it up to his neck.

He snapped the gloves used for the lunar surface

on over the gloves attached to the suit, then, turning, backed up against the heavy thirty-six-hour EVA pack which was still hanging on the wall. The pack snapped onto his shoulders and he pushed the wall release button. Even in one-sixth gravity he felt the weight sagging down. On Earth the load would be over a hundred and eighty pounds' worth of air, water, cooling and heating systems, but here it was a comfortable thirty pounds, with the suit weighing another twelve pounds in Moon gravity.

Matt came up to him, already dressed.

"Let's check you out," Matt said and leaning over, he reviewed the chest-mounted computer controls.

"Get your helmet on, Justin."

Justin took his helmet and snapped it in place. Matt turned on the suit's power and Justin felt the cool air circulating in.

"Everything checks."

Justin did the same for Matt and finally gave him the okay sign.

"All you guys suited up?" Vanderberg asked and he looked around the room.

He clicked on to another radio circuit and seconds later the rear door opened and the girls came back out, suited up as well.

"Everybody receiving me?" Vanderberg's voice whispered through Justin's headset. "Count off by your numbers and give me an okay if your suit checks out. If you are not one hundred percent on line with all equipment, you are to stand down. If I find out your suit isn't ready and you go out anyhow, I'll boot your tails straight back to Earthside on the next shuttle, so be honest with me. This isn't a game."

Inside Justin's helmet was a full array of instruments which could project information onto the inside of his helmet's visor and he double-checked his readouts which showed green.

Justin gave his number, declared everything was okay and listened as the rest of the group reported in, including a very dejected Pradeep who reported that the pump for his liquid food supply was on the blink.

"Sorry, cadet, you'll stay with the ship for this one."

"I don't need to eat, sir, it's only for a day. Hell, I'm used to fasting! I do it half a dozen times a year on holy days!"

Vanderberg chuckled.

"Sorry, cadet, I'll make sure you go out with one of the other squads at the start of the next semester. Who's your partner?"

"Tanya, sir."

"Cadet Leonov, you'll have to triple team with ..." he hesitated for a moment, "with Bell and Everett."

"Do I have to, sir?" she moaned, and Justin fought to suppress a curse.

"That's an order, cadet. Form up with them."

"Yes, sir."

Justin turned his eyes to the upper right corner of his helmet and blinked twice. The laser scanner which was focused on his eyes instantly followed his orders and switched him to the prearranged private radio circuit with his partner.

"Just great, we get stuck with her. I think Vanderberg did it just to mess with us," Justin groaned.

"I heard that, cadet," Vanderberg said. "I expect you to cooperate with her and that's final," and Justin gulped as Vanderberg clicked out of their circuit and back to the open line.

"Now listen up, people." Vanderberg continued, speaking again on the open circuit.

"We'll be out for twenty-four hours. The hike will start us off past the historic site, and then up to the top of a nearby mountain peak. I want you to keep a sharp eye out on your suit monitors for overheating. If you go a degree above 80 you're to sing out. If your suit should overheat and your visor fogs up, you're in big trouble, both survival-wise and with me personally.

"And another thing. I know it's embarrassing but your suits are designed to handle going to the bathroom. So don't hold it till we get back, or you'll all be turning some rather unpleasant colors. There've been emergencies where people have had to live in EVA suits for up to ten days. It might not be pleasant, but it sure is better than dying. Do we understand each other on this?"

Justin nodded, though he felt rather foolish and embarrassed with the EVA diaper and other hook-ups to handle this situation.

"Suits fully pressurized."

Justin looked at the computer console projection in his helmet, punched the activation button on his chest, and again the cooling air started to whisk around him. His chest board showed green, matching his helmet display, and he looked around at the others, waiting while Vanderberg ran a final check.

Matt double-checked Justin's chest instrument monitor. Justin did the same, and the two friends gave each other the thumbs-up sign.

Vanderberg went over to a control panel, making sure that the hatches up to the topside of the ship were fully secured and then started to bleed the air out of the lower deck. Justin felt his suit expanding ever so slightly, the sounds from outside of his suit dying away into silence. Soundlessly, the airlock door opened and Vanderberg went out. Justin lined up with the others and finally stepped out onto the Moon's surface.

The view was of a magnificent desolation, the gray-brown landscape standing out crystal clear, long shadows cutting across the surface from the high mountain peaks.

Vanderberg went around to the side of the ship and opened a cargo hatch. A surface vehicle was inside and he climbed aboard, driving it out onto the surface, pulling up alongside the group.

"Sorry I've got to ride, folks," Vanderberg said, "but there's no sense in hauling all the emergency equipment on our backs. On the way back down I'll give each of you a shot at driving.

"Stay with your EVA partners. I don't want anyone wandering off. Now let's roll it."

The group started off, and over the main channel came the sound of excited laughter as they took long bounding strides across the surface, dust swirling up around them. Justin felt as if he was almost floating, each step taking up half a dozen feet. As they crested a low rise, a squat spiderlike ship appeared straight ahead and he looked at it with awe.

Vanderberg stopped his vehicle and got out.

"You know the rules for historic sites. You can look but don't touch. At least for this one, we can get up close, unlike Apollo Eleven which is entirely sealed off and covered with a dome."

Vanderberg led the way and the group walked up to the spacecraft which stood alone upon a high plateau. An old fifty-star American flag stood bright against the black sky, the instrument packs around the ship still standing duty, as if waiting to be powered back up to life.

Justin walked to the side of the ship and looked up. Beside the ship was a historical marker explaining the background of Apollo 17, the last of the Moon missions launched in the 20th century.

On the side of the ship was a small plaque bearing the names of the astronauts and the president of the United States all the way back in 1972 when this, the last of the first interplanetary exploration vessels, had landed.

"You're looking at a wonderful piece of history here. This is the landing stage of Apollo Seventeen, the last of the Apollo ships to land on the Moon," Vanderberg said quietly. "Why, I bet if Professor McCain was with us, she'd give you every boring detail of this ship and its mission," and the group chuckled.

"But more seriously, though. It's also a lesson in how shortsighted we can sometimes be. Here it was 1972 and Americans were landing on the Moon."

"We, I mean the old Soviet state, sent an unmanned mission at nearly the same time," Tanya interrupted.

"Yeah, but Americans walked here first," Madison replied good-naturedly.

"We all got here together," Vanderberg interjected. "Remember, there was a U.N. flag aboard the first Apollo. But the main point is that here the United States was on the Moon in 1972. They could have been to Mars by 1985 and had hundreds of people living and working in space by 1990. But they dropped the ball. It's sad, some of the problems that hit the world at the beginning of the 21st century could have been avoided, and we could have been years ahead of where we are now. The energy shortage and pollution would have been defeated long ago rather than getting taken care of in my generation. They might have even been able to head off the series of nuclear attack incidents. Some of the people back then kept saying there were too many problems at home to worry about space. Foolish of them to even think that way. We still hear those voices today. That's why I wanted you to see this ship. The astronauts who flew her started something that will never stop. We're going for the stars, and it all started right here."

Vanderberg walked over to the ship and stood before it, staring at it with a near reverent awe.

"Come on, let's get hiking."

The group turned away from the bottom half of the Apollo landing module and started out across the plateau. Justin pointed out to Matt the wheel tracks of the original Apollo electric car, which stood parked by the side of the ship. He was almost tempted to go over to the car, climb into the seat and see if it still worked.

"Say, Justin, how goes the Astro-Navigation?" Tanya asked.

"Thanks for reminding me," Justin replied.

"You know there's even a betting pool going on as to whether you'll flunk it or not."

"Thanks for the comments," Matt interjected.

"Just wondering, that's all."

"So you can figure out which way to bet, is that it?" Justin asked coldly.

"I already have my bets down," she said, her voice edged with a too sincere cheerfulness.

"Look, Tanya, just because we're teamed up doesn't mean we have to speak with each other."

"Hey, I didn't want to be assigned to you guys anyhow."

"Well, we're the unlucky ones on that count," Matt retorted, "so just knock it off and let's save our breath."

The ground started to climb upwards and as Vanderberg called a ten-minute rest Justin went over to sit against a boulder. He took a deep drink of water from the suction tube which was just below his chin and then swallowed a bit of his liquid meal. The taste wasn't all that bad, almost like a beef broth, but he found himself wishing for a genuine hamburger with all the trimmings, a meal that would be rather impossible to eat at the moment. There was the other problem as well that was starting to bother him. With all the money spent on space suit design, no one had yet to figure out a way to scratch yourself, and right at the moment he'd have given anything to nail the itch right in the small of his back. He knew that if he thought about it, it'd drive him batty, so he tried to force the thought out of his mind.

"Let's move it," Vanderberg announced and the group pressed on. They continued to climb up a steep slope and Justin found it to be a curious sensation. On Earth, he would have been leaning in against the side of the hill, even scrambling on all fours, but in the low gravity it was almost like a casual jaunt. They reached a shelf on the side of the mountain and paused for a moment. Justin looked back down. The mountains of the Moon stood out in a clear sharp light, with no atmosphere to soften the view. Earth rode a hand span above the horizon, and over his shoulder the blinding sun shone. And most curious of all was the fact that the stars were out as well, though dimmed by the reflected glare. It was silent, totally silent, except for the sound of his breathing and the thin hum of static in his radio.

"Incredible view," Matt whispered. "I've seen space from Saturn's rings down to Venus and it still leaves me in awe."

For a moment all the anxiety that had been troubling him went away. So often he would go out into the countryside, find a quiet place and just lie back and watch the clouds roll across the fields of Indiana, or at night stretch out behind the barn and watch the Moon. And now it was reversed as he stood on the slope of a mountain and looked back across space to Earth. He thought the view from the dome back at the Academy was awesome, but this beat it. He had heard how some people, when they got on the Moon, were hit by a case of the willies, that the place was simply too desolate. He found it to be the exact opposite. The view was hauntingly beautiful and it made him realize just how much he could love living in space. The only thing on Earth that could even begin to compare was the southwestern United States, but that paled in comparison to the spectacle laid out before him.

"Let's keep it moving," Vanderberg announced, and the group continued on, weaving their way through boulder fields and following the mountain upward.

Even in the low gravity Justin soon found it to be hard going and he looked over enviously at Matt, Tanya and the others who bounded along with seemingly effortless ease. He started to feel a bit clumsy and noticed that his suit's temperature gauge was creeping up to eighty and that he was starting to sweat. He plodded along, struggling to keep up. Vanderberg drove up beside him in the buggy.

"How's it going, Bell?"

"All right, sir."

"Care to drive the cart a bit?"

"I can handle it, sir," he replied, not wanting to admit that he was becoming thoroughly pooped.

"All right then, cadet, but if your gauge goes any higher you're driving for a while."

"Please, sir, I'd rather walk."

"Okay, Bell, just keep up with the group, remember no more than ten meters from your buddy."

Vanderberg drove ahead, zigzagging the cart around a series of boulders, and continued up the sharp thirty-five-degree slope, dust kicking out behind him.

Suddenly Justin noticed that the group had stopped and, breathing hard, he came up to join them. They were at the top of the mountain. There was a small flat plateau at the top, several dozen meters across. He slowly walked around it, letting his breathing get back to normal, the temperature in his suit starting to drop away. On the far side of the plateau was a steep slope that dropped down to a cliff. The low angle of the sun cast a shadow across the edge of the drop but he could easily see in the dim glow of Earth shine that it was a sheer cliff with a valley thousands of feet below.

He felt a sense of triumph and he turned in a full circle, looking out over the canyons and valleys below. It reminded him a bit of Death Valley, but Death Valley looked like it was blooming with life in comparison. Far off in the distance he saw the tiny speck of their shuttle craft and the sight of it gave him a vague sense of uneasiness. If anything should go wrong, seriously wrong, it was a long way back down, and there was no place where the ship could take off and land to pick them up.

He knew that in the cart there was more than enough emergency equipment: extra air, food, water and an inflatable solar storm shelter in case there was a sudden flare on the sun and they were forced to get under cover before the high dose radiation hit. He stilled his fears.

"All right, folks, who's making the campfire?" Madison quipped and the group laughed.

"Ivan and Miko, no going off alone into the bushes, you two," Matt chimed in and everyone laughed along with him to the discomfort of the couple from Sharon's squad.

The two senior cadets were not along on the trip with their squads and everyone was grateful for that. A curious fact seemed to be coming up, however, in regards to their squad commanders. Everyone in first squad hated Sharon, the same way everyone in second squad hated Brian. But to hear the members of first squad tell it, Brian was an all right guy, friendly, willing to listen and offer advice. The information caused hoots of derision from Justin and his comrades and they found that their friendly comments about Sharon were treated the same way. The whole thing was a bit of a mystery.

The group settled down on top of the peak, sprawled out in a loose circle. Vanderberg started to regale them with stories about his thirty years with the service, rounding it off with a couple of traditional ghost stories about haunted ships and spirits lurking in the Martian tombs. Matt added several tales about solar sailing, including the famous *Comet's Tail*, which was the Flying Dutchman of space, a lost ship that would appear like a ghost and then disappear from view. It was believed that whoever saw the *Comet's Tail* would die on his next voyage.

"My uncle Dan once saw her," Matt said. "He was standing watch as first mate aboard the old *Queen of the Solar Wind*, which was out prospecting asteroids.

"He said it appeared like a ghost as he was coasting around an asteroid. Why, that asteroid was just loaded with nickel iron, a real haul it was, maybe a couple of million tons of high grade ore and they were going to stake a claim on it."

He paused for a moment, and Justin could almost imagine his friend puffing on a pipe, sitting on a dock with an old sailing ship anchored behind him.

"So why isn't he dead?" Tanya chimed in.

"Easy enough," Matt replied softly. "Now don't go jumping the gun on me there, you Earther."

"Yeah, pipe down, Tanya," half a dozen chorused in.

"Well, as I was saying. My uncle Dan was braking in, setting up a close orbit on that asteroid. A tricky job that is, orbiting something that small. When from around the lee side of the rock comes the *Comet's Tail*. Dan said his hair just stood on end. The ship was there, but then again it wasn't, you could see right through it. Its sails were all in tatters, its communications dish just popped full of micrometeor holes. It was comin' straight at him and Dan, why, he popped on the reverse thrusters, burning up fuel like mad. He said his finger was just about frozen to the throttle he was so scared.

"Well, that *Comet's Tail* came right across his bow, not a hundred meters away, its number three sail yard just scraping by, missing his ship by inches. And then he got a look inside her. Up there in the forward pilot's booth he said he could see the ship's captain as clear as you can see the Earth right now."

He paused for a second and more than one cadet

turned to look back at Earth which was hanging low on the horizon.

"He snapped up a pair of binoculars and took a close look and said that as long as he lives he wishes he hadn't have done that."

"How come?" Madison asked, her voice soft.

" 'Cause he saw the pilot, he did, Captain Thaddeus B. Nelson, the first solar sailor of them all. There he was sitting, hands on the throttle and furling boom controls."

Matt paused for a second to build up the effect.

"He was a skeleton, he was. He turned and looked at my uncle, his eyes like two red coals of fire, but the rest of him all bleached and white, as white as the Martian icecaps. He looked straight at my Uncle Dan, raised his hand and pointed."

"So what did your uncle do, wave back?" Justin asked, half joking but half scared as well.

"Wave back? Like hell. He started screamin' his bloody 'ead off. The captain of the *Queen* was already coming up on deck, shouting and cursing at Dan for using up fuel and then he saw old Thaddeus and he set to screaming, too.

"And then it just disappeared into vacuum. The ship was gone, melting away into nothing. The last thing to be seen was the skeleton of Nelson still pointin' at them."

"So, like I said, why's your uncle alive?" Tanya interjected, though this time her voice was a bit more nervous.

"I'm gettin' there. Well, they hightailed it out of there, pulling in their sails and burning fuel. And I tell you, a sailor doesn't burn fuel unless he's got a really important reason for burning. It's a matter of pride, it is. A sailor will take a week to do something by sail that a ten-minute burn would do just as well. So they beat it back to Ceres, didn't even bother to file a claim on that rock they'd been prospecting.

"Now Dan, Dan was so darned scared he swore he'd never sail again. Got right off the old *Queen*, and took up as a miner and believe me a sailor becoming a miner is like a lion turning itself into a mouse."

"Hey, my dad's an asteroid miner, so don't knock it," Ali, a scrub in Sharon's company snapped. "He always said you sailors were a bunch of drunks and bums anyhow."

"No offense intended," Matt replied, "but without us sailors you'd never get your rocks anywhere."

"The story, finish the story," several cadets shouted, knowing that if they didn't Ali and Matt would square off and carry on one of the old traditional arguments of sailors versus miners for hours.

"All right, all right," Matt said quietly. "As I was saying, Uncle Dan jumped ship right there, even gave up his contract, and bonus. Said he was never gonna sail again.

"His captain had a fit. The captain wanted to quit as well, tried to sell the ship, but no one would touch it since it was now jinxed. Half the crew jumped as well. Anyhow, he finally had to pull out on a contract run to Mars."

Matt paused for a moment.

"He never got there. A tracking station on Phobes

claimed they picked up a signal, it was the captain screaming, screamin' his bloody head off. And then, well he just plain disappeared, nothing, not a bit of wreckage, a distress beacon, anything. Just plain disappeared forever."

"Naw, no one disappears like that," Tanya said quietly.

"Ask Commander Vanderberg about it," Matt replied.

"Yeah, is this true?" several cadets chimed in.

"It's like he said," Vanderberg replied, his voice serious. Justin looked over at the instructor but the reflected glare of the sun on his faceplate kept him from seeing whether Vanderberg was grinning or not. "It's in the record files, check with Uncle if you want when you get back. The *Queen* disappeared with all hands on the Ceres to Mars run back in '59. Never found a trace of her. It's still a mystery."

"You think it was the *Comet's Tail* that got her?" Madison asked quietly.

"Don't think we'll ever know," Vanderberg replied, his voice still serious.

"What about your Uncle Dan?" several cadets asked, turning back to Matt.

"He didn't sail for nearly eight years, until the accident on my parents' ship. He figured then that he had to keep up the family business."

Justin looked over at Matt. His friend had only mentioned what happened once, the memory of it still evidently painful. The truth of it was that Matt was the only survivor of the meteor hit to *Corona* which ruptured the hull integrity of the main cabin.

Matt's mother had thrown him into the rear cabin and slammed the door shut, while she and her husband stayed on the other side. Matt claimed that she didn't have the strength left to get through with him but that wasn't the whole story. Checking in Uncle's files later Justin figured the rest of it out. In the few seconds which Matt's mother had when the cabin had undergone explosive decompression, she must have realized that there would be barely enough air and supplies in the back room for one person to stay alive until help arrived. She deliberately stayed on the other side to give her son a chance at surviving. Matt was only seven when it happened, and Justin could sense just how terrible those three weeks must have been for him, trapped in the small room, his dead parents floating just on the other side of the door, clearly visible through the viewport. It was three weeks before his uncle arrived aboard a commandeered ship. Matt had already slipped into unconsciousness, with the air supply nearly exhausted. They buried his parents in space, patched the *Corona* and then sailed on.

As Justin looked at his friend he found himself wondering yet again what had formed Matt. There was the self-assuredness, the boastful swagger, and the friend who had already evolved into the natural leader of the squad. Yet he could sense the deeply hidden fears as well, remember the several occasions when Matt would wake up in the middle of the night with a painful cry, tears in his eyes. He would fumble around, embarrassed, mutter a curse if Justin asked what was wrong and then settle back down. But Justin knew that for the rest of the night Matt would not be able to sleep.

There was a moment of silence and Justin was glad no one asked for any details.

"So Dan figures that old Captain Nelson was satisfied with snatching the *Queen* and decided to let him go. But I'm telling you, that old ghost ship is still out there and if you ever see it, you'd all better turn in your commissions and just quit this here Space Service."

There was a round of nervous chuckles and a couple of jokes which fell rather flat. The group was silent for a moment, a few of them looking around nervously, and Madison suggested a song.

They started out with the usual line of Academy songs but soon shifted to some of the current hits and then went back to the songs they had learned in the Scouts when they had sat around campfires back on Earth. As the group sang it all seemed so strange to Justin, there was no campfire, no chirping of insects or the smell of the wood smoke. Instead their voices drifted on the open radio link, the silence of the vacuum of space wrapped around them, the air inside the suit antiseptic and cool.

Matt was the star of the performance, half singing, half chanting old solar sailing songs, which he explained came from sea songs of earth when sailing ships once filled the oceans, their canvas sails like clouds on the horizon. The songs also had a more modern link, tied to the American songs of the late 20th century about truck drivers on the road.

The conversation finally started to turn towards

the current crisis with the Martian colonial government, which was threatening to vote for secession from the United Nations. The talk immediately started to heat up until Vanderberg cut it off, ordering that talk of politics was forbidden for the rest of the trip.

"Well, cadets, time to turn in," Vanderberg finally announced. "Remember, don't lie down in the shade, it's two hundred below there. Your suit heater takes a lot more energy than the cooler. More than one person has been killed when his moisture exhaust vent froze over and his humidity scrubber overloaded, so be careful."

Vanderberg got up, went over to the buggy, found a spot between a couple of boulders and lay down.

Justin looked around at the group and instantly decided that this was definitely weird. First off, they were a group of sixteen-year-olds camping out together and there was no ushering of the girls off to their tents, although it was impossible for anything of a romantic nature to go on. There were plenty of rumors floating about Ivan and Miko violating the rules regarding getting a bit too physical in a relationship and sneaking off together late at night, but out here if they ventured to crack open their pressure suits for a quick kiss it was a guaranteed trip home in a box.

But beyond that, there was no campfire, no tents, no sleeping bags, nothing. They were just supposed to lie down, and it wasn't even dark.

Justin paced around for a minute with Matt and they found an area relatively free of boulders, pushed the smaller rocks aside and lay down.

"Tanya, we've got a spot right here between us for you," Matt said, attempting to put on a seductive voice.

"Shut up, Everett, I'm bunking next to Madison and Sue."

Matt and Justin laughed.

It was definitely weird, Justin realized. Here he was, lying in a space suit, out in the vacuum of space. He started to think about all that could go wrong, from a massive solar flare, right through to a micrometer impact. Beyond that, it was decidedly uncomfortable. It was impossible to lie on your back with a pack still on, he immediately realized. He rolled over onto his side and then onto his stomach, turning his head to one side, since his helmet projected forward and pushed his head back when it was pressed into the lunar surface.

He heard mumbled curses on the main circuit which grew more numerous until Vanderberg told everyone to shut up or get a demerit.

He felt like hours had passed, but a look at his chronometer display inside his helmet told him it'd been only twenty minutes since he lay down. Then he started to watch the chronometer as it ticked off the passing of each second until he finally looked straight at the display and blinked three times, thereby telling his computer to shut it off.

Then the sound of his own breathing started to get to him, followed by the eerie silence of space.

He closed his eyes, trying to will himself to sleep.

✧   ✧   ✧

Justin opened his eyes, and came to the conclusion that it was simply impossible to sleep. He looked to where the chronometer display was and blinked twice and it came back on.

He'd been asleep for nearly four hours. He sat up and looked around in surprise. A couple of the other cadets were sitting up as well. Matt was beside him and he clicked over to their private channel to hear his friend snoring away.

"Can't sleep, Bell?"

It was Tanya and he looked over to where she was sitting up.

"Kind of strange trying to do this in a space suit."

"I'd give anything for a shower right now. I'm starting to feel really gross in this suit," she sighed.

"Yeah, along with a cold soda and a pizza."

"With sausage and mushrooms on it?"

"Pepperoni."

"Will you two knock it off?" Matt groaned. "You're on my channel too."

"Sorry," Justin replied, glad that Matt was awake, and a bit surprised that he and Tanya had actually gotten through half a minute of conversation without getting into a fight.

"Let's take a walk," Madison chimed in.

"I thought it was sleep time," Justin replied.

"Ah, come on," Tanya replied, the edge of a taunt in her voice. "Vanderberg didn't forbid that and we've had four hours of sleep. Let's take a quick walk to check things out and then we'll bed back down."

They stood up and a couple of cadets from the other squad clicked into their channel.

"Mind if we come along?"

"Come on then," Tanya said, and she pointed out a high pinnacle a hundred meters away.

The group set out, walking along the narrow crest of the mountain. Justin looked down the steep opposite slope which dropped away for at least a thousand meters into the dark valley below. He found the shadows and light of the Moon to be fascinating. Since there was no atmosphere to diffuse the light, any place blocked from the direct light of the sun, or not lit up by Earthlight or reflection from the surrounding hills was as black as the depths of space. With the sun low on the horizon the high peaks of the mountains stood out like skeletal fingers, rising up out of the darkness.

They reached the edge of the crestline and gazed down into the sheer drop-off of a canyon below. The ground before them sloped away at a forty-five-degree angle for a couple of dozen meters and then dropped down into a sheer cliff. Justin picked up a small rock, tossed it out over the rim, watching it turn end over end, disappearing over the edge and into the blackness.

"Let's count how long it takes before we hear it hit bottom," Madison quipped and the group laughed.

"Let's head back, guys," Matt said quietly. "A little too treacherous here."

"All right," Tanya replied and they turned to head back.

Even as it started to happen Justin thought the whole thing had a strange dreamlike quality to it. One second Tanya and Sue were standing atop a boulder on the edge of the precipice and then in the next second they weren't. But they didn't fall the way he was used to seeing people fall. It was slow, almost graceful, the boulder they were standing on shifting, tumbling down the steep slope in slow motion, the two girls going over the edge with it.

Justin didn't even think about his actions. He cried for Matt to follow him then bounded up to the edge and leaped over after them. He started to slide down the slope, slowly building up speed, heading straight for the cliff. It all felt unreal. Tanya was not two meters ahead of him, still falling, Sue above her, and then they went into the shadows at the edge of the cliff and disappeared.

He slid into the shadow after them.

He looked up to the top of his helmet, blinked twice and his helmet lights snapped on. He blinked once more, setting them on wide beam, and he saw Tanya hit the ground directly ahead of him, right at the edge of the cliff, dust and gravel spraying up.

For the first time he heard voices, someone screaming, and then another voice crying, gasping. In the wide angle beam of light he saw the boulder continue to roll down the slope, bounce, and then pitch out into space, curving downward, and disappearing over the edge of the cliff.

He continued to slide down and with a cold sickening horror realized that he was going to go over the edge as well. He slid up against Tanya who was thrashing and flaying.

"Grab hold of my legs!" Justin shouted and he rolled onto his stomach extending his arms, desperately trying to grab hold of something, anything.

He saw Matt beside him, still on his feet, moving fast, catching up to Sue. Matt leaped forward, tackling her around the shoulders, and then slammed down onto the ground, even as her legs shot out over the edge of the abyss.

A small outcropping of rock drifted into view and desperate, Justin reached out and grabbed hold. He felt his legs going out of the edge of the cliff, gravel underneath him sliding out, spilling into the darkness and disappearing, falling straight down.

He heard Tanya screaming and felt her clutching him around the waist.

"I'm losing air, I'm losing air!"

He let go of the rock with one hand and reached down, hooking a hand under her shoulder and pulling her up by his side. Even as he pulled her up he was amazed that he could do it.

For a brief second he saw her face inside her helmet, her eyes wide with panic, her mouth open.

He kicked his way up, knees scraping against the edge of the cliff, the gravel underneath still flooding away. He felt the rock he was holding on to starting to shift.

"Grab hold of my shoulders, I've got to let go of you!"

"Don't!" And her voice was filled with panic.

"Grab hold or we're both going over, damn it!"

He felt her hands reach up around his helmet, blocking his vision. He latched on to the rock with both hands and pulled hard. The rock started to shift even more and as he scrambled up over it, the rock rolled out from underneath and fell into the darkness. His knees were now up on the edge, Tanya still clinging to him, and he crawled half a dozen feet back up the slope. The gravel underneath started to shift and he felt as if the ground would just simply slide out from under him if he continued to go up the slope.

"Tanya, you still with me!"

"Air!" Her voice was rasping, distant, as if coming from far away.

He rolled onto his side and broke her deathlike grip and then he saw the tear in her suit's arm.

"Hang on!"

He reached down to his emergency kit strapped to his thigh, tore it open and pulled out a patch. Ripping the plastic cover off he slapped the sticky side over the tear in her suit, pressing down hard with both hands.

"Damn, that hurts," she gasped. "I think it's broken."

"Well, either it hurts or you get spaced," he snapped.

He felt a shower of rocks banging against his helmet and looked up to see several of the cadets up on the edge of the slide, trying to form a human chain down to where he was.

"Get back to Vanderberg, he must have rope on board the buggy," Justin shouted. "You might start a slide and push us over the edge."

"Just hang on," Madison cried, "we'll be right back."

"Don't hyperventilate," Justin said. "The patch

should be holding, check your pressure gauge."

"It's all right," she gasped, "it's all right."

"You two okay?"

"Where are you, Matt?"

"To your right, buddy."

He breathed a sigh of relief. In the seconds after he grabbed hold of Tanya he thought that Matt and Sue might have gone over the edge. Justin looked over his shoulder and felt his blood go cold. Matt was hanging half over the edge of the cliff, the other cadet's arms wrapped tightly around his shoulders.

"Say, do you always act like this on your first date?" Matt quipped.

"For God's sake, don't let go!" she shouted.

"Not on your life, Sue."

"Matt, Justin, can you two get back up?"

Justin looked to the top of the slope and saw Vanderberg and a knot of cadets gathered around the edge.

"Kind of a rough go, sir," Matt replied. "This rock I'm hanging on to feels like it wants to give out any second."

"Don't let go!" Sue cried.

"Look, I'm afraid if we try to get down, we might set off a slide," Vanderberg said, his voice sounding strangely calm. "I'll work a couple of ropes down."

He disappeared from view and was back a minute later. With an expert toss he dropped the first rope straight on top of Matt, who finally convinced Sue to let go with one hand, work it around her waist and clip it to her suit's waist tool belt. Vanderberg tossed a second rope to Justin and he clipped it onto Tanya's waist belt.

"Up we come. Be careful not to snag on any sharp rocks."

With teams of cadets on the ropes, the two girls started to slide back up, Matt and Justin hanging on to their waists.

"You two seem might friendly all of a sudden," Matt joked.

"If Sue wasn't on your line I'd cut it," Tanya snapped.

"Still the same old Tanya," Matt replied.

"I'm starting to lose air again," Tanya suddenly gasped.

"Hang on, Tanya," Vanderberg said, his voice still calm. "Don't try to hold your breath, exhale. If you don't, you might damage your lungs."

Justin took one hand off of her waist, clamped it down tightly on her arm and she cried out again from the pain.

They continued to slide up the slope and he could hear her voice getting weaker as her suit's pressure dropped off.

Justin switched his radio channel.

"Vanderberg?"

"Here, Justin."

"Hurry it up, we're losing her!"

"We've got time, son. If you can hear her breathing, she's still got some air left in there."

Justin clamped down harder and saw a corner of the emergency patch flapping up and down as air bubbled out of Tanya's suit. He moved his hand up, placing it over the opening, and squeezed, feeling the air pressure bubbling out now from the other side of the patch.

They hit the top of the crest and Vanderberg knelt down by Tanya's side, tearing open a large emergency patch.

"All right, Justin, let go now!"

Justin released his grip and the patch he had put on blew off. As if from a great distance away Justin could hear Tanya's scream. Behind her faceplate he saw her looking up at him, eyes wide with fear. Vanderberg, working with lightning speed, lifted Tanya's arm up and wrapped the patch around her arm.

"Give me that cuff!"

A cadet handed over what looked like a plastic hose, which Vanderberg slipped up over Tanya's arm, covering the patch. He pulled a small D ring attached to the sleeve which instantly inflated, pressing the patch down tightly while also supporting the arm.

"Tanya, you still with us?"

She was silent.

"Air cylinder!"

A cadet passed a cylinder over and Vanderberg hooked it into her external air port and opened it up, while watching her suit monitor.

"Where are we?" she gasped.

"Oh, just cruising around on the surface of the Moon," Vanderberg replied, the relief in his voice evident.

"Damn, my arm, *Bozhe moi*," and she lapsed into Russian.

Vanderberg picked her up, took her over to the moon buggy and put her in the back. He came back to the group and took a minute to thoroughly inspect Matt, Sue and Justin to make sure their suits and gear were all right.

"I'm taking her straight back to the ship. The rest of you hike down. Everett, you're in charge of the group. Take it cautiously, stop every fifty minutes for ten. Follow your tracks from yesterday back down."

"Yes, sir."

Vanderberg bounded back to the car and started straight down the slope.

Justin suddenly realized that everyone was talking, patting him on the back, helping him up to his feet. He looked over at Matt and Sue, who was still clinging to his side.

"You did all right, buddy," Matt said. "Hell, and for Tanya no less."

Justin nodded and turning, looked back down the slope. Suddenly he felt very weak indeed, his knees turning to rubber. He found that there was a terrible feeling building up in his stomach and he was afraid he was going to throw up. He fought the urge down. People had survived vomiting inside their suits, but it was an experience he didn't want to try out.

Light-headed, he sat back down on the ground, putting his head between his legs.

"Feeling okay, buddy?" Matt clicked in on their private channel.

"Think I'm going to throw up."

Matt laughed, came over and sat down beside him.

"For God's sake, Justin, heroes don't throw up after their heroics."

"Well, this one feels like it," Justin gasped.

"Breathe deeply, just relax."

He gasped for air, realizing that he was doing what he had told Tanya not to do, hyperventilating. He looked back down the slope and the drop-off beyond and felt a cold shudder of fear.

What the hell did I just do? he wondered. *I risked my neck for Tanya?*

The shaking finally started to pass, the terrible pressure in the back of his throat died away and he finally stood back up.

"Let's go home," Justin said. "I've had enough adventures for one day."

❖   ❖   ❖

"Deck fully pressurized."

Justin unclipped his helmet and took it off, grateful for the fresh air after twenty hours of breathing recycled suit air, which was starting to get a little too gamey. The hatch to the upper deck popped open and Vanderberg climbed down.

"How's Tanya?" half a dozen cadets asked at once.

"Simple fracture to the lower arm and some light lung damage from the depressurization. We've got to get her back to the Academy hospital but don't worry, she'll be up and around in time for her finals."

A happy cheer went up and Justin again found himself to be the center of attention.

"Change, shower up, and let's head for home," Vanderberg announced.

Justin peeled off his suit, dropped his undergarments into the disposal storage chute and queued up for a quick one-minute shower. Changing back into his class C coveralls he went back up to the main deck and looked around. A knot of cadets were at the back of the deck, gathered around a row of seats that had been converted into a bunk. He started to go back, then stopped and turned to head to the front of the ship to take his assigned seat.

"Justin?"

He looked back and saw Tanya sitting up, looking at him.

Feeling nervous, he went aft and the cadets who had been chatting with her drifted away. Madison passed him and flashed a quick smile.

He stopped by Tanya's side and she looked up at him, her features pale, her left arm in a sling, a small breathing tube clipped to her nose and a bio monitor hooked up behind her. He looked at it quickly and hoped that all the lines squiggling across it meant that she was okay.

"Have a seat."

He sat down, not sure what to say.

"I owe you one, Bell."

"It was nothing, don't worry about it."

She laughed softly.

"Don't worry about it. If you hadn't grabbed me I'd be a bloody smear. . . ." Her voice trailed away.

He looked at her and she tried to smile, forcing back tears.

"I've been a real crud to you since we got here. I've been thinking about that all the way back. I don't know why I acted towards you like I did. Maybe I saw you as a threat."

"Me, a threat?"

"Yes, you, Justin Bell. You think you don't fit in somehow. That you're different. Maybe I saw it differently."

She stopped for a moment.

"Hell, I don't know, but thanks for my life."

To his astonishment she leaned up, kissed him lightly on the lips and then shyly pulled back.

Unable to speak, he stood back up, mortified to realize that Madison, Matt and quite a few others had seen what had just happened.

Tanya looked up as well.

"This doesn't mean anything's going on between us," Tanya said quickly.

"Suu-u-re, it doesn't," Madison replied teasingly.

Justin, unable to speak, looked at Tanya and then fled to the front of the ship and settled into his seat.

Matt came up and joined him.

"You're redder than Mars," Matt said with a laugh.

"Just shut up," Justin said through his teeth.

"Sure, sure, to think though that you'd actually let Tanya Leonov kiss you. You amaze me sometimes, Bell, simply amaze me."

"Everyone strap in for liftoff," Vanderberg announced, and he came out of the forward flight deck and walked down the length of the ship, checking up on the cadets. As he came back forward he stopped by Justin and Matt, leaned over and shook their hands.

"You two showed some quick thinking and real

guts. I'm noting that in my official report which will go into your records and recommending both of you for the Silver Star for saving another's life while risking your own."

"Thank you, sir," Matt replied quietly.

Justin was unable to reply and Vanderberg flashed a smile and went back forward.

"We are cleared for takeoff, people. We'll be back aboard the Academy in four hours and twenty-seven minutes."

The ship lifted up, turned and started to climb, the Apollo landing site briefly visible through Justin's window.

He settled back in his chair and closed his eyes as the ship accelerated up to three gs in its climb out from the Moon's gravitational field.

Just what the hell had he done? He couldn't even explain it to anyone, let alone himself. There had been no contemplation, no real understanding of the risk. He had simply leaped after her, as if by instinct, and felt no fear until after it was all over. Even as he thought about it, he was afraid that Matt would see his legs starting to shake.

Without any real warning it all started to flood over him and he quickly reached for the sick bag strapped to the back of the seat in front of him and promptly lost what little food he had managed to consume over the last day.

Terribly embarrassed, he looked around and saw that Matt was leaning forward, coughing loudly, and Justin realized that his friend was covering for him so that nobody would hear or see what was going on.

He leaned back in his seat and weakly looked over at Matt.

"Some hero we've got here," Matt said with a smile.

"Yeah, right."

"Don't worry about it, buddy. I feel exactly the same way about it all. I was scared to death the whole time."

"Really?"

"Bet on it."

Sighing, Justin put the bag under his seat, leaned back, closed his eyes and promptly went to sleep in spite of the g's and the weightlessness that came afterwards.

✧ **Chapter VII** ✧

"Ship's company attenshun!"

The assembly of over two thousand cadets and ship's personnel snapped to attention as Rear Admiral Thor Thorsson entered the room and strode down the main aisle. Justin, standing to one side of the podium, looked out nervously at the assembly.

The assembly room, located down in the half-gravity zone of deck level Z-5, was capable of holding all ten thousand personnel that lived aboard ship when the regular September to May session was on. Though the room was barely a quarter full, Justin could tell that Matt was looking at the crowd with gape-mouthed amazement. He was seeing more people in one place than he had ever encountered before.

Thorsson gained the podium, turned and faced the assembly.

"Stand at ease, be seated."

Thorsson looked out over the audience.

"I've called this special meeting for two purposes."

He made a flourish of picking up a sheet of paper and then started to read off a letter of commendation, for Matt, Justin and four second-year cadets who had spent the summer on the Moon. Only three were present. An empty seat with a class A uniform shirt and cap placed upon it was between Justin and the other three cadets, who had helped in a rescue operation when a Shepherd transport crashed landed. The fourth cadet never came back, sacrificing his only remaining air cylinder to keep an infant alive.

Thorsson continued on with a brief description of what Matt and Justin had done, along with the acts of the four other cadets. When he was finished Matt, Justin and the other three stood up. Thorsson came over, shook their hands and presented the first three with the Silver Star. He moved to Matt and, smiling, pinned a Silver Star to Matt's shirt and then approached Justin.

Justin felt his heart pounding and tried to stare straight ahead as Thorsson pinned the medal to his shirt. He raised his hand up to salute and Thorsson returned it. To Justin's surprise, Thorsson winked at him and then turned away to approach the empty chair.

"Cadet William Alexander Fawcett, for meritorious service, above and beyond the call of duty, with the sacrifice of your own life to save another, I have the honor to present to you the Medal of Honor."

Thorsson pinned the medal to the empty shirt, came to attention and saluted. Justin looked over at Thorsson out of the corner of his eye and saw tears in the old man's eyes. Thorsson stood silently staring at the empty chair. He bowed his head slightly and then turning, walked back to the podium.

"Be seated."

The room was silent and Thorsson stood looking out at the crowd. Justin immediately sensed that something was wrong, and after a long moment of silence there was a nervous murmuring in the room.

"Those of you who attempted to tune into outside broadcasts undoubtedly discovered that all communication off this ship was cut at 0700 this morning."

Justin nodded slightly, having asked Uncle for a news update and Uncle claiming that the commlink was off line, something rather unusual.

"I requested that Uncle cut such links because I felt it best to tell all of you directly what has just happened."

Thorsson reached into his breast pocket, pulled out a piece of paper and unfolded it.

"I received the following communication this morning at 0650 from United Nations Space Operations Command."

He held the paper and started to read.

"From U.N. SOC to Thorsson, commanding Academy ship *Star Voyager*.

"We have received confirmed information that effective at 2400 hours tonight, system standard time, the colonial government of Mars shall issue a declaration of secession. . . ."

A lone cheer rose up from the group and startled, Thorsson looked up as a cadet came to his feet and threw his cap in the air. A second later several others followed his example.

Thorsson said nothing, and the cadets looked around. Embarrassed, they sat back down.

"As I was saying, a declaration of secession from the United Nations Colonial Administration. The Colonial Administrator on Mars informs us that this, I repeat, this is not a declaration of war, but it is a declaration of political independence. The ruling council of Mars will act to seize all United Nations property on Mars and in orbit above it. The ruling council has requested that all United Nations personnel, including those serving with the fleet either sign a statement of noninterference or leave the planet within forty-eight hours."

He paused for a moment and there was a stirring in the room, many of the cadets breaking discipline to talk.

"Silence in the hall, please," Thorsson said quietly, and the room settled back down.

"Inform your personnel of this situation immediately. Those cadets who believe that, due to this crisis, they can no longer honor their oath of commitment to the service must leave United Nations ships and property on the next available transit."

Thorsson slowly folded the paper and put it back into his pocket.

Surprised, Justin looked over at Matt, afraid of what he might do.

Thorsson waited for a minute, letting those in the hall talk freely among themselves, and then he cleared his throat. The room fell silent.

"So, it has finally started," Thorsson said, his voice soft and distant. "All of you cadets are young, the seeds of this crisis were planted long before you were born. I fear that before it is done, you might find yourselves torn, pitted one against the other. Perhaps you might even find yourselves as enemies, required to kill those whom you once called friends.

"I hope not, I pray that it never comes to that. And if it should, try to remember that there was once a time, here, when you were friends, and let that temper how you act, so that when the crisis has finally passed, all of us can go on together, to fulfill the path that we together embarked upon."

He cleared his throat again.

"If there is anyone present here, who feels that honor must bind him to the course that the Parliament of Mars has embarked upon, and that he or she can no longer serve in a United Nations uniform, they are free to go. A shuttle to Earth Orbital Three leaves here in two hours, and from there you can catch transit back to your home."

The room was silent. The cadet who had stood up and cheered came to his feet and looked at Thorsson. Coming to attention he saluted, then stepped into the aisle and walked out of the room, his footsteps echoing. A dozen other cadets stood up after him. Justin was saddened to see that one of them was

Jenkins, their leader in the falcon fighting championship game. All but one of them saluted Thorsson; the last cadet just looked at him defiantly and walked out.

Justin looked over at Matt, not sure of what he would do. Justin knew that his best friend was in full sympathy with the separatist cause, even though he was not from Mars. Matt looked at him, obviously torn, and for a second Justin feared that he would stand up. Matt finally shook his head slightly and then settled back in his chair.

There was a stir down in the front of the room where the faculty sat and, to Justin's surprise, Vanderberg stood up.

"Sir, do I have your permission to withdraw?" Vanderberg asked, looking up at Thorsson.

Thorsson, unable to speak, merely nodded a reply.

Vanderberg saluted Thorsson. He looked over at Justin and Matt, gave the barest flicker of a smile and then turned and walked out of the room.

Thorsson waited in silence until he was certain that no one else would leave.

"If anyone here should decide later that their loyalties are with Mars, feel free to come and see me for transit back home. Good luck in your exams and God protect all of us in the days ahead."

Thorsson left the podium and the assembly came to attention. As he left the room a senior cadet stepped forward and faced the room.

"Dismissed."

Justin stood up and looked over at Matt. The feeling of pride and excitement he felt, not only for himself, but for his friend, had been washed away with the announcement of secession.

A number of cadets came up to shake hands with Justin and Matt, and they drifted through the crowd to the back of the room. Heated arguments were already breaking out, and Justin overheard more than one cadet announce that anyone who backed the Martian secession movement was a traitor and should be put up against the nearest wall and shot.

They headed back to their room and closed the door.

"Uncle, are we hooked back up to outside yet?"

"Signal came back on five minutes ago."

"Give us the news channel."

Justin and Matt sat down and a moment later Pradeep came in to join them.

It wasn't good, Justin could see that. Three people had already been killed, one a fleet officer, the other two colonists, in a barroom brawl that broke out in the Martian city of Bradbury. That incident had heated things up even further, with two members of the U.N. Colonial Administration calling for armed intervention.

Justin finally looked over at Matt.

"Are you going to join up if fighting starts?"

Matt sat silent for a moment.

"I guess I'll have to," he finally said. "I've gotta put my money where my mouth is. What will you do?"

"Me, I'm from Earth, same as Pradeep," Justin finally replied.

"I know that, but what will you do?"

Justin looked over at Pradeep and his friend sighed.

"Sure the U.N. is a great idea," Pradeep said, "but I still define myself as coming from India first. We need secured resources even more than most, and if the outer colonials set up a blockade, it'll be chaos. Matt, I'll have to stand against you."

Matt simply nodded his head in understanding.

"It always comes down to that in the end, where we come from, what we think our people need. I know it's still tough in parts of India, but it's just as tough in the outer colonies. The taxation is ruinous."

"Remember the colonies were created to help get Earth out of its economic mess, to stop the wars, to help keep people from starving," Pradeep replied.

"Sure, I know that," Matt replied. "Hell, I'm pulling an A in Space History just like you. But let me just ask you one question, Pradeep."

"Go on then."

"How do you feel about India declaring its independence from Britain? I think the British were far better colonial administrators than most. They even tried to do the right thing by India whenever possible, but in the end British interests came first and your people decided it was time to make the break."

"I think that's different."

"No, it's not, it's not a damn bit different," Matt replied sharply.

"Hey, guys, I think we're all friends here, aren't we?" Justin interjected.

Matt and Pradeep looked at each other for a moment. Matt finally started to smile and extended his hand.

"Still friends?" he asked. Pradeep smiled in return and took Matt's hand.

"Still friends."

Matt then looked back at Justin.

"And what do you think?"

"I just wish it hadn't come to this," he said, "not yet. I still need time to think about it. Earth is home to me, I just can't forget that. Win or lose in the finals, in three days I'm going back there, either for a furlough or for keeps."

"Just for the furlough, buddy, and am I still invited?"

"Sure, why the hell not?"

"I don't know," Matt said quietly, "from the news, I guess colonists might not be too welcome down there at the moment."

"The hell with the news, and besides, like Thorsson said, the declaration of secession wasn't a call to war."

"Good," Matt said with a smile. "I've never seen a river before, or blue sky, or a forest, and I've never heard a bird, except for the parrots some of the miners keep and usually they aren't singing, they're swearing. I didn't want to miss seeing Earth, it might be my only chance."

"And you won't."

"But what are you thinking about all of this?"

"Like I was saying, Earth is home to me. It's where I was raised. The farm has been part of my mom's family for over two hundred years."

He paused for a moment. Again there was that haunting feeling as he thought of home. He couldn't wait to head down to Shades Park, throw a canoe in on Sugar Creek, starting at the Deer's Mill covered bridge, and take Matt down the river through Turkey Run Park. That was paradise, drifting by the sandstone cliffs, shooting the rapids, and pulling over to take a dip in a clear crystal-like pool of icy water.

There was the other side, however, which now haunted him as well. The memory of space was now part of him as well. Now he could understand what had crept into the blood of his grandfather, and why his father could no longer stay earthbound, in spite of his mother's pleas. He knew that in the end, he would be the same, if he could survive the exams coming up. He knew that there would be a day when he could very well turn his back on Earth and never come home again.

"I think in the end, I'll be with you, Matt. But for now, I hope it doesn't come down to a choice because if it does I'm afraid it will tear me apart."

❖   ❖   ❖

"Justin, might I suggest that you consider getting some sleep? It's two thirty in the morning."

"Just shut up, Uncle, and give me the next problem."

"Cadet Bell, studies have shown that sleep deprivation will result in diminished performance after only . . ."

"Uncle! Just give me the next problem."

The computer sighed, a trait which made Justin almost forget that he was in fact talking to a machine.

"Listen, Justin, I can read your bio scan easy enough. You're exhausted. This morning is finals day not only in Astro-Navigation but in your other courses as well.

I don't think you can physically stand up to it."

"Don't tell me what I can and can't do," Justin snapped.

"All right then," Uncle said. "I'll up load the next problem. But don't say later that I didn't warn you."

"Hey, Justin."

Startled, he turned in his chair and saw Tanya standing in the doorway, her arm still in a sling.

"What the hell are you doing here?" Justin whispered, afraid of waking up his two roommates.

"Couldn't sleep and was up studying. Mind if I come in?"

"Tanya, if you're caught in a guy's room after hours, we're all homeward bound."

"The study lounge is open though."

"Okay, wait for me outside."

"I'll talk to you in the lounge, Uncle."

Justin grabbed his notebook computer and went out into the hallway where Tanya was waiting.

"How's the Astro-Navigation?"

"Not good," he said, looking at her curiously, and the two went to the nearest lift and dropped down to the lower deck where the study lounges were located.

"You feeling okay?"

"Fit as a balalaika," she replied with a smile. "How come you didn't drop by for a visit?"

"Well," and he wasn't sure what to say. He was still a bit taken off guard over the kiss. After all, until the accident she was his most hated enemy.

"I did want to say thanks again."

"You don't have to," he replied shyly, looking down at the floor.

She laughed softly, her eyes sparkling.

"I can well imagine what you thought of me at times. I guess I was a bit of a heel. Back home my family name means 'hero.' It wasn't just my great-grandfather, it was my dad as well, and my grandmother who was a famous ballerina. Everyone kept expecting a lot from me."

"I know what you mean," Justin said quietly.

"I guess I should have realized that. I knew about your dad—who doesn't?—and I think I was taken off guard when I first saw you and you were so damn space sick. I was expecting to meet some sort of super cadet."

She laughed and he found himself actually smiling.

"I couldn't resist poking some fun, and then it just kind of made me feel better somehow so I kept on doing it."

He didn't reply and continued to look at the floor.

"I didn't know who was saving me at first. When I hit the ground I knew my arm was broken, and then I just kept on sliding right for the edge. I really thought it was all over. Funny though, when I suddenly saw that it was you doing the saving my first thought was that you were actually trying to help me go over the edge, and I didn't blame you."

"Really?"

She laughed again.

"No, silly. I was scared to death. I hung on to you for dear life and was damn grateful you were there. And amazed at just how brave you were."

"It's okay. But do you want to know something?"

"What?"

"I really can't remember that much about it. I mean, the jumping after you part. I just moved and thought about it later. After it was all over I was petrified and I even threw up on the ship afterwards."

"Yeah, I heard about that."

"You did?" and he was suddenly mortified.

"Sure, we couldn't help but hear you."

He was absolutely horrified. He thought Matt had covered for him and everyone kept looking at him now as something of a hero.

She looked at him and put a hand lightly on his shoulder.

"No one thinks the less of you for getting a bit shaken up afterwards. It's normal."

"Really?"

"Sure it is. I had the shakes all the way back and if you had taken a close look at Matt you would have seen him shaking a bit too, so don't worry about it."

They stopped at the lounge door.

"I need to go over some astro-navigation problems. Would you mind reviewing them with me?"

"Thanks, it sure would help."

They went into the lounge, which was nearly filled with cadets doing last-minute cramming. At the sight of the two of them coming in together a buzz went through the room, with more than one cadet turning to sneak a quick look.

"All right, guys, knock it off," Tanya snapped and a chuckle went through the crowd. They took a seat together at the far corner of the room, next to the viewport. Down on Earth, they could see dawn was streaking across western Russia.

"This was my favorite time of day back home," she said almost wistfully. "Did you ever see the White Nights of Saint Petersburg?"

"No, but I heard about them."

"It's wonderful. At midnight in late June the sky's streaked with the colors of twilight, the sun barely setting on the northern horizon. The whole city is up and tens of thousands of people are out walking along the Neva River. Nobody sleeps. They only open the bridges across the river at night, and all the ships start to move, gliding along, the river reflecting the colors of the sky. It's lovely.

"Do you miss home?"

"A lot. I missed seeing the White Nights this year, but it'll really be strange not to be home in October when the first snow starts to fall." She paused. "That is, if I make it back in for the next semester."

"I'll miss that, too," Justin said softly, "especially walking through the woods on a snowy day, the world so quiet, as quiet almost as space."

He thought about that for a moment. If he didn't pass the test coming up, it wouldn't be a worry. He'd see snow again. The problem was that he knew it'd never be the same. Every moment he spent down on Earth, he realized now, would be a torture, especially at night when the stars were overhead. He could see that in his grandfather, and now he knew why the old man would sit on the back porch at night, looking up, dreaming of past glories.

He looked over at Tanya and saw her looking at him.

"Maybe we should get to work," she said a bit too quickly and she opened up her computer.

✧   ✧   ✧

He walked into the room, stopped next to his assigned seat and looked around. Matt was several rows forward and his friend turned, looked back and gave him a thumbs-up.

He knew he had gone past the state of simple exhaustion. He felt as if every muscle in his body was ready to simply fall apart and melt into the floor. He'd already gone through two exams so far today, but this one was the clincher.

Commander Xing strode into the room and they came to attention.

"Be seated."

He settled down into his chair and waited.

This was it. All the cramming of the last two months coming to its conclusion.

"Plug in your computers for a security check," Xing announced.

Justin hooked a jack into the main system and his computer clicked to life, with Xing's computer running a check to make sure no one had any personal note files hidden somewhere inside his system. That was something he had triple-checked before coming into the room. It was yet another way to earn a quick trip home, and an "I forgot," or "I didn't know it was in there" excuse simply would not wash.

They had all been cautioned with the tale of a senior cadet, taking the last of his finals, who was tripped up by this and was expelled. Hardly anyone believed he was actually attempting to cheat; those types never made it much past the first year anyhow, but the review board had voted to expel him anyhow, citing the fact that if he forgot to double-check something like that, he couldn't be trusted with command of a ship or base where a second's inattention might prove fatal.

To Justin's absolute amazement a high-pitched bell started to ring and everyone looked around nervously. A cadet in the first row suddenly stood up and faced Xing, extending his hands in a gesture of appeal.

"Cadet Murray, do not touch your computer. Leave the room and report to the Admiral's office at once."

The cadet, his features drawn, turned and walked out of the room, eyes straight ahead.

Justin watched him leave. At least it was over for Murray, he thought.

"There will be no talking during the exam. If you have a question for me, page me through your computer. You may begin."

Justin looked down at his screen as the exam appeared and swallowed hard. She had tossed twenty questions at them, some of them three- and four-parters. The first ten were easy computations. If you knew how to pull up the data from the accessible testing files, you could have each of them down in a minute or two.

He started in, first knocking off the easy ones that dealt with simple orbital mechanics. There was even a bit of a tricky question that used the ancient rockets of the Apollo days and traced out the emergency return of Apollo 13 after it lost its main engine due to the explosion of an oxygen tank in the command module with a tie-in question regarding the first landing on the Moon by Apollo 11. He smiled at that one, never having guessed that Xing would actually pull in some space history. If you already knew how the original astronauts did it, the question was a cinch. He accessed the general history file, pulled up the data on the thrust of the landing and command modules for Apollo 13, plugged the information in and in five minutes had the question knocked off.

He continued to plow through the test, his fingers flying across the keys, watching the screen and double-checking each formula as he moved along.

And then he hit question seventeen. It was purely hypothetical, dealing with a planet supposedly orbiting Betelgeuse, the red giant star in the shoulder of Orion. Xing had loaded all the necessary data regarding the imaginary planet into the question and all he had to do was plug in the necessary information in the main file system regarding the star. It was an aerobraking maneuver using a standard Aeroflot T-27 high speed transport. He was tempted to raise a question right there. The thought of a T-27 crossing six hundred and fifty light years was in itself absurd, but he didn't think he should call Xing on that point.

The planet had a thin atmosphere, almost equivalent to Mars, requiring a low sweep. He plugged the numbers in and within a couple of minutes had the answer roughed out. He double-checked it, realized he was on the mark and then pushed on to eighteen.

But there was something gnawing at the back of his thoughts. Seventeen was almost too simple, not like Xing at all. And besides, if she wanted a thin atmosphere approach why go to all the trouble of building a simulation of a make-believe planet, when Mars, Europa or Titan would have served just as well.

He looked up at the clock, he had thirty minutes left.

He heard several muffled groans and sneaked a look up at Xing who stood up and scanned the classroom angrily, returning the class to silence.

He hit questions nineteen and twenty and understood the groans. It was a killer, a linked question with nineteen being another aerobraking exercise, using Jupiter, with the data calculated from that taken into question twenty, where after the aerobraking you then went into orbit around the moon Europa. It was second-year stuff to be certain and he started to wade into the question. Ten whole points of the exam were tied into them, an absolute killer. If he missed here, he was out of the school. He plowed into the question, finally clearing nineteen and the first part of twenty and then looked back up at the clock.

He had used too much time! Only seven minutes were left and then he looked back at number twenty. The rest of the question was far too complex. Even if he threw twenty minutes into it, he still doubted if he would get it all right.

He closed his eyes and tried to clear his thoughts.

It was really starting to hit him just how much he really wanted to stay at the Academy.

He looked back at his computer, feeling crushed. He couldn't finish twenty in time. If he missed even a single part of the other nineteen questions he was out, for he needed at least a ninety-six in this exam to pull his average up to the minimal passing score of eighty.

"Xing always throws a curveball," Uncle had told him.

So where was the curveball?

Nineteen and twenty were no curves, they were just plain out hard. It had to be somewhere else. He looked back at the clock. Six minutes left.

Spend it on reviewing, it was the only hope left. He leaped through the questions one more time. The one on Apollo 13 was a bit tricky but if you knew history you were in. He looked back at the clock.

And then he came to number seventeen. There had to be something hidden in the question.

He looked at his figures, tracing an aerobraking maneuver down to fourteen thousand two hundred meters above the planet's surface and then rising back up to a standard circular orbit one hundred and eight kilometers above the surface. Bells started ringing in Justin's head.

Mars and crashing into Mons Olympus, the question Uncle had tested him on: it was too similar.

He pulled the imaginary planet's map up on his computer and punched in a request to show any mountain ranges above fourteen thousand meters.

A dark red line appeared straight across the planet's reverse side.

In a panic, he looked back at the clock. Two minutes.

He punched in a request for all mountains above

nine thousand meters and the red line barely shifted. Regulations stated an aerobraking could not come within five thousand meters of the ground!

The mountain range on this planet rose up clear through the atmosphere and out into space! An aerobraking maneuver around the planet was impossible!

If he went for a polar loop, would that do it? The mountains there were just under nine thousand meters over both poles. Shoot for a polar loop? He checked how fast the planet spun on its axis. It was a fast mover, completing a turn every ten hours, and he realized that due to centrifugal force a planet's atmosphere was ever so slightly thicker at the equator and thinner at the poles. If he shot for the pole, at fourteen thousand meters the atmosphere would be too thin and the braking maneuver would fail.

He looked back up. Forty-five seconds.

He took a deep breath and started to type.

He punched the delete button for his entire formula and quickly typed in "Aerobraking maneuver impossible due to planetary obstructions." The bell rang, shutting his computer down.

Justin sat back in his chair and closed his eyes.

The room was as silent as space as everyone waited for the results to be posted.

He opened his eyes and looked around, his stomach in a knot. Would this be the end of it all? he wondered. He could imagine himself homeward bound tonight, traveling with the other cadets on their seven-day leave, the rest of them laughing, joking, knowing they were coming back at the end of next week, while he was going home forever.

He stared at his computer screen, praying hard, and saw the numbers appear. For a brief second he thought it was all an illusion, a wishful dream; and then he was in the air, forgetting as he leaped up that the classroom was in the one-third gravity zone. He shot up half a dozen feet.

"I made it!" Justin started to scream, "I made it!"

"Cadet Bell!"

He floated back down and embarrassed, realized that the entire class was staring at him, including Commander Xing who was standing at the front of the room, glaring at him coldly.

He came stiffly to attention, though it was impossible to wipe the grin from his face.

"Cadet Bell, you will not be reporting back to this institution next week if you make another demonstration like that. Do you read me, mister?"

He saluted stiffly.

"Yes, sir."

She stared at him coldly and then returned her attention to the rest of the class.

"Heaven help our space program if this class is typical of the type of cadets we're recruiting today. I will see most of you this fall for intermediate level navigation. You are dismissed."

Justin looked down at his computer, suddenly afraid that he had somehow misread the information. But it was there. He had scored a ninety-six on his final, combined with his sixty-four for the midterm, homework and quizzes he had come out with an 81 average, just barely a B. It was an impossibly tight squeeze but he had made it. History and Procedures had been a breeze, and even Brian had given him a passing grade for discipline. He was coming back!

He picked up his computer, started for the door and found himself surrounded by his friends, Matt, Pradeep and Madison, who came up and slapped him on the back. As they headed out into the corridor even Tanya came up alongside him, put her good arm around his waist and hugged him.

"Now I've got to teach you how to really fly in the falcon games," she said.

"And he's got to teach you a little humility," Matt replied and she gave him a good-natured punch in the ribs.

Several of the senior cadets were hanging around in the hallway, looking up as the class came out, and Brian casually strode up to the group.

"From your stupid grin I guess that means I'm stuck with you this fall," Brian said.

"You're damn right he's coming back," Matt replied.

Brian looked at Matt coldly for violating the rules against swearing, but then a thin smile creased Brian's features.

"Congratulations, cadet, I knew you'd make it," and he extended his hand to Justin.

He then nodded to the thin silver strip above Justin's left pocket and then over at Matt's.

"And I'm proud to serve alongside you guys as well."

Taken aback, Justin was unable to reply. Sharon

was standing behind Brian and grinning, she gave Justin a thumbs-up and then turned to check on how her own cadets had made out.

"I'll see all you guys next week. Have a safe trip back to Earth," and he turned and walked off.

"Well, I'll be damned," Justin whispered, "he might be human after all."

Laughing, they continued down the hall and Justin saw a group of cadets coming stiffly to attention. Thor Thorsson was coming down the corridor, stopping, asking various cadets how they had done, nodding and smiling. Justin and his friends stopped as he approached.

"So, I take it from the grins I'll be seeing you people for the fall semester."

"Yes, sir," they all chorused in reply.

Thor smiled approvingly.

"Matt, Justin, the Academy's proud of how you two handled yourselves on the Moon, it was an action in the finest tradition of the Academy. If ever two cadets earned the silver medal it was you two," and he looked down approvingly at the silver bars which he had pinned over their left breast pockets the day before.

"I'm rather glad about it too, sir." Tanya said.

He shook Matt's hand and then turned to Justin.

"I'll see you in the viewing lounge again sometime, Justin and we'll talk some more."

Justin smiled and then Thorsson continued on.

"He's incredible," Madison whispered.

"Yeah, I wish everyone here was like him," Pradeep replied.

"You know, I almost forgot, we're stuck with the Terminator again this fall," and everyone groaned as they continued down the hall, devising ways in which they would love to see her spaced.

Thorsson turned to watch them go, catching the tail end of their conversation, and he laughed softly to himself. He went into the classroom where Commander Xing was closing up her computer.

"Glad the summer session's over?" Thorsson asked.

She looked up at him and nodded.

"It's tough, Thor. You see these kids and sometimes it almost breaks your heart."

He sighed and sat down on the edge of her desk.

"I just saw Murray. Too bad. He was in tears when he left my office to pack his gear."

"He was a good kid. He wasn't cheating. I think he was just too tired and forgot to dump his files before coming here. Isn't there some way to give him a second chance? He had the third highest average out of all the scrubs here."

"You know the rules, Mary. We did that boy a favor. It's better to wash him out now over this, than have him kill himself further down the line. Remember, there are no second chances in space. He got too cocky. Everyone kept telling him how great he was and he started to believe it. With a head like that, someday he'd skip part of a preflight check, figuring he knew it all, and wind up killing not only himself but a hell of a lot of others as well. That's why we have the rules that we do."

"It's still hard to watch it though, and I'm the one who winds up being your, what are they calling me now, 'the Terminator.' Thanks to you I'm the most hated person here."

He opened Xing's computer back up and punched up the grade files and looked them over.

"He certainly squeaked through."

"Who?"

"Cadet Bell."

Xing started to smile.

"I almost had to throw him out, he let out a yell and jumped halfway to the ceiling when the grades were posted."

Thor smiled.

"Old number seventeen almost nailed him. I was tuned into his computer and watched him reason it out. I almost died when he got it wrong at first and damn near went up and kissed him when he turned it around at the end."

"He'd have dropped dead if you had," Thor said with a laugh.

"You really like him, don't you?" she asked.

"He reminds me of his dad."

"Funny, I expected some sort of super hero to come through the door. When I first looked at him I couldn't believe this was Jason Bell's son."

"They're all awkward at sixteen," Thor said with a smile, "even Jason was, and even you, Miss Xing, if I remember correctly. By heavens, those old-fashioned braces that you were wearing were simply awful."

She laughed softly and shook her head.

"Yeah, I guess I was."

"Come on, let's go get a cup of coffee. In seven days the entire school's reporting back from summer training and we've got a lot of work to do before then."

"It's going to be a tough semester coming up, especially with the Mars crisis."

Thor nodded and looked over at her.

"You know, Vanderberg turned in his resignation this morning. He's taken a commission with the Martian colonial defense forces."

"Damn." She shook her head sadly.

"What are you going to do?" Thor asked.

She lowered her head.

"I called Mars home for ten years. I buried my husband and children there." She paused for a long moment and Thor reached out to touch her hand.

"Hell, Thor, what are you going to do is more the question. You helped found that colony."

"I have to stay here."

"Why? You don't care for the government any more than I do."

"Because I have to stay," Thor said quietly. "But we're not talking about me, what are you going to do?"

She shook her head.

"I don't know yet, I just don't know."

Thor tried to smile.

"Stick with me for a while longer, Mary. This crisis is only beginning. There'll be plenty of time yet for all of us to make our decisions."

The shuttle plane taxied up to the ramp at Lafayette's airport and shuddered to a stop. Standing up, Justin grabbed hold of his bag and looked over at Matt, offering him a hand as he struggled to his feet.

"This gravity's a killer," Matt groaned. "How do you stand it all the time? It was bad enough in the exercise room with Malady kicking us around."

"You get used to it, spacer. Just take it easy."

They made their way down the aisle, and Justin was aware of the fact that the class A uniforms that he and Matt were wearing certainly drew attention. An elderly woman in the row across from them had spent hours telling them about her grandson who had graduated the year before and was now a project engineer with the Mars terraforming program, giving them every detail from the base of the skyhook tower at Rio, all the way up to Chicago and now on the transfer flight out to Indiana. A couple of passengers started to give her a hard time on the flight to Chicago, calling her son a traitor. Matt and Justin leaped to her defense and a near fight seemed imminent until the flight stewards broke it up, threatening everyone with arrest for disrupting a commercial flight.

"Come over for tea, boys, you have my address," she chortled as they left the plane.

"I can't promise, ma'am," Justin said politely, glad to finally be escaping, though he knew that Matt was rather taken with her and chances were they would at least drop by.

As they stepped out of the plane into the early evening twilight Matt looked around in wonder, breathing deeply. They walked into the small terminal and started for the door when Justin suddenly felt his heart skip over. Standing in the corridor were John Ellington and four of the other guys from high school who had taken such delight in giving him a hard time. He felt a strong desire to just turn around and find another way out, but he knew he couldn't avoid it.

He kept his eyes straight ahead and continued on with the crowd, hoping they wouldn't see him.

"Well if it isn't the space cadet."

He felt his heart sink, and he slowed down and looked over. Ellington was slouching against the wall, a sick sort of grin on his face. He stood up and started to move towards Justin, his buddies following in his wake. The five moved to block Justin's way.

He felt himself go cold. He came to a stop and from the corner of his eye he saw Matt sizing the situation up, his friend's eyes going narrow. The presence of Matt snapped something inside of him. This was the first real friend in his life, a buddy who had risked his life alongside him to save two others. There was no way he would let someone like Ellington push them around. And damn it all, they were cadets in Star Voyager Academy.

Ellington slowed and Justin detected an uncertainty in his old bully's eyes. He knew the Academy had changed him, that had become obvious when he had tried on one of his old civilian shirts just before leaving and found that it now barely fit.

"Were you talking to me?" Justin snapped. He let his bag drop and he easily moved into a comfortable fighting stance and stared straight into Ellington's eyes.

"Who are these greasy-looking punks, garbage sweepers for the airport?" Matt interjected, a light touch of laughter in his voice.

"They're not worth our time," Justin replied and he actually found himself starting to laugh.

Ellington looked at him, his mouth open.

"You can't talk to me like that," Ellington finally replied.

"I just did, now make something of it," Justin replied.

Ellington started to open his mouth.

"Come on and just try it," Justin said softly, staring straight into Ellington's eyes. "If you do, I promise you they'll carry you out of this building on a stretcher."

He imagined Malady standing to one side watching and he shifted ever so easily into an attack stance, ready to lash out if Ellington moved.

There was a frozen moment, Ellington looking at him in astonishment.

"Come on, let's get out of this place, we've got better ways of wasting our time than picking on these guys," Matt said and he picked up Justin's bag.

Justin kept staring into Ellington's eyes and then saw the flicker of uncertainty.

Justin started forward, letting his shoulder slam up against Ellington, forcing him to step back. He half expected to suddenly get sucker punched from behind but nothing happened. He heard a curse, but he continued on and actually started to laugh. One of the bigger fears of his life had become insignificant.

"Glad we didn't have to fight," Matt whispered. "It's a lousy way to start a vacation, though I bet Malady would have taken them apart just for the fun of it."

"Besides, it might have gotten our uniforms dirty," Justin said with a grin.

They stepped out into the evening air. Matt broke away, going over to a small park on the other side of the magnetic levitation train stop. He walked into the grove of trees and touched one, running his hands over the bark, looking at the soaring green canopy overhead.

"It's incredible," Matt sighed and Justin was amazed to see tears in his friend's eyes.

"I know how you feel," Justin replied.

"What do you mean?"

Justin was looking up as well, but not at the trees. Overhead the stars were coming out, the Moon red and full, low on the western horizon.

"Tomorrow I'll take you down to Sugar Creek," Justin said. "You'll see a real river and we'll take the canoe and shoot some rapids."

"Really?"

"You'll have the time of your life, buddy."

"It's just incredible. I couldn't imagine that the world would be this beautiful."

"I feel the same way about space," Justin replied and he looked back up, knowing that in seven short days they'd be going back to start another semester — at Star Voyager Academy.

ABOUT THE AUTHOR

William R. Forstchen lives in Black Mountain, North Carolina, with his wife, Sharon, and their one-year-old daughter, Meghan. William is an Assistant Professor of History and Education at Montreat-Anderson College and is completing his Ph.D. at Purdue University with a specialization in the American Civil War. He has published over fifteen science fiction and fantasy novels including *The Lost Regiment* series. His interests vary from whitewater rafting and scuba diving to historical reenactments of the Civil War.

PRAISE FOR
LOIS MCMASTER BUJOLD

What the critics say:

The Warrior's Apprentice: "Now here's a fun romp through the spaceways—not so much a space opera as space ballet.... it has all the 'right stuff.' A lot of thought and thoughtfulness stand behind the all-too-human characters. Enjoy this one, and look forward to the next."   —Dean Lambe, *SF Reviews*

"The pace is breathless, the characterization thoughtful and emotionally powerful, and the author's narrative technique and command of language compelling. Highly recommended."   —*Booklist*

Brothers in Arms: "... she gives it a geniune depth of character, while reveling in the wild turnings of her tale. ... Bujold is as audacious as her favorite hero, and as brilliantly (if sneakily) successful."   —*Locus*

"Miles Vorkosigan is such a great character that I'll read anything Lois wants to write about him.... a book to re-read on cold rainy days."   —Robert Coulson, *Comics Buyer's Guide*

Borders of Infinity: "Bujold's series hero Miles Vorkosigan may be a lord by birth and an admiral by rank, but a bone disease that has left him hobbled and in frequent pain has sensitized him to the suffering of outcasts in his very hierarchical era.... Playing off Miles's reserve and cleverness, Bujold draws outrageous and outlandish foils to color her high-minded adventures."   —*Publishers Weekly*

Falling Free: "In *Falling Free* Lois McMaster Bujold has written her fourth straight superb novel. ... How to break down a talent like Bujold's into analyzable components? Best not to try. Best to say 'Read, or you will be missing something extraordinary.' "   —Roland Green, *Chicago Sun-Times*

The Vor Game: "The chronicles of Miles Vorkosigan are far too witty to be literary junk food, but they rouse the kind of craving that makes popcorn magically vanish during a double feature."   —Faren Miller, *Locus*

MORE PRAISE FOR
LOIS MCMASTER BUJOLD

What the readers say:

"My copy of *Shards of Honor* is falling apart I've reread it so often.... I'll read whatever you write. You've certainly proved yourself a grand storyteller."
—Liesl Kolbe, Colorado Springs, CO

"I experience the stories of Miles Vorkosigan as almost viscerally uplifting.... But certainly, even the weightiest theme would have less impact than a cinder on snow were it not for a rousing good story, and good storytelling with it. This is the second thing I want to thank you for.... I suppose if you boiled down all I've said to its simplest expression, it would be that I immensely enjoy and admire your work. I submit that, as literature, your work raises the overall level of the science fiction genre, and spiritually, your work cannot avoid positively influencing all who read it."
—Glen Stonebraker, Gaithersburg, MD

"'The Mountains of Mourning' [in *Borders of Infinity*] was one of the best-crafted, and simply best, works I'd ever read. When I finished it, I immediately turned back to the beginning and read it again, and I can't remember the last time I did that."   —Betsy Bizot, Lisle, IL

"I can only hope that you will continue to write, so that I can continue to read (and of course buy) your books, for they make me laugh and cry and think ... rare indeed."   —Steven Knott, Major, USAF

What do you say?

Send me these books!

Shards of Honor 72087-2 $4.99 _____
The Warrior's Apprentice 72066-X $4.50 _____
Ethan of Athos 65604-X $5.99 _____
Falling Free 65398-9 $4.99 _____
Brothers in Arms 69799-4 $5.99 _____
Borders of Infinity 69841-9 $4.99 _____
The Vor Game 72014-7 $4.99 _____
Barrayar 72083-X $4.99 _____
The Spirit Ring (hardcover) 72142-9 $17.00 _____
The Spirit Ring (paperback) 72188-7 $5.99 _____
Mirror Dance (hardcover) 72210-7 $21.00 _____

Lois McMaster Bujold:
Only from Baen Books

If these books are not available at your local bookstore, just check your choices above, fill out this coupon and send a check or money order for the cover price to Baen Books, Dept. BA, P.O. Box 1403, Riverdale, NY 10471.

NAME: _____

ADDRESS: _____

I have enclosed a check or money order in the amount of $ _____.